STRANDED WITH THE RECLUSIVE EARL

Eva Shepherd

MILLS & BOON

First Published in Great Britain 2021
by Mills & Boon, an imprint of HarperCollins*Publishers* Ltd,
1 London Bridge Street, London, SE1 9GF

www.harpercollins.co.uk

HarperCollins*Publishers*
1st Floor, Watermarque Building,
Ringsend Road, Dublin 4, Ireland

Stranded with the Reclusive Earl © 2021 Eva Shepherd

ISBN: 978-0-263-28419-5

08/21

MIX
Paper from
responsible sources
FSC™ C007454

This book is produced from independently certified FSC™ paper
to ensure responsible forest management.
For more information visit www.harpercollins.co.uk/green.

Printed and bound in Spain
by CPI, Barcelona

After graduating with degrees in History and Political Science, **Eva Shepherd** worked in journalism and as an advertising copywriter. She began writing historical romances because it combined her love of a happy ending with her passion for history. She lives in Christchurch, New Zealand, but spends her days immersed in the world of late Victorian England. Eva loves hearing from readers and can be reached via her website evashepherd.com and her Facebook page Facebook.com/evashepherdromancewriter.

Also by Eva Shepherd

Breaking the Marriage Rules miniseries

Beguiling the Duke
Awakening the Duchess
Aspirations of a Lady's Maid
How to Avoid the Marriage Mart

Young Victorian Ladies miniseries

Wagering on the Wallflower
Stranded with the Reclusive Earl

Look out for the next book, coming soon!

Discover more at millsandboon.co.uk.

To Liz and Pat,
thanks for your continued support and encouragement.

Chapter One

～～～

Cornwall 1890

Lady Iris Springfeld was an enigma. Everywhere she went, the whispers exchanged behind gloved hands and fans were always the same. Why wasn't she married? After all, she possessed the necessary qualities a man looked for in a wife. She was beautiful, graceful, sweet-natured and was known to come with a sizeable marriage settlement.

During her first Season, when she turned down several proposals, no one thought anything was amiss, as an attractive daughter of an earl could have her pick. She must be waiting for a better offer, everyone assumed. By the end of her second Season, with still no marriage prospects, a few eyebrows were raised, a few questions were asked, but most expected a marriage announcement to happen some time soon. But now that she had reached the advanced age of twenty-three, in the middle of her fifth Season, and still no ring on her finger, Society ladies were avidly discussing the situation.

Something *must* be wrong with Iris Springfeld.

What the gossips didn't know was that Iris harboured a closely guarded secret, one she had only shared with her two sisters, Daisy and Hazel. Unlike most members of the British aristocracy, Iris Springfeld was determined to marry for love. Until she met a man she truly loved, one she knew for certain loved her for who she really was, not her pretty face and not her social status, she would remain single.

And that man most certainly would not be Lord Pratley. Iris shuddered and pulled her jacket more tightly around her arms to try and protect herself from the inclement weather. Lord Pratley had been taking full advantage of Iris's presence at Lady Walberton's house party to pursue her relentlessly, so relentlessly he had driven her to take the dramatic action of feigning a headache and telling her mother she needed an early night.

She didn't like lying to her mother, but what

choice did she have? It was the only sensible course of action she could take under the circumstances. She was sure if Lord Pratley had given her one more compliment she would have forgotten every lesson that had been drummed into her on correct etiquette and how a young lady must conduct herself in Society, and would have given him what for.

Iris wiped away the raindrop dripping from her nose. If Lord Pratley could see her now, she doubted if he would be complimenting her on her beauty. Not when that thick blonde hair, which he admired so much, was no longer piled on top of her head in a carefully structured coiffure but hanging in a bedraggled mess down her back. He most certainly would not be describing her now limp locks as like spun gold or silken sunlight. As for her eyes, the ones he had said were as blue as cornflowers, and designed to capture a man's heart, they were now hardly visible as she squinted through the increasingly heavy rain.

And it would be stretching the truth to say she was graceful and elegant, certainly not in her present circumstances. With her fashionable blue hat flopping around her face like a damp rag, her pale blue skirt now splattered with mud and her boots full of water, she looked more like a tramp than a fashionable young lady. She giggled to herself, wishing he could see how she looked. On second thoughts, she was sure he would still be able to think of some fawning comment to make, even about this state of dishevelment.

Her giggle turned to a grimace as wet mud flowed over the top of her ankle boots. She looked down to discover she was standing in the middle of a puddle, and her once cream silk boots were now a dirty brown. Extracting herself from the sucking mud, she tried not to think about the damage she was doing. Her lady's maid was not going to be happy when she finally returned home and all this bedraggled clothing had to be washed and mended.

Perhaps it wasn't the most sensible thing to do—go for a muddy walk in clothing designed for spending a comfortable evening in a warm drawing room and light footwear that had never been expected to withstand the rigours of country paths.

Claiming to have a headache so she could retire to her room had seemed like a good idea at the time. As had her plan to quickly escape from the house so she could have a quiet walk. All she had wanted was to enjoy the sunset and a few moments' peace away from

Lord Pratley's flattery. How was she supposed to know that the weather in Cornwall could change so quickly?

If Iris were superstitious, she would see this drenching as the price she had to pay for telling her mother a white lie. Could a small white lie really cause the gods to make the wind howl, the rain to pelt down and to turn what had previously been a cloudy but otherwise pleasant early evening into a raging tempest just to punish Iris for telling lies?

As if the gods were listening in on her thoughts, the rain fell harder. She pulled her sodden hat more tightly down onto her head. 'All right, all right,' she said to the all-powerful gods. 'You've proved your point. I shouldn't have lied to Mother.'

And to make matters worse, it appeared she was now completely lost. She paused in her trudging along the path to look around. All these fields looked exactly the same, so how was she expected to get her bearings? And she was sure she had passed that barn already. Or did all barns in the Cornish countryside look identical?

What was becoming increasingly obvious was she had no idea how to get home and she needed help. While getting a thorough drenching was perhaps preferrable to an evening in Lord Pratley's company, it was starting to get dark, and even his company would be better than being stuck out in the countryside in the middle of the night during a storm.

She looked ahead, turned and looked behind, and pulled her jacket more tightly around her shoulders. Either direction could be the way back to the Walbertons' estate, and either way could also take her further from her destination. There was only one thing for it. She hadn't passed a single soul on the path since the rain started, so there was unlikely to be anyone from whom she could get directions. Apparently, the sensible people of Cornwall did not go out walking in storms, so she was going to have to seek help at the very next house she came to.

It was unacceptable behaviour for a young lady to approach an unknown house, uninvited and alone, but what choice did she have? Staying out in this weather all night long was the only other option, and that was no option at all. Surely the rules of etiquette could be abandoned under these conditions.

She took another look behind her, flicked up her jacket collar and made a decision. There was no point retracing her steps. It was better to just keep walking and stop at the very next house she came to, and if no houses appeared before it got dark, she would shelter in one of those identical barns.

At least it was an adventure, she tried to console herself as she walked, or, more accurately, squelched along the muddy track, but it was an adventure she would like to come to an end, sooner rather than later.

She turned the corner, looked in every direction but still saw no houses.

'All right,' she called out to anyone who might be listening, including the weather gods. 'I've been suitably punished for lying to my mother.' She placed her hand on her heart. 'I solemnly swear that I will never lie to my mother again. If you return me safely to Lady Walberton's house, I will never, ever misbehave again. I will conduct myself in an exemplary manner throughout the rest of the house party. I will smile politely, laugh at the men's jokes, listen to the women's gossip and even join in with my own titbits of information. And I will never tell a lie, never, ever again.'

She waited for the rain to stop falling, the wind to settle down, and a sign to appear pointing her in the direction of the Walbertons'. None of these things happened, so she continued trudging along the path, muttering her annoyance at herself.

Just as she was starting to think that Cornwall was an uninhabited part of the British Isles a large house appeared in the distance. Looking up at it, while holding her hat on her head so it wouldn't be whipped away by the wind, she said a silent thank-you.

Trying to avoid the worst of the mud, she walked towards the house, then stopped at the start of the long driveway.

'Please be home, and please be kind,' she muttered under her breath as she took in the rough stone exterior. Crenellated battlements ran along the top edge of the building and round turrets stood proud and tall at the four corners, showing that it had once been a castle before being converted to a manor house. It was a somewhat forbidding exterior, one originally designed to repel intruders.

But this was not the Middle Ages, she reminded herself as she traipsed up the driveway. It was the eighteen-nineties, not the fourteen-nineties. It was a time of steam trains, electric streetlights, even underground railways—certainly not the Dark Ages, when a man's home really had been his castle and he had defended it with all the might at his disposal. She paused in her walking and looked up at the building. No, this was not the Middle Ages, a time when young maidens could be held captive in turrets.

She gulped down her trepidation. Now was not the time to get fanciful and be intimidated by the look of a house. On a sunny day it probably looked welcoming and friendly. It was surely just the storm that was making it look like something from one of those gothic novels she so loved to read.

And what choice did she have? She could hardly wait until a friendly cottage appeared with roses round the door and a welcoming mat at the doorstep. No, this intimidating castle would have to suffice.

She approached the house and scanned the windows for lights but found none. Did that mean no one was home? Hopefully, that was not the case. The rain was now falling even more heavily, and the wind was getting stronger. The storm was giving no impression of being about to settle down at all soon and the last thing she wanted was to continue wandering aimlessly around the countryside.

At least the doorway was covered. Finally, she could shelter from the rain. She took off her rather useless blue hat and wrung out the water. The hat was the height of fashion, with its ostrich feathers, lace and bows, but it had been useless at protecting her from the elements and now looked rather sad and pathetic. She brushed down her skirt, trying to remove some of the mud from the bottom, and did her best to straighten her hair.

If her mother could see her now, she would be horrified. Not only was Iris doing something almost unforgivable in approaching a stranger's door unaccompanied, but she was doing it while looking like a complete fright. Escaping from the party really had been a mistake. One that must never be repeated, she reminded herself. She raised her eyes skyward, hoping the gods were still listening to her remorseful thoughts and would take further pity on this poor, drenched creature and ensure that the owners of the house gave her a warm welcome.

She took hold of the brass ring in the mouth of a rather stern-looking lion, and pounded on the solid black wooden door, praying it would be heard above the sound of the storm.

Then she waited. And waited.

Please, please, someone be at home.

She pounded again, harder, with more

desperation. Was she going to have to spend the night sheltered in this doorway like a beggar?

Bolts scraped open. Locks clanked as keys were turned. Iris was tempted to run from the ominous sound, then covered her mouth to suppress a nervous giggle. What was she expecting? That the Frankenstein monster was living in Cornwall and was about to attack her? That a ghostly apparition was going to appear before her?

She really did have to stop reading those gothic novels.

The door opened and a rather pleasant-looking, smartly dressed butler peered around the half-open door, the stub of a candle flickering in his pewter candle holder.

'Good evening,' she said in her friendliest voice, as if appearing on someone's doorstep uninvited, in the middle of a storm, looking like a drowned rat, was a perfectly normal thing for a young lady to do. 'Would you please inform the lady of the house that Lady Iris Springfeld would like to visit?'

The butler continued to stare at her, but his look was bewildered rather than threatening.

'I'm afraid I'm lost,' she said, this time hoping to elicit his pity, 'and, as you can see, rather wet. Would you please tell the lady of the house that I am in need of some assistance?'

The butler stood back to let her in. 'There is no lady of the house, but I will let the master know of your situation. Please come in.'

Iris entered the home, which was in near darkness, apart from the scant light coming from the butler's candle and a few candles burning in sconces on the wall. It really was starting to appear as if she *had* stepped back in time. Or was it simply that the master was a miser who did not want to waste money on keeping his home well lit?

'Please wait here,' the butler said and disappeared up the dark hallway.

Iris placed her sodden hat back on her head and tried to straighten up her clothing, then looked down at her muddy boots, which were leaving damp footprints on the oriental rug. She quickly stepped off it and onto the stone tiles. Her eyes adjusted to the dim light and the hallway came into view. This part of the house appeared to be modern, with a large domed window that would let in light during the day, elegant marble pillars, and an expansive divided staircase at the end of the hallway. She looked up at the walls, lined with large portraits glaring down at her through the gloom.

'His Lordship will see you now.'

Iris emitted a small yelp. It was the butler's voice she had heard, not one of the painted ancestors coming to life. To cover her embarrassment she gave a small, nervous laugh.

'Please follow me to the drawing room,' he said, politely ignoring her rather peculiar behaviour.

'Thank you,' she replied, pretending that neither the yelp nor the laugh had actually happened.

The drawing-room door creaked loudly as the butler opened it. Was this house deliberately trying to act as if it was the setting for a horror novel? Was the master going to be a hobgoblin, or some depraved being from the underworld? Right now, she was so desperate for shelter she'd take her chances with a hobgoblin, provided it meant she could get out of the rain.

She entered the room, and the master stood up while the Irish wolfhound lying at his feet raised its head and looked in Iris's direction.

No, definitely not a hobgoblin. Unless hobgoblins were over six feet tall, broad of shoulder, long of leg and wore dark grey tailored suits.

'Good evening,' she said in her sunniest voice as she bobbed a small curtsy. 'I'm Lady Iris Springfeld. I was caught out in the storm and got rather wet in all that rain.' She pulled a mock frown and gestured to her wet skirt.

Then she waited for him to say something reassuring. No response came.

'I'm afraid I also got rather muddy.' She looked down at the foot of her gown, then sent him another small, apologetic frown. 'I'm sorry about that.'

'Come closer to the fire,' the man said.

His voice wasn't exactly friendly, but nor was it the voice of a diabolic, depraved creature from the underworld. Not that she *actually* knew what diabolic, depraved creatures sounded like, but she was sure they would not have deep, masculine voices that were rather pleasant to listen to.

'Thank you.' She approached the fire, which was providing the only light in the room, and relished its warmth, while trying to ignore the way her clothing was starting to steam slightly.

She looked around the large yet sparsely furnished drawing room. It was obvious he did not receive guests often. Not only did his rather unfriendly manner suggest that, but also all the furniture had been pushed to the edges of the room, with only one leather armchair in front of the fire.

'That's much better,' she said. 'Being beside a warm fire is so much better than being out in that weather.'

She looked up at him and smiled. His face was slightly turned away from her, but in the subdued light he appeared to be much more attractive than the average hobgoblin. Her gaze moved down to his jacket. One lapel was slightly tucked under. He must have pulled it on in haste when she entered the room, and she was tempted to straighten it for him. Instead, she continued to smile, hoping he would smile back and show her she was welcome.

'And who do I have the pleasure of addressing?' she finally asked, when it became obvious he had no intention of doing the honours himself.

'I am Theo Crighton, the Earl of Greystone.'

She bobbed another curtsy and waited for him to say something, anything else. Was he deliberately trying to make her feel uncomfortable? If that was his intention then he was succeeding.

'The lady perhaps requires a change of clothing, my lord,' the butler said. 'She is soaked to the bone.'

Iris would have thought that was obvious and not something that His Lordship needed to be informed of, but she said nothing, merely nodded her thanks in the butler's direction. At least he had some manners, even if his master didn't.

'Yes, see to it, Charles,' the taciturn Earl said. 'And will you please provide the lady with a chair?'

'It's very kind of you to invite me in,' Iris said, trying to keep her voice light and friendly, as the butler dragged a matching leather chair from across the room.

The Earl really had no choice, but manners would dictate that he at least pretend he was pleased to assist. And it certainly wasn't the way most men treated her. If she stumbled into Lord Pratley's home in a state of distress and needing rescuing from a storm, he would be moving heaven and earth to make her comfortable and would have behaved as if she was doing him a great honour by allowing him to assist her.

The butler arranged the chairs beside the fire. 'I've moved your chair two feet to the right, my lord.'

'Thank you, Charles. And would you also

bring some tea for Lady Iris and something for her to eat?'

He turned to nod to the butler, the side of his face that had been in shadow now exposed in the fire's flickering light.

Iris's hand shot to her mouth and she was suddenly ashamed of herself and everything she had thought about the Earl. It was all now so obvious. The dim lighting, the pushed-back furniture, even, dare she admit it, his failure to act the way most men did when in her presence. He was blind. Scarring covered his forehead and one eye, and the other eye was lifeless, suggesting it too had either limited or no sight.

Iris was tempted to apologise, although she wasn't sure what for. Perhaps it was for her uncharitable thoughts about the bleakness of the unlit house, or for her unwanted intrusion, or for whatever had caused the scarring on his otherwise handsome face.

And it *was* a handsome face. Black hair framed chiselled cheekbones and a strong jawline, which was bearing evening stubble. As she continued to stare at him, for some unknown reason she was tempted to run her finger along the small cleft in the middle of his chin.

Her hand continued to cover her mouth, as if caught in an inappropriate act, and she quickly looked away, surprised at her own boldness, even if it had only been a thought.

The butler bowed and left the room. Iris sank down into the soft leather, trying to push out any thoughts of cleft chins, strong jaws or high cheekbones.

'Please, won't you sit down?' she said, indicating the chair opposite, then withdrew her hand, realising it was a pointless gesture if he couldn't see her.

The Earl reached out behind him to the arm of the chair then sat down and picked up his glass of brandy.

'Would you like a brandy or would you rather wait for tea?'

'Actually, a brandy would be rather nice,' she said with a polite smile. 'Just to warm myself up a bit,' she added.

Certainly not to steady my nerves.

His gruff *humph* suggested he did not believe her, but he crossed the room and took a glass from the sideboard, then poured her a brandy from the cut-glass decanter and steadily handed it to her. As her hand lightly touched his, the strangest sensation shot up her fingers, her arm, and into her chest, where her heart did a peculiar jump.

That was odd. Touching a man's hand had never had that effect on her before. It had to be the effect of this rather disconcerting day that was causing her nerves to behave in such an unusual manner. She took a quick gulp of her drink and coughed as the woody alcohol caught her in the back of the throat, then burnt its way down to her stomach.

Oh, for goodness' sake, Iris, behave yourself. You accidentally touched a man's hand. That's no reason to become so flustered.

She closed her eyes and drew in a slow breath to steady herself, took another sip of her drink and smiled at her host.

'I'm so pleased I stumbled upon your home,' she said, keeping her voice light and friendly. 'Otherwise I'd probably still be wandering around in this storm. And I saw no one during my walk, so I couldn't ask for any directions to get back to Lord and Lady Walberton's house.'

He said nothing, just nursed his drink and stroked the head of his dog. The animal growled with contentment, looked up at Iris with its liquid brown eyes then went back to sleep.

'That's where I'm staying. At the Walbertons' estate,' Iris continued. 'For a house party. My mother and I. We're both staying there. All week. But I decided to go for a walk. Silly, really.'

He still said nothing.

'I didn't think the storm would come up so quickly,' she burbled on, trying to fill the silence. 'One minute the sky was clear. Well, not exactly clear. It was cloudy, and there were a few dark clouds on the horizon, but still, I didn't expect the sky to open up and for there to be such a downpour. And as for the wind, my goodness, it can certainly blow here, can't it?'

Her prattling was making her sound like a ninny, but what choice was he giving her? This uncomfortable silence had to be filled, and he wasn't doing much to help. Iris was not used to anyone sitting in her company and not speaking. At home there was always constant chatter from her mother, brother Nathaniel and sister Daisy, along with her older, married sister Hazel during her frequent visits. And when she was at social events people always made conversation with her, especially men. But this one, this Earl of Greystone, looked as if he was as sparse with his words as he was with his candles.

'I mean,' she continued after she had given him enough time to reply, time which he chose not to use, 'who would expect the weather to change so quickly?'

'Anyone familiar with English weather, I would have thought.'

Iris laughed, even though the expression on his face suggested he was criticising her, not teasing.

They sank back into an awkward silence, broken when the butler re-entered with a pile of clothing. Iris smiled at him, so grateful for the interruption.

He looked down at the clothing, blushing slightly, an unusual sight as servants were usually well-trained to keep their faces impassive under all conditions. 'I'm afraid the maids are all somewhat shorter than you, my lady, so their dresses would be rather immodest if you wore them. I hope these will suffice, my lady.' He blushed a slightly darker shade of red.

Iris took the clothes from his outstretched hands. 'I'm sure they'll be perfect,' she said, trying to reassure the uncomfortable servant. Then looked down at the clothing and frowned. He had handed her a pile of men's garments.

'I'm sorry, my lady,' he rushed on. 'We tend

to retire early in this house, and the other servants are already in bed, but I shall call for a maid to help you change.'

'Oh, no,' Iris said. 'I've caused enough inconvenience already. I wouldn't want to disturb the household any further.'

She looked over at the Earl, expecting him to contradict her, to say it was no inconvenience whatsoever, that her presence was not a disturbance.

No contradiction came, so she continued. 'Thank you for the clothing and I'm sure I'll be able to manage on my own.' Iris knew that the maids would have been working since the early hours of the morning and would have to be up again early tomorrow, so she was not merely being polite when she said not to disturb them. And how hard could it be to dress yourself in men's clothing? Iris didn't know but was about to find out.

'Very good, my lady,' the butler said with a bow. 'When you have changed, I'll take your damp clothing to be cleaned and dried.'

'You're very kind.' She smiled at the butler and was pleased that he smiled back. At least someone in this house was friendly.

The butler departed and the Earl rose from his chair. 'I'll give you some privacy and leave you to get changed beside the fire where it's warm,' he said, which was possibly the longest sentence he had said since she had arrived.

'Thank you. And I hope you'll be joining me for tea. I wouldn't want to drive you away from your room.' And what presumably was the only lit fire in this dark, gloomy house, she added to herself.

Instead of a response, he merely bowed and left the room, his dog trotting at his heels.

As she pulled off her damp dress and underclothes Iris tried to count her blessings. She was out of the storm. She had a fire to warm herself beside. Now she had clean, dry clothes to wear, and she wasn't in the company of a hobgoblin or a diabolic creature from the underworld. She smiled as she undid her corset. Although perhaps falling into the hands of a hobgoblin might have been a better outcome. Such a creature would probably be a better conversationalist than the morose Earl of Greystone.

Chapter Two

~~~~~~~~~~~~~~~~~~~~~~~~~~~~~~

Her damp, muddy clothes discarded on the floor, Iris looked around the room for a mirror, curious to see what sort of figure she cut in her gentleman's attire and to try to tidy up her dishevelled hair.

But there were no mirrors hanging on the walls, which made perfect sense. What use would a blind man have for a mirror? She was going to have to do her best with what she had. Taking the brush Charles had kindly left her, she tried to tame the mass of wet, tangled hair and clip it up off her face. It was a lost cause. To restyle her hair was going to demand the skills of her lady's maid, and every attempt resulted in the hair falling back to her shoulders in a damp mess. Eventually she conceded defeat and pulled it over her shoulder into an untidy plait.

She looked down at her peculiar attire. Wearing a man's shirt and trousers, she knew she looked ridiculous, but it would be nice to know just *how* ridiculous. Without a mirror there was no way of knowing. She twisted and turned to see how she looked from behind, but that was about as successful as her attempt to style her hair.

But she was sure the view from the back would be no less unflattering. How could anyone look attractive wearing trousers that were so long she'd had to turn them up at the bottom, and so baggy she'd had to pull the belt in to the very last hole, a white shirt that swamped her and hung down to her mid-thigh and had sleeves so long they had to be rolled up numerous times before her hands could reappear?

Oh, well, she consoled herself. She might not look particularly elegant or fashionable, but at least she was dry and comfortable, and no one would see her in this rather outrageous costume. And even if the Earl could see her, she doubted he would care what she looked like and he certainly would not pass comment. To do so would require him to actually speak to her, something he was apparently loath to do.

She rang the small silver bell on the table

beside the Earl's chair to signal that she was now respectably dressed and the Earl could re-enter his drawing room. Well, that was perhaps an exaggeration. Her attire might be considered respectable for a pantomime character but certainly not for a fashionable young lady.

She brushed down the soft linen shirt and wondered about the clothing. The cut and quality of the material marked it out as gentleman's attire, so presumably it belonged to the Earl. She was wearing his clothing. Iris was unsure how she felt about that.

She looked towards the door and listened to see if anyone was approaching, then lifted the shirt and gave it a tentative sniff. Still staring at the door, fearful that someone might burst in and catch her in such indecorous behaviour, she inhaled again, deeply and slowly. The clothing was freshly laundered, but it still held an underlying masculine scent, deliciously musky with a hint of lemon, presumably from his soap. Briefly she closed her eyes and drew in another deep breath as that same unexpected sensation she had experienced when she had touched his hand once again rippled through her body. Tingly, unsettling but not unpleasant. Definitely not unpleasant.

The door opened. She dropped the material

and quickly sat down, fire erupting onto her cheeks. The Earl entered, the wolfhound padding along behind him. He sat in the chair he had occupied before. The dog curled up at his feet, and with a small, satisfied grunt closed his eyes to sleep.

'I look a fright, I know,' she laughed, lifting her hands to indicate her shirt and trousers. The heat on her cheeks intensified. She was such a numbskull. He couldn't see what she looked like.

He merely nodded.

'But thank you so much for providing me with clean, dry clothing. I feel so much better now,' Iris said through her embarrassment.

Instead of answering he took a sip of his brandy and scratched the dog's head.

Iris waited for him to say something, anything. He continued to pat the dog, saying nothing. She coughed, to remind him of her presence, in case he needed reminding that he was not alone. He still said nothing.

She lightly tapped her fingertips together as she looked around the room, trying to think of something, anything to say that would engage this antisocial man in conversation.

The door opened and the butler entered. Iris turned and beamed a smile at Charles, so grateful was she for the interruption to the interminable silence.

He bent down and removed her pile of clothing.

'Thank you, Charles,' she said, even though it wasn't her place to thank the Earl's servants. 'I'm so sorry about the state of my clothing. I did get rather caught out in the weather, and the paths became so muddy, so quickly.'

Charles merely nodded. He at least had the excuse of being a servant for not engaging her in conversation. 'I'll do what I can to clean your clothing and get it back to you as soon as possible, my lady,' he said with a bow.

As he departed, Iris noted one of her muddy silk stockings was trailing out behind him and heat rushed to her cheeks. She looked over at the Earl, hoping he hadn't noticed, then remembered he would not be able to see. It did not matter that such an intimate piece of clothing had been on display, but that did nothing to quench the fire burning on Iris's cheeks.

If her mother knew that she had allowed her underwear to be on display in such a manner she would be outraged. Just as she would be horrified to see Iris sitting in front of a fire with a man she had not been formally introduced to and dressed as a gentleman.

But her mother couldn't see her and would never know. No one would ever know. Iris smiled to herself. She was dressed as a man. No one could see her and no one cared, certainly not the Earl. Really, she owed it to herself not to let this opportunity go by and to enjoy the novelty.

She looked around the room as if proving to herself that it was true, that no one she knew would ever know that she had spent an evening dressed as a man. Still smiling, she moved from sitting on the edge of the seat as young ladies were expected to do and slouched against the back of the armchair.

Such a relaxed posture could never be achieved when wearing a corset, which demanded the body remain completely upright. Relishing the freedom, she unclasped the hands folded neatly and decorously on her lap and placed one on each arm of the chair, then crossed one leg over the other, placing her ankle on her thigh, the way she had seen many a man do.

This was glorious. It was so comfortable, and she almost felt powerful. Smiling to herself, she tilted back her head and pretended she was smoking a large cigar and puffing out smoke rings to the ceiling.

She could get used to dressing like this, although she knew she would never dare to do so if anyone could see her.

The door opened and she quickly resumed her usual ladylike manner of sitting ramrod-straight at the edge of her chair, with her hands neatly folded in her lap.

Charles entered and placed a tray of tea and sandwiches on the side table.

Her heart thudding with guilt, she nodded her thanks and without comment he departed.

She was so naughty. It really was not right for a woman to behave in such a manner, even if no one could actually see her. Even though it had just been a bit of childish fun, the sooner her own clothes were returned to her the sooner she would be able to leave and stop misbehaving.

'I do hope Charles is able to dry out my clothing soon,' she said. 'I'm very grateful for the change of clothes, but I will have to change back into my own before I go home. If my mother saw me dressed like this she would be mortified.'

'You won't be going home tonight,' the Earl said, not turning from the fire.

Iris stared at him, wide eyed. What on earth did he mean? Was he going to force her to stay all night? Was he now about to turn into that depraved creature she had feared? Should she be scared? Making a run for the nearest door? A man she did not know was threatening to trap her in his home, and yet that unfamiliar sensation deep within her was not fear. She wasn't sure what it was, but it most definitely was not fear.

'This storm will not be over before day-break,' he continued. 'I will not risk my coach-man's life by sending him out in this weather.'

'Oh, I see.' She laughed to cover her embarrassment. Is that really what she thought he would do? That he was going to keep her captive in his castle so he could use her for his own licentious pleasure? She squirmed slightly in her chair and her naked toes curled up on the woollen rug. She really had been reading far too many gothic novels. *Held captive*, indeed. What a joke.

'No, I wouldn't want to put anyone's life at risk,' she said, hoping her voice didn't betray her overreaction.

He humphed his approval. 'We can only hope that your family are equally sensible and don't risk anyone's life either by sending out a search party in this weather.'

Iris shook her head. 'No, they won't. They

don't know I'm missing.' Her hand shot to her mouth as if to take back those words. Why had she told him that? He had already told her she would not be leaving until the morning. Did he really need to know that no one would be looking for her?

'Well, I'm sure they will notice I am missing, eventually,' she continued. Why did she keep imagining he was about to imprison her in his castle? Lock her up in the turret? If anything, he had given her every impression that she was here under sufferance, and if there weren't a storm outside he would be tossing her out at the first opportunity he got.

'I'm sure they will,' he said, his voice sounding bored as he stretched in his chair, drawing Iris's gaze to his long legs.

Thank goodness there wouldn't be a search party. She wouldn't want to put anyone to any trouble, but more than that, it would all be too embarrassing to be caught out in a lie and to be found in her present awkward situation. Her eyes flicked back to his face as her cheeks reddened. But her mother thought she was tucked up safe and sound in her own bed, behaving herself as a proper young lady should, and hopefully would not be tempted to check on her daughter before morning.

'I've asked Charles to prepare a room for you, and the coachman to take you home first thing in the morning, weather permitting.'

'Thank you,' she said.

They fell back into silence. Iris looked around the room for something else to talk about. Nothing came to mind. Her gaze returned to the untouched tea and sandwiches. Although neither hungry nor thirsty, she poured herself a cup and added a dash of milk. At least that gave her something to do, which was preferrable to sitting in silence or desperately trying to make strained conversation with the austere Earl. And perhaps tea and sandwiches would distract her overly imaginative mind from inappropriate thoughts about ravishment and imprisonment.

'The butler has only brought one cup. Shall I ring for another?'

'I don't drink tea,' he said.

And you don't believe in making polite conversation either, or in putting your guests at their ease.

Picking up her teacup, she looked over at him, sitting slouched in his chair, his long legs stretched out in front of him. He really was the most inhospitable, grouchy man she had ever met. Perhaps whatever had caused his scarring had also caused him to become cantankerous. She supposed that being blind could make a person bad-tempered and bitter.

She chewed on her bottom lip as she continued to stare at him. But it didn't have to. Her Uncle Henry was blind, but he was still a friendly, lovely man. But then, like herself, Uncle Henry was surrounded by a warm, happy family, not living alone with only servants and a dog for company.

Although, surely that was his choice and if he didn't like being alone he should just change it. And he did have a lot to be grateful for, such as this wonderful home, plus, despite his scars, he was still an extremely handsome man. Iris was sure she would not be the only woman to think so.

She continued to stare at him and wondered if he knew just how good-looking he was. His dark hair was thick and perhaps a little long for what was fashionable, but it gave him a certain rakish quality, like a buccaneer or warrior of old. She was tempted to reach over and smooth it down, or perhaps to ruffle it up even more with her fingers. She smiled. Wouldn't he be shocked if she did so?

Her gaze moved down to his strong jawline, which was shadowed by dark stubble. Perhaps he had not shaved today. Although, if he did not like having visitors, she wondered why he bothered to shave at all. He could grow a long, tangled beard like a hermit and who would care?

Yet it seemed he did care. His clothing was fashionable, clean and tidy, his boots were buffed to a high shine and his cravat was expertly tied. And he did wear his clothes rather well. Her gaze ran down his body, dressed in a dark grey suit. He certainly had a nice physique. Her scrutiny moved along his legs, where she could see the outline of his thigh muscles under the fabric of his trousers, then slowly back up his body, to his narrow hips, flat stomach under his white linen shirt, and broad shoulders. No, there was certainly nothing wrong with his body. And at over six feet, he'd be head and shoulders above her own five feet six.

Iris smiled to herself and sighed with satisfaction. Observing him like that had been rather pleasant. It was certainly nice to be able to stare at a man without his knowing or without causing any breach of propriety. She was usually the one on the receiving end of such scrutiny, as men weighed up her beauty to see if she was worthy of their attentions.

Now she was doing the same. And if she was in the market for a grumpy, rude, irritable recluse, his appearance would make him top of her list.

'So, have you finished staring at me?' he said, causing Iris to jump in her seat and her teacup to rattle in its saucer.

'How did you…? I was not staring at you.' She pulled her shoulders back in a demonstration of being affronted and placed the cup on the table with a defiant clink.

'I might be blind, but I'm not an imbecile. What else would you be doing, sitting there in silence, not moving?'

'I might have been staring into the fire? Or… Or…' Iris looked around the room for inspiration.

'Well, were you?'

She paused and turned back to face him. 'If you're so clever, can you tell what I am doing now?' She poked out her tongue and glared at him.

'No, but I suspect you are either pulling a rude face or making a rude gesture.'

'I would never make a rude gesture,' Iris said, completely taken aback.

'A rude face, then. What was it? Did you cock a snook, poke out your tongue?'

Iris crossed her arms, determined not to answer him.

'Well?'

'I poked out my tongue, if you must know. But it was nothing less than you deserved.'

He swirled his brandy. 'Is that always how you behave when someone takes you in out of the rain and gives you shelter? Or is it only when you're in the company of someone who is blind?'

'No, not usually,' she shot back. 'But it is how I behave when someone is rude to me.'

Iris wasn't sure if that was entirely true. As a young lady who had been taught to always behave with impeccably good manners in every situation, she had never poked her tongue out at anyone before, ever. But then, she had never met anyone who was so rude to her. Every other man she met socially did the opposite, going out of his way to try and impress her, to show himself to be an amiable, likeable young man. Whereas the Earl seemed determined to make her dislike him. And in that he was succeeding.

She waited for him to say something, to explain himself, to put an end to this embarrassing situation, but he said nothing. He merely took another sip of his brandy, as if there was nothing more to be said on the subject, and they sank back down into an even more uncomfortable silence.

Iris suppressed an annoyed sigh and stirred another sugar cube into her tea. The fire crackling in the grate and the occasional growl from the dog as he slept were the only noises breaking the silence. If he was going to continue in this manner, either not speaking, or when he did speak being insufferably rude, it was going to be a very long evening indeed.

Chapter Three

Theo ground his teeth together to stop a groan of exasperation from escaping. Having to spend the night in the company of this dizzy chatterbox was going to make this a very long evening indeed.

Not that all his evenings weren't long, but at least they were quiet. Just as he liked it. He scratched Max's head. The dog grunted his contentment. Max was all the company he needed. He did not need pretty young things coming into his home with their irritatingly sunny dispositions and mindless prattle.

He looked in the direction of the teaspoon clinking against the teacup. It was easy to tell that she was young and pretty. The swish of her skirts when she had first entered showed the quick, lithe movements of a young woman. And the tone in her voice was that of a woman who was used to being admired. It was obvious that when she spoke to a man she expected him to respond with rapt attention and flattery. Well, that was wasted on him. He had no time for young ladies who wanted men to shower them with compliments and fall under their spell every time they fluttered their eyelashes or pursed their pretty lips. The one good thing that had come from his injuries was that he would never again fall prey to such coquettishness.

'What's the dog's name?' she asked, her voice still holding that grating sing-song quality.

'Max.'

At the sound of his voice, Max stirred and sat up.

'Oh, aren't you a beauty?' Max's head moved from under his hand, and his paws padded across the floor to Lady Iris. 'Oh, yes, you are, you're quite the beauty.'

To Theo's disgust the traitorous Max's tail started thumping on the floor, encouraging her in her flattery and caresses. Unlike himself, Max was not immune to the attentions of an attractive woman.

'I've got a pug dog at home called Sookie. She's lovely too. Isn't she? Yes, she is. Oh, yes, she is. I think you and Sookie would be the best of friends, wouldn't you?'

The childlike tone of her voice made Theo wince, but the dog's yelp of encouragement and the increased vigour of his thumping tail suggested Max found nothing wrong with being doted on and spoken to as if he were a two-year-old child.

'She's a lovely, lovely dog…just like you, Maxie-Waxie.'

Theo clicked his fingers. 'Heel, Max,' he ground out. The dog was a noble Irish wolfhound, not a frivolous little pug dog, and should not be treated in a manner that undermined his dignity.

Maxie-Waxie, indeed.

Max slunk over to Theo and with a small groan of annoyance settled down at his feet. Theo scratched the dog's head in consolation, wishing he could explain to the animal that pretty women who owned pug dogs were to be avoided at all cost. They were frivolous, flighty and not to be trusted with anyone's heart, man or beast.

He also wished this damn storm would settle down so this Lady Iris Springfeld could be placed in a carriage and removed from his presence. But the howling in the trees, the scratching of the branches against the windows, and the persistent hissing of rain on the roof made it clear that the storm would not be over this night. He could only hope that tomorrow the roads would not be waterlogged and that she would not be forced to stay another day. Theo doubted if he could stand it.

A rhythmic tapping drew his attention back to Lady Iris. It seemed she was now drumming her fingers on the side table.

'This really is a rather lovely room.' He heard her stand up and move away. It was no longer the swish of a skirt that moved around the room, but the gentle rub of fabric from her trousers as she walked. When he had been standing beside her, he had estimated her height as about five feet six, so she must be swamped by his clothing. But the confident way she strode round the room suggested that she was not in the slightest bit embarrassed about being attired in such a manner. But then, there was no one to see her, was there? No real man to feel embarrassed in front of. No one whose opinion she should worry about. Only him, a man who was no threat to any woman.

He lifted his glass to throw back his drink but discovered the glass was empty. That irritating woman was driving him to drink, at least to drink even more than he usually did.

'In fact, the whole house is rather splendid. When was it built?' Her voice carried from across the room.

Was she taking an inventory? Weighing up his obvious disadvantages against what he was worth? If she was, she was wasting her time.

He drew in a deep breath before answering. 'The original castle was built in the mid-fifteenth century, but it has been added to constantly over the years.' Hopefully that would satisfy her.

'Yes, I noticed the castle ramparts when I was coming up the driveway—very scary, especially in a storm.' She gave an annoying little laugh.

Not scary enough to warn you off though, unfortunately, Theo wanted to add.

'This room I would guess is early Georgian. Spacious, ornate ceiling, large floor-to-ceiling windows, and that chandelier is rather magnificent. I wonder what it looks like when it's lit up.'

'I wouldn't know,' he said, hoping his terse manner would make her be quiet.

'No, I suppose not,' she said, her voice gentle, causing a small spark of guilt to erupt deep inside him. Of course he knew what the room was like, knew exactly how magnificent the chandelier looked when it was fully lit. How it sent light sparkling round the room. Hadn't he hosted many a social event in this very room before his accident? Hadn't he enjoyed seeing the house full of elegantly dressed people, all partaking of his hospitality? And hadn't he, most of all, enjoyed seeing Estelle dressed in all her finery? His beautiful fiancée had always been the most attractive woman in the room. And hadn't he relished the look of envy on every man's face?

But that was before he knew what beautiful young women were really like. That was before the world had turned its back on him. He poured himself another brandy, and furiously swirled the aromatic drink round in the glass.

She returned to her seat and said nothing more. Perhaps now she was actually going to be quiet. But no. Within a matter of seconds the relentless drumming of the fingers started again, until it felt as if the noise was crashing into his skull and drowning out the sound of the raging storm.

He reached out to still the noise. His hand covered hers, the skin soft and warm against his palm. Momentarily he froze, his mind swamped by unwanted sensations, then his hand jerked back as if scalded.

'Stop doing that. It's annoying,' he snapped with more force than he intended.

'Oh, sorry. I didn't mean to… I, um… What exactly was I doing?'

Her constricted voice sounded as confused as he was feeling.

'You were drumming your fingers on the table.'

'Oh, was I? Sorry.'

Why did she have to make him feel like such a brute? He was in his own house. Surely if he didn't want her making that infernal racket, he had every right to stop her. And why did touching her hand have such a profound and unexpected effect on him? He made a tight fist to try and crush the lingering imprint of her silken skin.

'I'm surprised you could hear it above the sound of the wind.' She gave another annoying little laugh, stood up and resumed walking round the room. He tried not to listen to the sound of the trouser legs rubbing against each other. The last thing he needed to think about was young women's legs.

Fabric rustled loudly as she pushed back the curtains. 'The rain's coming down even heavier now and the wind is so strong the rain is almost horizontal. Thank goodness I found your house when I did. I'd hate to be still wandering around in this weather.'

She was doing it again. Making him feel like an inhospitable brute. But then, that was exactly what he was. He was inhospitable because he did not want guests in his house. And the accident had turned him into a brute, a man that Estelle couldn't bear to look at.

But the unwelcome visitor was right. She had needed refuge from the storm and had not chosen to invade his privacy. Presumably if given a choice of where to take sanctuary it would not have been with him. He had no right to treat her like the enemy simply because circumstances had thrown them together. And tomorrow she would be gone. Then he could forget all about her. All he had to do was endure this one night and try and remember how he was supposed to behave when hosting a guest.

'Yes, it was lucky you found this house,' he said, trying to sound less irritated. 'There are no other houses for miles around.'

The curtain rustled back into place as she dropped it and walked back to her chair. She emitted a small sigh, the leather creaking slightly as she sat down, then those fingers started drumming again. Theo clasped his hand tightly around his brandy balloon so he would not be tempted to touch her one more time.

'Oh, sorry,' she said. 'I forgot. You don't like that noise, do you? Well, if you don't want me to keep annoying you by tapping my fingers, you're going to have to make conversation.'

'Am I?' Theo was unsure which would be the greater annoyance.

'Yes, you are. And if you don't want to talk to me, then you're going to have to listen to me talking to you. You've probably noticed that I'm not very good at keeping silent.'

'Yes, I had noticed,' he said, his voice bearing an uncanny resemblance to one of Max's growls. But it did not have the intended effect. Instead of being cowed she gave another of those exasperating laughs.

'So, shall I tell you all about myself and my family?'

He made no response.

'All right, if you insist. As you know, my name is Lady Iris Springfeld. I have an older sister called Hazel, who is married to Lucas Darkwood. They have a beautiful little daughter called Lucy. I also have a younger sister called Daisy, and an older brother called Nathaniel.'

She stopped talking. Hopefully she had exhausted all she had to say. No such luck.

'So, any questions so far?'

He made no response.

'No? All right, then, I'll continue. We live in London—Belgravia—but have a family estate in Dorset. My mother and I are visiting Lord and Lady Walberton for their house party. Lady Walberton is one of my mother's oldest friends—well, I don't mean she's really old, but they've known each other for simply ages. Do you know them? The Walbertons, I mean.'

She waited for his response. 'Yes,' he finally said.

'Oh, good. They're rather delightful, aren't they?'

Theo shifted in his seat. He had attended many parties at the Walberton estate. They were a regular part of the local social calendar and provided an opportunity for men who were seeking a bride to inspect what was on offer that Season. That had been where he had met Estelle.

He moved on his chair to try and find a more comfortable position and to drive out all thoughts of his previous life. 'If they are so delightful, why did you decide to escape their house party and go wandering around the countryside on your own?' Theo said, his annoyance directed as much at his memories as at this babbling young woman.

'Hmm, well, that wasn't because of Lord or Lady Walberton.'

'Pray tell, what would be so dreadful as to send a young woman out into the wilds of Cornwall during a storm?' He could hear the sarcasm dripping off his voice. Had she been trying to teach some besotted young man a lesson? Was she piqued because she wasn't getting enough attention? Were there other young women at the party who were prettier than her, or had nicer gowns and she needed to draw attention back to herself?

'Well, there wasn't a storm when I set off and I didn't realise the weather could get quite so wild, quite so quickly, but I suppose, well, I was a tiny bit bored. Balls and parties are such fun at the beginning of your first Season, but this is my fifth, and, as much as I like socialising, sometimes they can get tiresome.' She released a small sigh. 'When I was first presented at Court I had such romantic notions of what the Season would be like. It was like a dream, doing my curtsy in front of Princess Alexandra. She's Queen Victoria's daughter-in-law, you know.'

He said nothing. Of course he knew that, but he did not want to encourage her in her ramblings.

'Then I attended my first ball and I loved every moment of it—it was like being in a fairy tale—but now, well, if I'm being terribly honest, it is starting to lose a bit of its sparkle.'

'So why haven't you married? Isn't that what Seasons are for?' he asked, then mentally castigated himself. He did not care one iota and had no desire to hear more of her relentless chatter.

It was her turn to remain silent. All he heard was the slight movement of clothing, as if she was shrugging a shoulder.

'Whatever your reasons, you're probably better off single,' he said in consolation.

'Like you,' she said, then gasped. 'Oh, sorry. That was rude and rather personal. You too probably have reasons why you're not married that you don't want to discuss with a stranger.'

He turned to face her. Was she as blind as him? Was the reason why he was single not staring her in the face? Could she not see his scars? Surely when she had scrutinised him earlier this evening she had not failed to notice just how disfiguring they were. She must realise that he had a deformity that would cause any sensible woman to immediately reject him.

'My younger sister, Daisy, vows and declares she won't marry either,' she continued as if oblivious to his appearance. 'Daisy says that marriage is enslavement for a woman. But Mother and Father are very happy together and no one would ever describe my mother as Father's slave. If anything, it's quite the reverse.' She laughed at her joke. 'And my older sister, Hazel, has never been happier since she married Lucas.'

He turned his face back to the fire, not wanting to hear about her family's happy marriages.

'But then, they all married for love.'

A contemptuous scoff was out of his mouth before he realised it. Love? That fickle emotion. Was that what she was waiting for? Was that why she was yet to marry? Well, she was in for some disappointments and harsh life lessons if she was pursuing that particular fantasy.

'Now, don't be like that. I saw how Hazel blossomed when she fell in love with her husband, and how happy she is. Real love is a wonderful thing.'

'And how do you know if it's real?' he retorted. What on earth was he doing? Discussing absurd romantic notions with this vacuous young woman? He needed to stop this. Now.

'I'm sure I'll know when it happens.'

He shook his head in disbelief. 'Pray tell, how are you going to know when it happens?' This frivolous young woman knew nothing. Hadn't he thought he had once been in love and been loved? And hadn't he been wrong?

'Well…'

She paused and he could hear a finger tapping, presumably on a chin or a cheek, as she contemplated the question. He should never have asked. He had no interest in this young woman's opinion on anything, especially not love, but her optimism had angered him and he had spoken before thinking.

'Hazel said she knew she was in love with Lucas when she couldn't stop thinking about him, when all she wanted was to be with him, that he had become the centre of her world.'

He scoffed again. 'That sounds more like a mad obsession.'

'Hmm, yes, perhaps. That's what Hazel said as well. She said it was a bit like going slightly mad. But she also said it was rather a wonderful madness that made you giddy with happiness.'

'And were none of the men at the Walbertons' house party causing you to go mad or giddy?' Not that he cared.

She laughed again, proving his point.

'Well, yes, some of them were driving me rather insane, but I'm pretty sure it wasn't love.'

'Driving you so mad you had to flee into a storm.'

'Yes, rather silly of me, I know.'

'So if you're already mad and giddy, how are you going to tell the difference and know when you're in love?'

Another rustle of clothing as she shrugged. 'Well, I'm just hoping that when it happens I'll know—just as Hazel said I would.'

'Then I wish you luck in finding a man worthy of your giddy madness,' he said, neither caring nor believing that she would ever find that illusory state.

'Thank you,' she replied, her voice equally sarcastic as his own. 'I assume you've never been giddy yourself?'

Theo recoiled at the absurdity of this idea. This young woman really was quite mad.

'I'm only joking. You don't strike me as the giddy sort.'

That had to be an understatement. 'Indeed, madam, I am not given to flights of giddiness.'

'No, I don't suppose you are. I imagine you're always completely sensible. And a man who doesn't believe in love would never allow himself to become giddy and certainly not to go mad over a young lady.'

Theo placed his brandy balloon on the table with more force than he intended. Why he was allowing this woman to blather on about love he had no idea. It was not a subject he wished to talk about or even think about. While young ladies may still harbour romantic illusions, love was something he had given up on six years ago. He even knew the exact date when all such delusion in that direction had disappeared from his mind, when reality had literally crashed down on him. Despite being left blind, his eyes had been opened to how fickle love was. But Lady Iris would have to discover that for herself.

As if unable to sit still for more than a second, she stood up and wandered around the room. He tried to ignore the sound of her picking up items and placing them back down again. She was obviously bored, but he had no desire to engage her in further conversation. Not if it led to ridiculous discussions on the nature of love. If she wanted entertainment she could find it herself—he certainly wasn't going to provide it. But Max had other ideas. He stirred at Theo's feet and padded across the room again to join their guest.

'You must feel trapped by the storm as well, don't you, Maxie-Waxie?' she said, to the accompaniment of a thumping tail. Max's obvious pleasure suggested that he, for one, did not mind being trapped inside during a storm with Lady Iris.

'Well, the room's big enough. Shall you and I go for a nice walk?'

Max yipped his approval, and their footsteps faded as they moved to the far end of the room. Theo tried not to listen. As long as she wasn't bashing his ears with her endless chatter she could walk around the room to her heart's content.

Eventually, after much childish talk about Max being a clever dog, a handsome dog, a friendly dog, they returned to the fire and Max chose to sit at her feet, his tail continuing its happy thumping. Theo braced himself for more mindless conversation. She said nothing. Good.

'Now you're doing it,' she said as her soft hand touched his.

'What?' he barked out in surprise.

'Drumming your fingers. I thought you said you didn't like the noise.'

Theo had been unaware of his actions, but it was impossible to not be aware of the warm hand encasing his own. Nor could he ignore his own reaction, that jolt that shot through his body, the fire that erupted deep within him, the craving for more, that was all but consuming him.

He tugged his hand away. Young ladies did not touch gentlemen in that way, and surely she must know that. Her actions were merely further proof that she did not see him as she saw other men. If he needed evidence of how this Lady Iris regarded him, as something less than a real man, then that touch would provide it.

'I'm merely getting tired,' he lied, his voice annoyingly constricted. 'I believe it is time to retire.' At least it was time he retired from her unsettling company. He reached across to grab the bell. 'I'll ask Charles to escort you to your room.'

He rang the bell vigorously. 'Weather permitting, the coach will be waiting to take you home tomorrow morning when you rise.' *Please,* he said in silent prayer, *make sure the weather is indeed permitting*.

'You rang, my lord,' Charles said as he appeared.

'Yes. Please show Lady Iris to her room,' he replied.

Hearing her rise from her chair, Theo stood up.

'Goodnight, then, and thank you once again for your hospitality.' There was no note of sarcasm in her voice, but surely she could not consider his behaviour hospitable.

'Goodnight, Lady Iris,' he said with a bow.

As she walked from the room, Max rose from the floor and began padding after her.

'Max, heel,' he called, shocked at the animal's easy disloyalty.

'Goodbye, Maxie-Waxie,' she said. 'At least someone will miss me when I leave tomorrow,' she added before the door closed behind her. Max emitted a small whimper then settled down on the rug in front of the fire where he liked to sleep at night.

Theo stood for a few minutes, still turned away from the fire, staring at a door he couldn't see. It had been an unexpectedly disturbing night. As soon as he had resumed his usual equanimity he too would retire to his bedroom and put all thoughts of Lady Iris and her silky, smooth skin out of his mind.

Chapter Four

~~~~~~~~~~~~~~~~~~~~~~~~~~~~~~

Iris followed Charles up the stairs and along the hallway to her bedroom, pleased to see that candles had been lit along the way. It was amazing what a difference a bit of warm light could make. The house was now not as intimidating as when she had stood outside, looking up at those forbidding turrets. The hallway was like those in the homes of virtually every other aristocratic family she knew. Rich carpets underfoot, walls adorned with paintings, and an abundance of antique furniture decorated with a seemingly endless array of vases, and silver, porcelain and ceramic figurines, presumably collected over the many years the family had inhabited this grand home.

Several lit candelabra had been placed in her bedroom, which was also pleasant and welcoming, with pale blue silk-lined walls, a canopied four-poster bed, a crackling fire and comfortable furniture. Despite the Earl being unsociable, it was apparent that the servants continued to maintain the home and keep it clean and well-aired.

'Thank you, Charles. For everything,' Iris said, meaning every word. He, if not the Earl, had made her feel that she was not intruding.

'You're welcome, my lady,' Charles said, turning down the edge of her bedding. 'It's nice to have a guest in the house. It has been far too long.'

Iris tilted her head in question, but Charles, the loyal servant that he was, merely bowed before leaving. She wasn't going to get any more information out of him.

On the bed a neatly folded nightshirt had been left for her. Iris picked it up and frowned.

A nightshirt.

She shook it out and shrugged. It was no more than she should expect. Charles could hardly go into the sleeping maids' bedrooms and remove their nightclothes for an unexpected guest.

She held it against herself. Just like the trousers and shirt, it was much too big, and the high quality of the finely woven linen suggested it belonged to a gentleman. She would be sleeping in Theo Crighton's nightshirt. It was a strangely intimate thing to do, and, if she had to admit, rather exciting.

That surprising little shiver rippled through her body.

What was this odd reaction to the Earl she kept having? Men never affected her the way he did. Since she made her debut five years ago, men had been endlessly attentive, at times more attentive than she would wish, but none had caused her to be so conscious of herself. None had caused her skin to tingle or her heart to flutter. Perhaps it was merely the challenge presented by a man who paid her no attention. Or perhaps it was because he was unlike any man she had met before—aloof, mysterious and rather intriguing.

She took a tentative sniff of the nightshirt, trying to once again detect his lingering scent. There it was, just a hint under the smell of the laundry soap. And there it went again, that little shiver that was now almost a familiar sensation. It made her want to close her eyes and sigh in response to the feelings that were engulfing her. She looked around the room. No one was present. He would never know. No one would know. So what harm was there if she did exactly what she wanted to? No harm at all. She buried her face in the nightshirt, inhaled deeply, then did indeed sigh loudly. It was delicious and, if anything was going to make her giddy and slightly mad, his masculine scent would.

Giggling at her somewhat improper behaviour, she removed her shirt and trousers, pulled the nightshirt over her head and wondered if the next time he wore it he would be able to detect her scent on it. It was impossible to imagine the Earl doing something as silly as burying his face in his nightshirt and breathing deeply. He was far too controlled for such frivolous behaviour.

She snuffed out all but one of the candles, climbed into bed and sighed again. The everconsiderate Charles had thought to have a bedwarming pan run over her sheets. Lovely.

Blowing out her bedside candle, she snuggled down into the warm bed and stared at the crackling fire.

It had been a long time since she had gone to bed this early—not since before her coming out. Usually she was up dancing at a ball to the early hours of the morning, or going to the theatre, taking a late supper, or attending one of the many other dazzling Society events held throughout the Season. But after such an eventful day she had to admit she was tired, and, as her nanny would have once said, an early night never did anyone any harm.

But, despite her physical fatigue, her brain was still wide awake, and sleep would not come. Her mind continued to whirl with images of everything that had happened during her adventurous day.

When she had left for her walk she never thought her day would end with her dressed in a man's nightshirt, sleeping in the house of a strange earl. And he *was* strange, in more than one way, not just because she had not been formally introduced to him and he was unknown to her family. He was quite decidedly a most unusual man.

Iris knew she should be concerned about her situation. If anyone found out it could ruin her reputation, and possibly destroy her chances of making a good marriage. But, surprisingly, that was not worrying her as much as it should. It would upset her mother, and for that she would be deeply sorry, but, as she had not yet met a man she could truly love and whom she knew truly loved her, marriage still seemed like an unlikely prospect.

Love.

She pulled her bedcover up to her eyes, as

if someone could see her blushes in the darkened room. Why had Iris actually talked about love, and to a man like him? Someone who was quite clearly scornful of such things? He must think her such a flighty featherbrain. But she did believe in love, even though she had never actually experienced it.

She wondered if the Earl had been hurt in love and that was why he was so cynical, then dismissed the possibility. Such a man would be incapable of any tender emotions, and no woman could possibly fall in love with such a morose man. She certainly couldn't. She rolled over in the bed as if to emphasise that point.

As intriguing as he was, and as much as he elicited rather unusual and rather thrilling reactions from her, he was not the sort of man she could ever see herself married to. She liked to have fun, to laugh, dance and enjoy herself, while the Earl looked like the sort of man who didn't know the meaning or point of having a good time.

The wind continued to howl against the side of the house, making its way down the chimney and causing the flames to flicker in the grate. Iris snuggled deeper under her warm bedcover. Yes, the Earl was a strange man indeed. He was decidedly different from every man she had ever met. His stern, handsome face entered her mind, and she couldn't help but wonder how he had got his scars. Presumably the same terrible event that had scarred him had also left him blind.

Was it some awful accident that had caused him to be so brooding, alone in his castle? Or had he always been such a misery? Whatever it was, he did not need to be that way. No one in Iris's family was ever miserable, at least not for long. Her mother would not tolerate it. She tolerated most things, but never self-pity. Everyone was expected to buck up and count their blessings.

Someone should give the Earl a good talking-to and her mother would be the perfect person to do it. But her mother would never meet the Earl. Unfortunately, tonight's adventure would have to remain Iris's little secret if she was to protect her reputation.

Iris sighed. That meant the Earl would remain just as he was, hidden away in his castle, cut off from the world and nursing his grievances.

Such a shame. Such a waste. She yawned more loudly than was entirely proper for a well-brought-up young lady. There must be someone out there who could make the Earl smile and realise that there was still joy in the world. Maybe even teach him that love really did exist. It just wouldn't be her.

With that thought in mind, she drifted off into sleep, only to have it torn away from her when a scream ripped through the air. She sat up in bed and looked around. The dying fire was still burning slightly in the grate, providing some light, but there was no sign of what had caused that chilling sound.

Was it the wind? It was still howling outside, but no more so than it had when she fell asleep. Was it part of her dream? Was the castle haunted? She bit her lip and reminded herself that ghosts did not exist and castles were never haunted except in gothic novels.

Then she heard it again. A man was screaming out as if the hounds of hell were ripping him apart. It was no dream. Nor was it a ghost—it sounded very real and very distressed.

Her heart pounding hard against the wall of her chest, Iris climbed out of bed and with shaking fingers lit her candle. Holding the candlestick holder out in front of her, she tentatively opened the bedroom door then stopped. She had no idea where the cry had come from, did not know the house and did not know what she would do if or when she found the source of the cry, but she had to do something. She could hardly go back to bed and pretend that scream had never happened.

Slowly, she edged her way down the now dark hallway, the candlelight flickering against the walls, her shadow appearing large and unsettling.

Then she heard it again, that mournful, painful cry coming from behind her. She turned and edged her way through the semi-darkness in the direction from which the cry had come. There were so many rooms in this large house, and the darkness was making her disorientated and confused.

The cry came again, louder, more plaintive, and it was definitely from the room at the end of the hallway. Placing her hand over the lone candle so it would not be blown out, she moved swiftly in the direction of the scream.

Her hand clasped the doorknob. She stopped and took in a deep breath. She had no idea what she was about to confront but there was no other option. A man was enduring some sort of torture. She looked back up the dark hallway and wished someone else, anyone else, was about who could help, but there was no one. The servants' quarters would be at the top of the house, too far away for them to hear. It would be so good to have the ever-reliable Charles with her, but in the darkness she would never be able to find his room. And even if she could it would waste time. No, it was all up to her now. Pushing open the door, she braced herself for whatever horror she was about to confront.

Chapter Five

Iris was unsure what to expect, but her imagination had spun off into wild flights of fancy. If she were in a gothic novel, then inevitably the Earl would be under attack from a supernatural demon and she, the romantic heroine, would have to save him. As unpleasant as that would be, it was still a much better option than his being attacked by a human demon, against whom Iris suspected she would stand no chance.

Slowly she opened the door and peeked around the edge. There were no demons of any kind, human or otherwise. The only occupant of the room was the Earl, thrashing about in the bed, the bedclothes tangled around him, his face contorted but his eyes closed.

A nightmare.

Her first reaction was to breathe a sigh of

relief. Just a nightmare. Then she admonished herself for being so selfish. The man *was* being attacked by demons, neither supernatural nor human, but demons of his own making. How could she possibly feel relieved about that, just because it meant she was in no danger? Although in reality he too was in no danger, in his head, whatever demons he was wrestling with were very real. As was his agony. He still needed to be saved and there was no one else around to do it.

She looked back up the dark corridor, then slipped around the door.

This was much worse than arriving unannounced at the home of someone to whom she had not been formally introduced. Worse than visiting a man's house alone. Even worse than staying the night in a man's home without a chaperon. What she was about to do bordered on the scandalous.

She was unmarried. This was a man's bedroom. They were alone. It more than bordered on scandalous—it was the very definition of scandal. But what choice did she have? And the reality was, they *were* alone. No one would know what she was doing. Breaches of propriety only became breaches when they became public knowledge. And scandalous behaviour couldn't become a scandal unless people were talking about it.

Iris nodded to herself, pleased with her logic, and quietly walked further into the room. She stood at the side of the high, wide bed, the Earl still thrashing about in the centre. There was nothing for it. She was going to have to join him on the bed if she was to free him from his torment.

Reminding herself that it was only a scandal if people knew and were talking about it, she placed the candlestick on his bedside table, gathered up the folds of the voluminous nightshirt and climbed onto the bed.

What would her mother say if she could see her now? Iris hated to think. While she might be commended for her concern over someone in distress, she knew her mother would not be able to excuse her daughter from joining a man in his bed.

But your mother is someone else who will never know.

The Earl continued to twist and turn, his head tossing from side to side on the pillow. She reached down and wrapped her arms around his shoulders, which were slick with sweat. He turned towards her and clung on like a drowning man. He needed help, needed her, so to hell with propriety. No matter what anyone might or might not say, Iris knew she was doing the right thing.

She pulled him closer to her body, placed his head on her shoulder, and gently stroked his hair. That was what her mother had always done when she was a child and having a bad dream, and it had always provided such comfort.

'There, there, you're safe now,' she said in the same soothing voice her mother had always used. 'I'm here now. Everything is going to be all right,' she added. It was also what her mother would have said.

His thrashing became less intense and she smiled. Yes, she was doing the right thing, and surely no one could disapprove, even if the Earl's chest was bare and he was possibly completely naked. She had no idea what state he was in under the twisted sheets, and, as a well-brought-up young lady, she should not even be speculating.

She gently ran her hand across his sweat-soaked brow, brushing back his damp hair.

His thrashing subsided further but he continued to gasp out *no, no,* repeatedly.

She tilted her head and leant it gently on top of his. 'There's nothing to fear,' she murmured. 'I'm here now and nothing or no one will hurt you.' Her lips were close to his forehead, so she gently kissed him, telling herself that she was merely doing what her mother would have done.

He relaxed in her arms, although his breathing was still laboured. He was mumbling, and she could feel his heart pounding in his chest. He needed her, needed to be comforted.

Her kisses moved down slightly to his cheek. Just to comfort him, of course, for no other reason. Then her lips lightly skimmed his lips. That was purely to still his fevered mutterings in the best way she could think of, for absolutely no other reason.

And it worked. Proving that she had nothing to admonish herself for. His breathing settled down and he relaxed completely in her arms, his still head resting on her shoulder, his chest pressed against hers.

She should go now, gently lower him back onto the bed and quietly slip away. The demons had left him and there was no reason for her to remain.

But she stayed, enjoying the feeling of having this muscular man in her arms. Loving the sensation of holding him. She placed her hand on his chest. His heart was still rapidly pounding. That convinced her.

She needed to stay. It would be wrong to leave until he had completely settled down. Once she had confirmation that the demons had completely left his mind then she would depart. In the meantime, there was no reason why she shouldn't continue to have her arms wrapped around him, his head on her shoulder. It was only right and proper.

She nodded, as if, since she was alone in the room, there was no one else to give her permission, so she granted it to herself. Her hand continued to rest on his chest, feeling the strong pounding of his heart, then moved slowly across the sweat-slickened muscles of his chest, causing her own heart to increase its furious beating. In the warm light of the flickering candle, his skin appeared bathed in a golden glow, showing off his sculpted muscles to perfection. He really was rather magnificent. Her fingers traced a line over his shoulders, and she could sense their strength and power. It was as if he had been chiselled out of marble, except that he was warm and very much alive. She traced her finger along a prominent vein that ran the length of his upper arm, then back up again.

Slowly her hand moved up his neck, to his cheek, running across the dark stubble of his unshaven face. When she had first met him, she had been tempted to place her finger in the cleft in the middle of his chin. So that was what she did now. After all, she thought, smiling to herself, she might never get another opportunity.

His face was now completely composed. She placed her hand back on his chest, just to check that he was indeed settled. His heart had returned to a regular rhythm. She had her confirmation. There was no justification for staying a moment longer.

She paused and touched his chest one more time. His heart now pounded slowly and strongly under her fingers. He was completely recovered. It was all over. It was time she left.

As gently as possible she unwrapped her arms from around his chest and lowered his head back to the pillow. Then, moving as slowly as she could, making sure she caused no disturbance, she eased herself to the side of the bed, determined not to wake the Earl, who was now sleeping restfully.

But she failed.

He sprang up. Jumped off the bed and turned towards her, his body rigid.

'What? Where?' his panicked voice cried out. His arms flailed in the air, his breath coming in quick, harsh gasps. Then his arms dropped to his sides. His spine straightened and he pulled back his shoulders.

'What are you doing here?' he asked, his voice cold.

Iris wasn't sure if the *you* he was referring to was her or someone in his dream, but as she was the only other person present she decided she had better respond.

'It's just me. Iris Springfeld.'

'I know who you are. What are you doing here, in my room?'

'How did you know it was me?' After all, he couldn't see her and a few moments ago he thought he was being attacked by some invisible demon or other.

'Your scent. You smell of orange blossom, and the rosewater you presumably apply to your face.'

And you smell all masculine and lemony, Iris was tempted to inform him, but instead she bit her lip to stop that embarrassing revelation from escaping.

'Answer my question,' he said sharply. 'What are you doing in my room, in my bed?'

Good question. What was she *still* doing

here? She looked over at him and her hand shot up to cover her mouth, but not quickly enough to stop a small squeak of surprise from escaping. He was scowling at her, but presumably he didn't know he was completely naked.

She was in a bedroom with a naked man. Now, this really was scandalous. And what was even more scandalous was that she was staring at him as if she had every right to do so.

Her hands flew to her eyes to cover them from the sight they had just seen, something a young lady should never see before her wedding night. Then, as if with a will of their own, her fingers slowly splayed open and she peeped out at the naked man standing in front of her.

Her hands moved from her eyes, where they were serving no purpose, and covered her mouth to stop any further gasps from escaping. She should not be doing this. It was so wrong. But how could she not? He was standing in front of her. *Naked.*

'Well, are you going to answer me?' he demanded.

Iris tried to answer, but instead she merely gulped and continued to stare at him.

And she wanted to do more than just stare. The temptation to run her hands over him was almost overwhelming, and her fingers were actually itching to do so. She swallowed again, lowered her hands from her mouth and tucked them under her legs, as if they needed to be restrained from doing what they longed to do.

This really was a shocking situation for any young lady to find herself in. Her intentions on entering his room had been honourable, but some of her subsequent behaviour had been decidedly improper. If he was horrified to find her in his room, heaven only knew what he would think if he realised that she had stroked his cheek, his chest, his lips.

'I...um... I was just...'

He placed his hands on his hips, waiting for the explanation that she was finding herself incapable of forming.

Her mind was too occupied by what she was seeing. While she was trying to tell herself to behave, to answer his questions and leave as quickly as possible, the part of her brain that controlled her eyes was not listening. They continued their own unforgivable progress down his body, taking in the dark hair on his chest, which thinned out into a line as it moved down his flat stomach. Her hand flew back to her mouth to cover the gasp that threatened to escape as her gaze moved lower.

She should not be looking. She really should

not be looking. This was unforgivable for so many reasons, and not just because it was not the way young ladies behaved. She was taking advantage of him, and she should be thoroughly ashamed of herself for acting in such a wanton matter. Yes, ashamed, she thought as her eyes lingered. Then her gaze flicked back up to his face, which was contorted with annoyance while he waited for her answer.

Tell him.

'Um…you're probably unaware of this,' she said, then paused, 'but I brought a lit candle with me and you're…well, you're standing in the middle of the room…and you're completely…'

She tumbled to her side as the sheet was wrenched off the bed from underneath her. When she sat back up and looked in his direction the lower half of his body had disappeared behind white linen, the sheet draped around his narrow hips. But there was still his chest on display, and an emboldened Iris felt no compunction about feasting her eyes on that part of his anatomy. After all, if he hadn't wanted her to look, he should have covered himself up completely, she reasoned, or was that justified?

'You still haven't answered my question,' he barked at her. 'What are you doing here?

Or do you make a habit of this sort of behaviour, coming into men's rooms in the middle of the night? Uninvited? And climbing into their beds?'

Now that some of him at least was covered her brain was able to function a bit better and she could focus on countering his accusations.

'No, I most certainly do not.' She jumped off the bed and placed her hands firmly on her hips, even though the defiant stance was wasted on him. 'You were crying out in your sleep, if you must know.'

The anger on his face slowly subsided, to be replaced by a hard look of reproach, either for her or for himself.

'And what did you think you were going to do? Rescue me?'

Iris shrugged. 'I didn't know what to think. I didn't know why you were screaming out.' She looked up at him and remembered how he had been when she had entered the room, his handsome face distorted in pain and distress. 'You were having a bad dream,' she said gently.

'A dream!' he all but shouted. 'You came into my room because of a dream?'

'Well, yes. It was a very bad dream.' She indicated the tousled sheets, then remembered that he couldn't see them.

'But still just a dream,' he spat out.

Iris shrugged. 'Sometimes dreams can be just as frightening as real life, or even more so.'

He shook his head as if not believing her.

'And, as I said, it was a very bad dream. You weren't just crying out. You were tossing and turning…your heart was pounding hard.'

He tilted his head and Iris hoped he wasn't wondering how she knew about the rate of his heartbeat. She didn't want him to know where her touch had taken her.

'So I really couldn't leave you like that, could I?' she raced on.

He drew in a deep breath and exhaled slowly. 'Dreams cannot hurt you and I am not a child who needs comforting.'

He was wrong. Dreams could hurt you and he had quite clearly been in pain. Something terrible had caused his nightmare. Something or someone had hurt him. Something was causing his belligerence. Possibly the same thing that had caused him to cut himself off from the world, and she was curious to know what. But now was not the time to ask such questions.

'Everyone needs to be comforted at times,' she said instead, wanting to add, *And you, I suspect, more than most.*

Instead of arguing with her he merely huffed out his disagreement.

'Do you know what the dream was about?' she asked, keeping her voice low and soothing.

'I do not,' he barked back. 'Nor do I want to discuss it with you.'

'It's just that—' Iris raised a shoulder, undeterred by his fury '—whenever we had bad dreams as children Mother always got us to tell her what they were about. She said that talking about them was how the bogeyman lost his power.'

He said nothing. Merely remained standing in the middle of the room, his hands now back on his hips.

'So that's why I think you should talk about it, so it loses its power.'

'I...am...not...a...child,' he finally said, his words drawn out, his anger barely contained. 'I am not frightened of the bogeyman and I do not require mothering.'

'I know... I just thought...'

'Thinking is one thing that you do not appear to do much of, Lady Iris. Intelligence is clearly not one of your strong suits.'

Iris glared at him. That was what everyone assumed. Because of the way she looked, everyone thought she could not possibly have a brain in her head. Few people outside the family ever wanted to hear her opinions. All men ever expected of her was to look pretty, to laugh at the appropriate times, and to enjoy their attention and flattery. And the Earl was no different. Even if he couldn't actually see the way she looked, he was still making the same assumptions about her as every other man she had met.

'How dare you?' she seethed. 'Just because I tried to help you doesn't mean you have the right to insult me.'

'And just because you want to mother me doesn't mean you have the right to barge into my bedroom in the middle of the night.'

'I did not barge in. And I do not want to mother you.' She looked him up and down in defiance. Then looked him up and down one more time, somewhat less defiantly and somewhat more appreciatively.

'If you weren't here to save me, then what were you doing in my room? Why were you on my bed? And why are you still in my bedroom?'

Iris swallowed. It was a good question. The real reason why she had stayed in his room after he had calmed down had nothing to do with mothering him, but she could hardly tell him the truth.

She could hardly tell him it was because she wanted to look at him, that she wanted to hold him, to touch him, and that she had done just that. She could hardly inform him that she knew what his muscular chest felt like, knew what it was like to run her fingers over his stubbled cheek, to touch his lips with her own.

She clasped her hands together, as if they contained a memory of his hard body, his soft lips, his rough cheeks.

Then she reminded herself of just how rude he was being to her, when she had only wanted to help. He didn't know what she had done and had no right to rebuke her. Instead, he should be thanking her for trying to save him from whatever demons were torturing his dreams.

'You really are the most infuriating, un-grateful man,' she said, preferring to be angry with him rather than thinking about her own inappropriate behaviour. 'You can't even be grateful when someone tries to help you.'

'I don't need your help, or anyone else's.'

'Well,' she said, her hands returning de-fiantly to her hips in imitation of his angry stance, 'the next time you cry out in the middle of the night, don't expect me to come running.'

The edge of his lip curled, presumably in disbelief at her statement. Was he thinking the same as her? There would not be a *next time*. After tonight she would probably never see the Earl again.

'Well, I'll go, then, if that's how you feel.' She sent him a fierce glare, then remembered that even her best glare was wasted on him, and looked back at the tousled bed, where moments ago he had been uncontrollably thrashing around.

'Perhaps I should just straighten the sheets and covers before I go so you can get a good night's sleep.'

She moved towards the bed, but her progress was halted when he grabbed her arm and barked out, 'Leave it.'

He really was insufferably rude.

'I just thought...'

'You just thought that you'd mother me one more time before you left. I do not want your help and, as I have already said, I do not need your mothering.'

'Oh, very well,' she huffed out, still looking down at the messy bed and wanting to tidy it up. How on earth he thought he was going to get a good night's sleep in such tangled bedding she did not know, but if that was what he wanted, well, be it on his own head.

He released her arm. 'Just go,' he said.

She huffed out another disapproving sigh, but, as there was nothing left to do or say, there was no reason for her to remain in his room a minute longer.

'Well, you appear to be all right now,' she said as she picked up her candlestick. 'Back to your old grumpy self. So I'll leave you to try and get some sleep in your destroyed bed.'

Although he could not see her, she lifted her head high and swept out of the room, determined that her exit would be one full of self-righteous indignation. At the doorway she stopped and turned. Even in a state of self-righteous indignation she could at least indulge herself in one last look at that exposed chest. After all, as they both knew, there was not going to be a *next time,* and she was not going to be able to feast her eyes on him ever again.

Chapter Six

Unbelievable. There was no other word for it. It was unbelievable. She was unbelievable.

When he heard the door click closed behind her, Theo climbed back into bed and wrestled with the sheets and bedcovers, trying to get them into some semblance of order. He had no idea where his nightshirt was, having pulled it off some time during the night, and there was no point trying to find it now.

He tugged at the tangled top sheet and pulled it up over himself, still cursing under his breath about that infuriating Lady Iris. Just who did she think she was, coming into his room uninvited? The last thing he wanted was some interfering woman who thought she could save the poor, unfortunate blind man.

Could she be more annoying? He doubted it. And then she had the audacity to act all haughty and offended, when all he had done was express his objections to her presence in what was, to his mind, a very restrained manner.

What on earth was she expecting? That he'd be eternally grateful to her? He was not a child and he did not need some do-gooder trying to turn him into one, and she needed to realise that.

He tugged at the twisted sheet. What was wrong with her? It was just a bad dream, for God's sake. He'd had them before and he'd no doubt have them again. There was no need for her to get quite so dramatic.

As he lay down on the pillow vague memories of his nightmare drifted back into his mind, flames lapping at the edge of his consciousness. It was a familiar dream, one that had often resurfaced over the last six years, but tonight's dream contained something else. Something different. Something gentle and tender. A woman's caresses, her light kisses, her soft body.

Had she touched him, caressed his face, his chest, or was that just something he had conjured up in his fevered state? He must have dreamt it, because he was also sure he had felt her lips on his forehead. That would never happen. No one would ever kiss him there, not on those ugly, disfiguring scars.

Damn that woman. She was even starting to invade his dreams now. He sat up and punched the pillow, trying to make it more comfortable while exorcising some of his rage. He neither wanted nor needed her help, and certainly did not want her caresses or kisses, even imagined ones. He knew the danger of letting a pretty young woman like Iris Springfeld into his life. He knew how easy it would be to fall under her spell. As enticing as it was to consider repeating the same mistake, it was too high a price to pay. One he would not be paying again.

No, he was perfectly all right on his own. So what if he had the occasional nightmare? He was perfectly capable of coping with them without her trying to mother him. He had lost count of the number of times he had woken from a fitful sleep, his sheets in a tangle, his body drenched with sweat. It was something he was used to. It was something he had learnt to deal with in his own way, without any help from anyone else.

He rolled over and his senses were filled with her scent, lingering on his pillow, on his sheets. Damn her again. Even when she wasn't present, he could not get away from her. He inhaled deeply. Orange blossom and rosewater. Despite himself, he had to admit there was something comforting about that scent.

Rather than turn away he continued to inhale her perfume. With each inhalation his breath slowed down, his anger dissipated. Then he drifted off into sleep, a sleep that this time was filled with the sensation of being held, being healed, being loved.

The warmth of the sunlight coming through the curtainless windows woke Theo from a restful sleep. He stretched in the bed, feeling more relaxed than he had for many a year. It made a nice change to have a good night's sleep, and he wondered what had caused it.

He lay in bed for a moment longer, replaying all that had happened yesterday and last evening, each memory chipping away at his calmness until it had completely evaporated and that familiar sense of rage engulfed him.

While he was often angry, this morning there was only one target for his irritation. Lady Iris Springfeld. That interfering, chattering busybody with that relentless laugh.

And she was still in his house. He was going to have to face her again. A woman who was not only annoying but had also seen him at his most vulnerable.

He hated the thought that she had been witness to his night-time terrors. He did not want anyone to think he was weak, least of all any young woman, and in particular Lady Iris Springfeld. It infuriated him that she was under the delusion that his nightmares meant he needed help. He needed no one, and he particularly did not need an interfering little ray of sunshine who thought she could make everything all right with a few comforting words and gentle caresses.

He threw off the bedclothes, their tangled state insulting him with further memories of last night, of the disarrayed state in which she had found him. His anger continuing to simmer within him, he walked to the window and pushed it up, hoping the fresh air would cool his temper. The wind had stopped howling and battering the house. Birds were now singing in the trees and the air had the sweet scent of wet grass and leaves.

There was nothing to stop her from returning home and out of his life. Good.

Turning from the window, he wrapped himself in his robe and rang for his valet. As he waited, he paced the room.

She was going to leave, but unfortunately he would still have to see her again for one last time. For politeness's sake, he would need to say his goodbyes, but then that would be that. She would be gone, her meddling would be gone, her damn interference and any further attempts to comfort him would be gone.

His pacing halted. What was he doing? Why was he so angry with her? Did her actions really justify this level of condemnation?

He drew in a deep breath and released it slowly. Was he being unfair? Or worse, a complete cad? What had she actually done? She had heard his cries in the middle of the night and had come running.

Her intentions had been good, if misguided. And, despite his annoyance, he did have to admit it had been brave of her. She was in a strange house with a man she did not know, but still she had responded to what she thought was a person in distress. And he had repaid her bravery with anger and scorn.

Clenching his jaw tightly, he recommenced pacing the room. Damn her yet again. Now it looked as if he was going to have to further belittle himself by apologising to the lady for his ungracious behaviour.

The sooner he got that particular indignity

over, the better. Then she could be on her way and leave him in peace.

His valet arrived with a bowl of warm water and his shaving gear. Theo sat down and James ran the soapy shaving brush over his cheeks and neck. He continued to fume as the blade was swished along the leather strop to make it razor-sharp.

Why did she have to come into his room and make his life so complicated? Didn't she know that young, unmarried women were not supposed to, under any circumstances, enter a man's bedroom? Did she not realise how compromised she could become by such an action? That if anyone knew of what she had done they could be forced to marry? His seething ratcheted up a notch.

Did such considerations not even enter her empty little head? Or did she believe that she would be safe from such a fate because it was *his* bedroom she was entering?

That presumably was her thinking. Even if she had been compromised, no family would insist that a man like him must marry their daughter.

He tilted back his head as the valet drew the blade up his neck and over his cheek, and drew in a series of long, calming breaths.

Now was the time to put all thoughts of Lady Iris Springfeld out of his mind. The last thing he should be thinking about was a woman who made his blood boil. Not when a cut-throat razor was being run over his face and neck.

Still breathing slowly and deeply, he fought to stop that little minx from entering his mind again, with all her laughter, chatter and inappropriate behaviour.

When the valet placed a warm towel on his face, he breathed a sigh of relief. He had managed to survive his agitation without receiving the slightest nick. Although that was due more to James's skill than it was to Theo's ability to keep Lady Iris out of his thoughts. And now he was going to have to endure her company for a little longer and try his hardest not to let his annoyance show, something that was going to take a level of self-control he was not sure he possessed.

'Is Lady Iris awake?' he asked his valet as soon as the warm towel was removed.

'Yes, my lord. I believe the young lady rose quite early.'

'Good.'

'And she's now dressed in her own, dry clothing.'

He could hear the amusement in his valet's voice. Presumably, Charles had informed him that Lady Iris had been forced to wear Theo's clothing last night.

'And where is she now?' he asked as his valet removed his suit from the wardrobe.

'I last saw her in the breakfast room,' James replied, handing Theo his trousers and shirt.

'And has the coachman been instructed to take her home as soon as she is ready to go?'

'Yes, my lord.'

Theo nodded. All he had to do now was make a quick apology, say goodbye, put her in a carriage and then it would all be over. His life would return to normal.

Once the valet had helped him into his jacket and finished brushing it down so it reached a standard that James would be happy with, Theo walked the well-practised route from his bedroom.

He made sure that the routes he regularly walked were clear of all obstacles. While the rest of the house was decorated with an array of fripperies collected over the years by his ancestors, the corridor outside his room was as spartan as a military barracks.

He also insisted that no hinges or locks be oiled so he would always know when doors were being opened and people were entering the room. Such arrangements gave him the confidence to move freely about his own house, whereas in public he never knew what obstacle might trip him up and reveal his affliction to the world.

He gripped the banister. And yet, in his own house, that little miss had seen him at his very worst. No wonder he avoided company. No wonder he shut himself off from the world. He did not need her or anyone else pitying him.

Holding on to the banister, he counted each stair until he knew he had reached the ground floor. Then he paced out the number of steps that would take him to the breakfast room.

He reached the door, gritted his teeth together and paused, his hand clenching the doorknob. With a resigned sigh he opened the door, determined to get this over and done with as quickly and as painlessly as possible.

Chapter Seven

'Good morning,' came her sunny greeting from the direction of the dining table. 'It's a beautiful day, isn't it?'

He mumbled his good morning, sat in his usual chair, reached for the coffee pot but found only air. That annoying woman had moved it. Charles quickly stepped forward and moved the coffee pot into the path of his waving hand. He murmured his thanks, poured his coffee and resisted the temptation to inform Lady Iris that he had a place for everything and he did not like things moved about, nor did he like having to rely on others to do even basic things for him, like pour the coffee. But he held his tongue, reminding himself that he had an apology to make, and an apology should not start with a rebuke.

'You may go now, thank you, Charles,' Theo

said. He did not need anyone hearing what he was about to say. He suspected the servants already knew about his nightmares—after all, servants knew just about everything that happened in a house—but they did not need to know about Lady Iris's night-time activities, and Charles most certainly did not need to hear Theo abasing himself and apologising to this flibbertigibbet.

'It would be hard to believe there was a storm last night if it weren't for the sodden driveway and the fallen branches,' she continued in that bright tone. 'Although the gardeners are already clearing everything away and making it tidy again. I popped outside before I came in to breakfast to enjoy the fresh air and they were busy at work.'

It seemed Lady Iris's sunny disposition was just as cheerful in the mornings as it was in the evenings. Some people were morning people, some evening people, but Lady Iris appeared, unfortunately, to be both.

'Now that the storm has passed, you'll be wanting to get home as soon as possible,' he said, and took a sip of the reviving coffee.

Or at least I will be wanting you to depart, the sooner the better.

'Yes, it would be best if I returned to the

Walbertons' estate as early as possible. Hopefully, if I get home before anyone rises no one will know that I was even missing. Fortunately, they tend to retire late and rise late, so I should be safe.'

He nodded his head in agreement. Good, she would be gone soon. But there was something he had to do before she left. Something that gave him great pain. He had to make that apology.

He took another sip of his coffee, placed the cup back in the saucer, drew himself more upright, took in a deep breath and exhaled slowly. 'About last night.' He took in another deep breath. Who would expect a simple apology to be so hard to make? But then, Theo was not used to explaining himself to anyone, and he most certainly was not used to apologising.

'Oh, yes, about that,' she said as her coffee cup clinked into its saucer. 'I used to have bad dreams all the time when I was a child and my mother always used to hold me and stroke my brow until all the scariness went away.' She paused, then gave a small laugh that sounded awkward. 'So that's why I was in your room when you woke. Just doing what my mother would have done for me. Nothing else. Nothing more.'

Theo clenched his teeth together to stop himself from telling her again in no uncertain manner that he did not need mothering, not from her, not from anyone, but he was fairly certain that lashing out was also not how one apologised.

Then his breath caught in his throat as he took in the other part of what she had said. *'Hold me...stroke my brow'*? Was that what she had been doing? Were those feelings that she had held him, kissed him, caressed him, real rather than something he had conjured up in his dream? But even if they had been real, she had not held, caressed or kissed him like a woman embracing a man, but as a mother comforting a disturbed child. It was an insult, not an act of affection or attraction. He was a man, for God's sake, not a child.

She had been in his room. She should not have been, but she had meant well. What she had done when she had been in his room, and her reasons for doing it, were neither here nor there. What he needed to do now was to get this damn apology over and done with.

'I am sorry for being so rude to you last night,' he said, his still-gritted teeth making the words sound terse. He forced his jaw to relax. 'You were very brave to react the way you did when you heard…' He rolled his hand in the air, not wanting to say out loud that he had been screaming in his sleep.

'Brave?' she said with a small laugh. 'I'm not brave. Foolhardy maybe. I didn't actually think too much about what I was doing. I just reacted, I suppose. Heaven knows what I would have done if you actually had been under attack from an assailant or this really was a haunted castle.'

There she went again, prattling on. Did she ever stop? But he held his tongue on that matter. Again, he was not meaning to criticise her but to apologise.

'Well, thank you.' There. He had said it. Hopefully, that would be the end of it and now he could drink his coffee in peace.

'That was my first thought when I suddenly woke,' she continued, destroying his hope for silence. 'That the house was haunted—after all, it is an old castle. Then I imagined some ruthless assassin was wandering the corridors, causing mayhem, or a band of desperate brigands.'

He continued drinking his coffee, unsure how or if he wanted to respond to such absurdities.

'Did I mention that I like to read gothic novels, and they do tend to make my imagination go off on some wild tangents at times?'

'No, but you have now. And with those thoughts in your mind, it is a wonder you even left your bed, never mind entered my room.'

'Yes, I suppose so, but I'm always being told off about doing things like that.'

He lowered his coffee cup. 'What? Do you make a habit of going into men's rooms in the middle of the night?'

'No, of course not. Don't be silly. I'm always being told off for acting before thinking.'

'Oh, I see. Like going for a walk when there's a storm on the horizon.'

'Hmm, yes, I suppose so. And thank you again for taking me in. I don't know what I would have done if I hadn't stumbled upon this house.'

He took another sip of his coffee, pleased that he had got that apology out of the way, and for restraining himself from mentioning that he would have preferred it if she had stumbled upon some other house and inflicted her relentless happiness on some other poor sod, someone who appreciated it. But that was unfair. She hadn't chosen his house, circumstances had forced her to shelter in his home, and at any other home she would not have been woken in the middle of the night by her host's screaming.

Theo swallowed down his coffee, wishing he could erase the memory of last night from his mind, but instead he remembered something else he should apologise for, something that was perhaps even more sensitive.

'And I am sorry that last night you saw me...' He paused, trying to think of the best way to phrase this so he would save her blushes. 'I'm sorry you saw me in a somewhat less than formally attired manner.'

She laughed. 'Well, that's one way of putting it, I suppose.'

He could see nothing funny in this situation. She had entered a man's bedroom, unaccompanied, and had found him completely naked. That would have sent most young maidens shrieking from the room. But not Lady Iris. And his apology, rather than making her blush, had amused her.

Was that because she still did not see him as a real man? Even after seeing him completely naked? Could this be any more humiliating? That anger that he had fought so hard to suppress while he was making his apology started to ferment within him.

'But that was hardly your fault,' she contin-

ued. He detected some muffling of her voice,
suggesting she had placed her hand over her
mouth. At least she had the decency to show
some embarrassment about seeing a man without a stitch of clothing on.

'You're right, I shouldn't have rushed
into your room without thinking. I wouldn't
have done it if I'd known you were—' she
laughed again, the sound still holding a hint
of awkwardness '—less than formally attired.'

'Well, we've both apologised, so the less
said about it the better.'

'Yes,' she said quietly. 'We certainly
wouldn't want it getting out that I had seen
you less than formally attired.'

'Hmm,' he murmured, not wanting to
continue this conversation and wishing she'd
stop repeating that phrase. With the apology
out of the way, finally he could drink his
coffee in peace. He rarely ate breakfast, and
this morning he had even greater reason to
refrain. He had no intention of delaying Lady
Iris's departure any longer than was necessary.
Although she apparently liked to partake of
a hearty breakfast. Knife and fork scraped
against her plate, and the smells wafting across
the table suggested bacon, eggs, sausages and
freshly baked bread. Cook must have decided

the guest needed to be fed well before she departed.

Hopefully, she would eat quickly and refrain from talking while she did so.

'And your servants have managed to get my clothes dry and remove all the mud,' she said, his hope for silence dying an immediate death.

'You'll be pleased to know I'm now dressed like a lady again and not in gentlemen's attire,' she said, open amusement returning to her voice. 'Although they couldn't do a thing with my hat. It still looks like a poor, drowned creature. I don't know what I'm going to tell my mother. I'll have to think of some reason why my hat spent the night out in a storm while I was tucked up safely in my bed at the Walbertons'. Although I can't for the life of me think what that reason might be.'

'Are you always this cheerful in the morning?' Theo said, cutting through the chatter that threatened to go on without end.

'Yes, I am. Thank you.'

'That wasn't a compliment.'

'Oh, wasn't it?' She stopped talking and Theo hoped that would be the end of it, even though he now knew from painful experience that such a hope would be in vain.

'But it can't be an insult. After all, there's

nothing wrong with being cheerful, is there? Particularly on a morning like this, when the sun is shining, the birds are singing and everything has that lovely fresh smell you get after it's been raining all night. It's simply glorious and makes you glad to be alive.'

'Some people like silence in the morning, even on "simply glorious" mornings,' he said, making 'simply glorious' sound like the worst type of morning there was.

'Well, nobody *I* know likes to be silent in the morning. At least no one in my family. Well, my father is rather quiet, but he's never objected to my mother, my sisters and I talking while he eats his breakfast, and my brother, Nathaniel, is just as talkative as me. If you think I'm noisy you should meet the entire family. Then you'd realise I'm actually one of the quieter members.'

Heaven forbid he should meet more like Lady Iris. But fortunately he was never likely to have the misfortune of meeting any other members of the Springfeld family, and certainly not the entire family en masse.

'It's just a man likes to drink his coffee before he's hit with a barrage of such buoyancy,' he said, explaining something that he did not believe needed explaining in his own home.

'Oh, I see. Would you like me to wait till you finish your coffee before I hit you with the full force of my cheerful good nature?'

He made no reply, merely refilled his cup as a signal that he still wanted silence.

'And I could say the same thing to you,' she continued, not picking up on his signal. 'Are you always this grumpy in the morning?' She waited a mere second. 'No, don't answer.'

As if he were going to.

'I think I already know what you're going to say about your moods in the morning.' The trilling note in her voice suggested that, if anything, she found his mood to be a source of great amusement.

Theo reached out to the bell that always sat in the middle of the table and gave it a hearty shake, hoping to drown out her infernal teasing about his moods.

'Charles, has the coachman prepared the carriage yet?' he asked the moment his servant entered the room. 'Lady Iris wishes to return home as early as possible.'

'The coachman has been informed to make haste and to let us know the moment it is ready,' Charles replied.

'Good.' Theo wondered whether the servants were delaying Lady Iris's departure, because it did seem to be taking an inordinate amount of time. They couldn't be that disloyal, could they?

They had never shown disloyalty before, even following all the changes that had taken place after his accident. Their lives, as well as his own, had altered irreparably following that fateful night. He had once entertained regularly. While that meant additional work for the servants, it also meant they got to socialise with the servants from other households who stayed over so they could attend to their masters and mistresses. He suspected they missed that aspect of their work. He knew Cook missed being able to organise lavish dinner parties, and the butler and housekeeper missed running a busy household. But despite the changes in the way he lived, he had retained all the servants as part of his household. They now simply had much less work to do. Surely that was an improvement on the long hours that servants in most households worked, and they were happy with their lot. He was certain of that. At least, he had never before had any reason to doubt their loyalty.

No, he was sure they wouldn't be so impertinent as to delay Lady Iris's departure any longer than was absolutely necessary, not when it must be quite obvious that he wanted the woman gone. It was her—she was making him imagine things.

'Charles, would you please go and see what is holding up the coachman? The man has had ample notice to get the horses and carriage ready. Remind him that it is imperative that Lady Iris gets home as soon as possible.'

'Very good, my lord,' Charles said before departing.

'You really are anxious to get rid of me, aren't you?' Iris said. 'You must really like spending all your time completely alone.'

A sudden, painful contraction gripped his stomach, as if he had been drinking a noxious substance instead of coffee. 'I enjoy my own company,' he said, horrified to hear a constricted sound in his voice.

'Hmm.' Her reply sounded as if she did not believe him.

But what did he care if she believed him or not? He did not need to justify the way he lived to her or to anybody.

'We are not all the same, Lady Iris. Some of us enjoy solitude and quiet,' he said, trying to justify himself, even though he believed it was not necessary.

'And living in solitude and quiet is what makes you such a contented person, is it?' she said quietly.

How dare she? This really was outrageous. Was she expecting him to defend the way he lived, to her?

'You don't have to be on your own, you know,' she continued, her voice still quiet.

Theo was too astounded to speak. Did this slip of a girl really think she could give him advice on how he was supposed to live his life? She knew nothing of him. Knew nothing about anything.

'Your neighbours, the Walbertons, are very friendly, very welcoming people. And I've met some of your other neighbours at their house. They are all very nice people. Perhaps you should make more of an effort to spend time with them.'

'And perhaps you should keep your opinions to yourself.'

She really was the limit. He could inform her that he knew exactly what sort of people the Walbertons were. He had once spent a great deal of time in their home, and they had attended many social events at this very house. He had also once entertained his neighbours on a regular basis. But that was in the past. He lived a different life now and had absolutely no intention of changing the way he lived just because she did not approve.

He waited for her to continue with her relentless chatter. To give him another piece of unwanted advice. She said nothing. Finally, he had the silence he was craving, but damn it all, he had been rude to her again. Although this time it was no less than she deserved.

'Thank you for your advice on how I should live my life,' he said, fighting to keep the sarcasm at an acceptable level. 'I'll give your opinions the consideration they are due.'

'I'm sure you will,' she said with equally false politeness. 'And I'm sure we won't be seeing you at the Walbertons' or any of your other neighbours' very soon.'

In response he merely took another drink of his coffee.

The door opened. 'The carriage is ready, my lord, to take Lady Iris home.'

Thank God for that, Theo almost said. At least now this ridiculous conversation could come to an end, at least now he would not be subjected to her advice or have to put up with her laughter and unrelenting chatter.

'Very good, Charles. I'm sure Lady Iris will

be leaving soon, assuming she has had sufficient breakfast.'

'Yes, I have, thank you, Charles.' Fabric rustled as she stood up. 'I'll leave you to drink your coffee in peace, shall I?'

'No, I'll accompany you to the carriage.' Why had he said that? After being less than welcoming to her last night and snapping at her this morning, why the sudden compunction to be courteous? Was it guilt over his bad manners, or was it just that he wanted to make sure she really did get in the carriage and leave?

He followed the sound of her swishing skirts down the hallway and out through the entranceway. She was right about the change in the weather. The sun was shining warm on his face, the grass and the trees smelt fresh and the soil had a rich, loamy scent. It was as if the world had been born anew after last night's storm.

Counting the steps, he walked down the front entrance to where the carriage was waiting.

'Well, goodbye,' she said. 'And thank you so much for your hospitality.'

Hospitality. Surely she was jesting. He'd provided her with shelter, nothing more. He had done everything he could to be as inhospitable to this cheerful young thing as was possible, without being openly hostile.

'Goodbye, Lady Iris,' he said, with finality.

With much rustling of fabric, she entered the carriage. Then the coachman flicked the reins, the horses whinnied in reaction to the effort needed to get the vehicle moving, coach wheels crunched on the gravel, and the carriage left the house.

He remained standing at the entranceway, just to assure himself that she really had gone, then walked back up the stairs.

'Good riddance,' he said under his breath as he entered the suddenly quiet house.

Chapter Eight

Iris turned in her seat and looked out of the carriage window at the lone figure walking up the stone steps into his home.

It was unlikely she would ever see the Earl of Greystone again, but Iris knew she would never forget him, nor the night she had just experienced. He was certainly intriguing, and Iris could not remember any other time when a man had so piqued her interest.

She sat back on the leather seat. Now she would return to the endless round of balls, parties, picnics and soirées that constituted her life. It was just a shame none of the men she met at those social events were as interesting as the Earl of Greystone. Not that she would see him as a potential husband. The mere thought of it was enough to make her laugh. The man treated her with contempt and behaved as if enjoying oneself were a crime against nature. These were certainly not characteristics she was looking for in a potential husband.

She looked back out of the window, at the retreating house. He was grumpy, ill-mannered, and had chosen to cut himself off from the rest of the world. No, he was most definitely not husband material, and even if she were interested in him, which she wasn't, he most certainly was not interested in her. He had made that abundantly clear. This morning he couldn't push her out of the door fast enough.

But on the other hand, even though he was grumpy, at least he didn't fawn over her and treat her like a pretty ornament the way most men did. And yes, he was rude, but he spoke his mind to her, rather than treating her with kid gloves as if she were a sensitive, delicate little thing who was easily hurt. It had all been rather refreshing in an unexpected way.

And in an equally unexpected way she suspected she would not be able to forget Theo Crighton, the Earl of Greystone.

Just as she knew she would not be able to forget or stop worrying about those demons that tormented him in his sleep. The carriage turned onto the country road, obscuring the house behind a row of elm trees. What those demons were, Iris would now never know. It presumably had something to do with whatever it was that had caused his scars, possibly even his blindness. Would he be afflicted by those dreams again tonight, with no one in the house to help him, to hold him? He was such a physically strong man, and yet he could be reduced to a state of thrashing, sweating agony by something that invaded and possessed his sleeping mind. He needed help, but he had made it perfectly clear to Iris that he was not prepared to accept it, and certainly not from her.

She released a long, sad sigh. Why did he think he was so different from everyone else? Everyone needed the help of others. Everyone needed to be supported at times, to know that they weren't alone and that help was at hand should they require it.

But there was nothing to be done about it. Probably, that would be the last time she would see Theo Crighton, so she might as well try to put him and all her unanswered questions out of her mind, especially as she had other worries that should be occupying her thoughts. Right now, she needed to focus on returning to the Walbertons' house as discreetly as possible.

She should not be thinking about the Earl, his behaviour, his demons and she most certainly should not be thinking about how he looked when he was less than formally attired, as he had so euphemistically described it. Iris smiled and bit her bottom lip.

Less than formally attired, indeed.

She shouldn't be thinking about it, but she knew she would never forget what the Earl looked like less than formally attired, and really, why would she want to forget such a sight? He had been quite simply magnificent, a feast for the eyes, and she *should* have been ashamed of herself for doing exactly that, feasting her eyes on his beautifully formed body last night.

But it certainly wasn't shame that was causing that little tremor to ripple through her body. She sat up straighter on the bench, trying to suppress that strange feeling and reminding herself that she had to stop thinking about the Earl. She needed to keep her wits about her so she could creep into the house without anyone seeing her or asking any difficult questions.

They had not travelled far, but the surrounding countryside already appeared familiar. Iris twisted in her seat to watch a group of pretty thatched cottages perched on the top of a cliff overlooking the ocean pass by the carriage window. She had admired those cottages when she had first set out on her walk yesterday, a walk that had lasted several hours. And yet the cottages were but a short carriage drive from Theo Crighton's home. She must have been walking round and round in circles. No wonder the Earl had thought she was a ninny, getting lost so close to where she was supposed to be. If she'd only stuck to the road. If only she'd walked in the correct direction, she could have been back in a matter of minutes instead of wandering endlessly and aimlessly until she was hopelessly lost and disorientated.

The Walbertons' home soon appeared, looking grand and stately on the top of a hill. The curtains were all firmly closed in the upstairs bedrooms of the three-storey house. Good, no one had as yet risen from their bed. The coachman turned into the long gravel driveway that led up to the front of the house.

'Excuse me, driver,' she called out. 'Would you please drop me off here? I can walk the rest of the way.'

'Very good, my lady,' the driver said, pulling on the reins. He jumped down to help her out of the carriage and after thanking him Iris looked up at the house to reassure herself that it was still completely quiet.

As quickly as possible she walked up the long driveway, avoiding the puddles left by last night's rain. The servants would already be up and about their work, even if the guests were still sleeping off last night's entertainment. Hopefully if any of them did see her they would merely think she had been out for an early stroll and not mention it to their mistress or master.

As quietly as possible she entered the house, and on tiptoes ran up the stairs to her bedroom. No one was about. It had all been surprisingly easy. Smiling to herself, she entered her bedroom. Then stopped, her hand still grasping the doorknob.

Her mother, the last person she wanted to see, was standing in the middle of the room, staring at Iris's bed, its tucked-in corners and pristine silk cover revealing that it had not been slept in.

'Good morning, Mother,' Iris said, fighting to keep her voice as even as possible.

Almost before the words were out, her mother flew across the room and threw her arms around Iris, clasping her tightly and rocking her from side to side.

'Oh, Iris, I thought you were… I thought… I don't know what I thought. That you were kidnapped, maybe, or something else terrible had happened to you.' She stepped back and placed her hand on her heart. 'I am so relieved to see you.' Then she frowned. 'Where on earth have you been?'

Last night Iris had sworn an oath to the gods, that if they took pity on her and found her refuge from the storm she would never lie to her mother again. They had played their part, and now it was up to her to keep her side of the bargain.

She sent her mother a forced smile, trying to think of the best way to explain herself that would not be a lie but would also ease her mother's concerns. Her mother waited, her face contorted with worry while Iris tried to come up with the best way to say she had spent the night alone, with a man she did not know, had seen him naked and spent part of the night in his bed. There was no way to say any of it that wouldn't cause her mother an unforgivable amount of distress. Surely the gods wouldn't mind if she told one more little white lie… after all, it wasn't for Iris's sake, but for her mother's.

'Oh, I… I woke up early and went out for a walk.'

Her mother raised one suspicious eyebrow and slowly looked Iris up and down. 'You are wearing the same clothes you were wearing yesterday.'

'I didn't want to disturb my lady's maid, so I dressed myself,' Iris blurted out.

The suspicious eyebrow rose further up the forehead.

'And what happened to your hair?'

Iris looked down at the frizzy mess falling around her shoulders and tried to come up with a logical explanation.

'It looks as if you have been dragged through a hedge backwards.' Her mother reached out and removed a small twig that had lodged itself inside the plait. 'And what happened to your hat?'

They both looked down at the limp rag dangling from Iris's hand. How was she going to explain that? If she didn't stop now her little white lie was going to get decidedly grey. She had no option. She was going to have to tell the truth. At least some of it.

'Oh, all right, Mother. I'll tell you what happened, but you have to promise not to get angry.'

'I will make no such promises. But one promise I can make is that I will get very angry indeed if you do not tell me exactly what happened. And no lies, mind you.'

'I went out for a walk in the early evening and got lost.'

Her mother frowned as she looked towards the window, gesturing wildly with her hand. 'What? In that storm?'

Outside the window the sky was blue. All was calm and tranquil, as if such things as wind and rain did not exist.

She turned back to Iris, her brow furrowed as she waited for an explanation.

'Yes. It wasn't raining when I set out, but then it was, and I got very wet. Plus, I got lost. So, I took refuge at the home of the Earl of Greystone. He kindly allowed me to stay the night until the storm had passed,' Iris rushed out in one breath.

Her mother's furrowed brow smoothed over as her eyes grew enormous. 'You stayed at a man's home? Was there a Lady Greystone present?'

'It's all right, Mother, he was the perfect gentleman.' That perhaps was an exaggeration. He was bad-tempered and inhospitable. Then there *was* the incident in his room when he had been less than formally attired, but perhaps it would be better not to mention that.

'Does anyone else know?' her mother asked quietly, as if they could suddenly be overheard. 'Did you tell anyone you were going for a walk? Did anyone see you coming home this morning, dressed in the same clothes, looking like that?'

'No, no and no.'

Her mother exhaled slowly through pursed lips. 'Good. Hopefully this Earl of Greystone is discreet. Do you think he will be discreet?'

Iris nodded rapidly. 'Yes, I'm sure he will be.'

'Hmm, but I think I need to ascertain that for myself.' Her mother placed a thoughtful hand on her chin. 'After all, he now holds your reputation in his hands, and he could easily destroy it if he has a mind to.'

'I'm sure he wouldn't, Mother.' For a start, if he was going to gossip he would actually have to socialise with others, and that was unlikely to happen.

'I think we need to pay him a visit.'

'No, Mother, that won't be necessary,' Iris all but shouted. 'I'm sure the Earl of Greystone is the very soul of discretion,' she added, her voice now more neutral. *And I'm even more sure that the last thing he will want is another visit from anyone, least of all me and my mother,* she wanted to add.

'Hopefully you are right. But I am still going to pay him a visit.' Her mother nodded, her mind made up. 'After all, I should thank him for his kindness towards you. Heaven only knows what might have happened to you if he had not offered you refuge from that storm. Visiting him and thanking him in person would be the polite thing to do.'

'Perhaps you could just send him a thank-you note,' Iris said, starting to feel desperate.

'No, I want to see the man for myself so I can be certain that your reputation is safe. If all is well, then I will just thank him for his kindness. If not, then I will impress on him that it is in his best interest to keep this incident to himself.'

Iris's heart sank. This was getting worse. The last thing she wanted was her mother issuing threats to the Earl.

'So, as soon as you have changed your clothing, we will set off. Is it far? Do you now know the way?'

'No and yes. It's actually easily within walking distance.'

Her mother raised those eyebrows again,

as if to say, *So how did you get lost?* but thankfully said nothing.

Her mother left the room and a defeated Iris threw her ruined hat onto the bed. The Earl of Greystone was not going to like this, not one little bit. He had only just got rid of her, and now he was not only going to have to deal with another visit, but this time she would also have her mother in tow.

She could only hope that she had not been lying to her mother when she said that the Earl could be discreet. The last thing she wanted was his letting her mother know anything at all about how Iris had actually spent the night.

Chapter Nine

Iris's mother was waiting for her in the drawing room, dressed for a stroll in the countryside.

Iris's head was still aching slightly, having just undergone a period of torture at the hands of her lady's maid, who had furiously brushed her hair to restore it to a neat and tidy state. A disgruntled Annette had then taken her clothes away to the sound of much tut-tutting at the condition of her stockings, which still bore some signs of last night's ordeal.

But at least now she was sensibly dressed for her latest unwanted visit to the Earl. She had chosen her dark brown walking dress embroidered with black thread, a matching hat, which she felt gave her a jaunty look, and sturdy black button-up leather boots. It was how she should have been dressed last night, rather than wearing her cotton skirt and jacket and such impractical silk boots. Not that it would have made much difference. She couldn't imagine what sort of clothes you would have to wear to protect yourself from a storm. Certainly nothing she had packed for a genteel country-house party.

But at least today she felt a little more like a sensible young woman, rather than the dishevelled wreck who had washed up on the Earl's doorstep last night.

'Right,' her mother said slightly more loudly than was necessary as she picked up her parasol. 'A nice stroll in the country on a beautiful morning—what could be better?'

Iris merely smiled her agreement. The loud comment was not for Iris's sake, but so that anyone who might be listening would think it was a stroll with no purpose, rather than a mission to save Iris's reputation from possible ruin. Not that anyone else in the drawing room was paying much attention. The two elderly gentlemen sitting by the empty fireplace were perusing their newspapers, and the young couple in the corner were more interested in each other than anything Iris's mother had to say.

They set out along the country lanes that Iris had travelled earlier that morning, her mother keeping up a constant chatter the entire way, informing Iris of all that had happened during the evening while she was missing, commenting on the scenery as they passed and exclaiming on the pretty country roads, the delightful hedgerows and the lovely green fields dotted with white sheep.

Iris merely agreed with all she said, nodding and saying yes, it was indeed delightful, all the while worrying about the reception they might get at the Earl's home.

The house loomed up before them. Although today, with the bright blue sky as a backdrop, elm trees gently waving in the light wind and the stonework sparkling silver in the sunlight, it didn't look quite so forbidding.

Iris placed her hand on her hat and looked up. Only the crenellated roof and those proud turrets of the original castle suggested the owner wanted to repel any intruders. And that was exactly how the Earl was going to see Iris and her mother, as unwanted intruders.

'Simply delightful,' her mother said. 'It's almost medieval, is it not? Yes, quite delightful. If nothing else, seeing this ancient home makes it worth a visit. The Earl must come from a long line of very distinguished family members to live in a house such as this.'

Iris cared little for historic homes so could

not share her mother's enthusiasm, particularly as they were about to storm the Earl's castle, armed only with their unwanted good cheer.

Gardeners were still clearing away fallen branches as they walked up the driveway, and her mother sent hearty greetings to each workman as they passed. When they reached the door she gave it a resounding knock and stood back, still smiling.

The door was opened by the same servant who had opened the door to her last night, minus his flickering candle.

'Good day, Charles,' Iris said. 'My mother, Lady Springfeld, and I have come to visit the Earl.'

Charles nodded and smiled in greeting. 'Good day to you again, Lady Iris.' He nodded in the direction of her mother. 'Lady Springfeld. Please come in and I'll inform the Earl.'

'Oh, this really is lovely!' her mother exclaimed as they waited in the entranceway, and Iris agreed. It *was* lovely. Sun was streaming through the large domed window above the front door, lighting up the hallway, which last night had appeared to Iris as a creepy, dark passage leading heaven knew where. Today it wasn't the slightest bit scary and, she had to admit, rather welcoming.

'Just look at these tiles, Iris,' her mother said, scraping her boot lightly along the clay tiles underfoot. 'I suspect they are the original medieval ones. Marvellous. Simply marvellous.'

Iris looked down at her feet, where an Oriental rug partially covered brown and white tiles featuring swirls and intricate patterns. They were the same tiles Iris had dripped on last night, but she had had as little interest in the flooring then as she did today. Her mind was too occupied by the thoughts of what reaction they were going to get from the Earl.

Her mother looked at the portraits of who she presumed were his ancestors lined up on the wall. 'Oh, and I see I was right. The Earl does have a very distinguished family tree,' she said with approval.

'Mother, before we meet the Earl, there's something I must tell you,' she said quietly, placing her hand on her mother's arm.

Her mother looked up at her and smiled. 'Yes, dear, what is that?'

'The Earl's blind.'

Her mother's smile faded and she frowned. 'Oh, that is a shame.'

Iris nodded her agreement. 'Yes, but he copes splendidly. After a while you actually forget that he can't see.'

'But he will not be able to appreciate just how beautiful you are.' She gently touched Iris's intricate coiffure, which Annette had insisted on styling once she had finished furiously brushing out every last tangle and frizz. 'And you look particularly lovely today.'

Her mother went back to looking around the entrance hall, a satisfied smile on her face. Iris could almost see her mind working. An earl. A long-established family. Large estate. Unmarried. Her heart sank.

Please, please, Mother, no matchmaking, she silently begged. *The Earl does not want me. He doesn't want anyone.*

Charles emerged from the drawing room. 'Please, come this way,' he said with a bow.

They followed him into the same drawing room where Iris had found the Earl last night. The fire was no longer burning, but he was seated in the same chair. Did he spend his entire life there?

Max was once again seated at his feet and instantly sprang up and rushed to the door.

'Maxie-Waxie!' Iris exclaimed, bending down and rubbing the dog's ears. A gesture that was rewarded with some vigorous tail-wagging.

She looked up to see the Earl standing beside the fireplace.

'Lady Springfeld. Lady Iris,' he said with a bow.

Both ladies curtsied. Even though he couldn't see them, Iris now knew that he would be able to hear the movement of their clothing and know exactly what they were doing.

'Please, be seated.' He gestured towards a sofa, which Charles had presumably moved forward to accommodate the uninvited guests.

'So, to what do I owe the pleasure of this visit?'

And when are you going to leave? Iris suspected he wanted to add. But at least he was being more polite to her mother than he had been to her last night.

They made their way across the room, along with Max, and all three sat down, the two ladies on the sofa, Max at Iris's feet. She smiled down at him and continued to pat his head.

'I came to thank you for saving my daughter from the storm last night,' her mother said, smiling brightly, even though the smiles were wasted on the Earl.

The Earl waved his hand in dismissal. 'It was nothing. Anyone would have done the same. It was just unfortunate that the storm was too fierce to risk my coachman taking her home.'

'Yes, quite… And as only you, my daughter and I know about it, it might be all for the best if it remains our little secret.'

The Earl nodded. 'I have no intention of telling anyone, Your Ladyship.'

It was no less than Iris would have expected. She could no more imagine the Earl gossiping than she could imagine him smiling.

'That is very gracious of you, Your Lordship,' her mother said with a small bow of her head. 'As you probably know, Iris is not married, and such gossip could ruin a young woman's chances.'

Iris's heart sank down another few levels. Here it came. The marriage pitch. Well, it was wasted on the Earl, and wasted on her. They did not like each other and a less unlikely couple she could not imagine. She would rather marry Lord Pratley. No, that wasn't true. Even the Earl was better than him. At least the Earl did not bore her senseless.

'Although, as she is so sought-after, it probably would not do irreparable damage,' her mother continued. 'Why, even this weekend I have had several approaches from young men, all eager to court her, as I have done every Season. Unfortunately, my beautiful daughter is somewhat choosy.'

She smiled at Iris, who was clenching her teeth and glaring at her mother. At least the Earl would not be able to see her distraught face. Nor would he be able to see her chopping motions, signalling to her mother to stop this conversation. Now.

Her mother frowned at Iris, turned back to the Earl and continued smiling.

'Then I'm sure you will have no problem finding her a suitable husband,' he said, his voice dismissive, as if he too would like to bring this conversation to an end.

'You are quite correct, my lord. She just has to meet the right man.'

Iris nudged her mother to get her attention and shook her head vehemently. To her intense annoyance, her mother did not even look at her, but kept smiling at the Earl. What was wrong with her? Unlike most mothers, Iris's had never tried to foist her onto a man she did not want, no matter how large his estate, how big his income or how lofty his title. Her mother wanted her three daughters to be as happy in their marriages as she was in hers. She wanted them to marry for love. So why the sudden change? Why was she suddenly so interested in the Earl? Was her mother starting to feel desperate because Iris was unwed after five Seasons?

'Yes, I believe my daughter would make a perfect wife for a man who appreciates her gentle nature and sparkling wit. She is also known throughout Society as a striking beauty. The many men who have asked for her hand have not even enquired about her dowry, which is rather sizeable. No, they have all been too taken with her beauty to even think about money.'

'Perhaps we should have some tea,' Iris said, interrupting her mother. She did not want tea, and it was not her place to make such a suggestion, but she had to say something to cut off her mother's blatant attempt to try and pique the Earl's interest by mentioning how much she was worth. It was so unlike her mother and it lacked even a modicum of subtlety.

Her mother sent her a sideways glance, as if she too was surprised by Iris's ill-mannered behaviour, then smiled at the Earl. 'Yes, that would be lovely. Taking tea will give us all a chance to get to know each other better.'

Iris saw the Earl suppress a sigh, but he rang the small silver bell on the side table, and when Charles arrived asked if he could please serve tea.

'Although I am sure you and my daughter had a chance to get acquainted last night,' her mother said, her voice light, even if her intent were not. 'But not too well acquainted, I hope, or we'd be forced to read the wedding banns.'

'No, we hardly even spoke to each other last night, as I went to bed almost immediately after I arrived,' Iris blurted out, causing her mother to turn to face her and raise a quizzical eyebrow. To Iris's horror, warmth flooded her cheeks. 'After all, it had been a rather traumatic day, and I wanted to get up early in the morning,' Iris raced on, trying to cover her embarrassment.

It was bad enough that she had been alone with a man, all night. That in itself could be enough for a family to force a man into marriage. But it was much worse than that. She had been in his bedroom, for goodness' sake, had seen him less than formally attired.

Her mother continued to stare at her, her head tilted, her disbelieving eyebrows raised.

'So we didn't spend much time together,' Iris continued, her voice now sounding as defeated as she felt.

'Just enough time to get to know Maxie-Waxie,' her mother said with a hint of disbelief. At the sound of his name the dog looked at Iris's mother and recommenced wagging his tail.

Her mother looked from the happy dog to

the frowning Earl. 'Oh, well, that will not do, will it?' she said, a note of victory entering her voice. 'Especially as I am sure you two have much in common.'

The Earl's leather chair creaked as he moved uncomfortably and he coughed lightly. *We have nothing in common*, Iris wanted to shout out. *Can't you see? We don't even like each other.*

Her mother continued to smile as Charles entered and served the tea. The Earl's expression reflected Iris's and she was sure he too was hoping this whole embarrassing incident would be over as soon as politeness allowed.

'We are staying at the estate of my dear friend, Lady Walberton,' her mother chatted on, while stirring her tea. 'The Walbertons are your nearest neighbours. I imagine you are all the best of friends as well.'

Charles smiled at Iris as he handed her a cup, then placed the Earl's tea on the side table, deliberately making the cup clink so his master would know where it was.

'I have not visited my neighbours for some time,' the Earl said, ignoring his tea. Anyone other than Iris's mother would know from the tone of his voice that this was how he liked it and that this was not a conversation he wanted to have. But Iris knew her mother could be relentless when she had made a decision, even if she did cover her single-minded determination with a veneer of ever-so-correct politeness and unrelenting friendliness.

'Oh, that simply will not do,' she said. 'We shall have to put that to rights, will we not?'

'There's nothing that requires being put to rights,' the Earl said, which was almost word for word what Iris wanted to say.

The Earl's dismissive attitude, his sullenness, and obvious lack of encouragement would have deterred a less determined woman, but Iris knew it would not put off her mother. It wasn't just because she saw the Earl as a potential husband for her middle daughter. Her mother was by nature of a happy disposition and expected everyone else to be the same. She simply would not tolerate anyone wallowing in misery. The Earl should just surrender now, paste a smile on his face and give in to her mother's demands.

'Lady Walberton is one of my closest friends and I am sure she will be delighted when I inform her that I have invited you to join us for dinner tonight. Most of the guests are leaving today, so it will just be a small, intimate dinner party and it will give us all a perfect opportunity to deepen our friendship.'

The Earl's jaw clenched tighter and his spine became rigid.

'That will not be convenient,' he said, slowly enunciating each word so his intent would be clear.

'Oh, that's a shame,' Iris said, giving her mother a pleading look, even though she knew it to be a fruitless gesture. 'If the Earl is busy then he won't be able to come.'

'Nonsense,' her mother said. 'I doubt if it is anything that cannot be put off to a later date, and, as we are only staying at Lady Walberton's until the end of the week, I am sure you can make time this evening.'

'Lady Springfeld, I will not be coming to dinner tonight, or any other night. I do not socialise with my neighbours,' he said, the forcefulness of his voice in stark contrast to her mother's cheerfulness.

'Well, that needs to change, does it not?' her mother said, unaffected by his tone. 'And tonight will be the perfect time for that change to occur. Shall we say eight o'clock? Then you will be able to partake in a sociable drink before we dine.'

He made no answer.

'You might as well know, my lord,' Lady Springfeld said, still keeping her voice light as if they were merely having a pleasant chat, 'that I do not give up. It is much easier just to do as I ask.'

'That is something I am becoming aware of, madam,' he said, not bothering to stifle a huff of exasperation.

'But if you are unable to come to this one dinner party tonight, then I am sure I can arrange to visit you again with my daughter each day before we leave. And I am sure there are many other guests who would be just as delighted as I am to see this house. Perhaps you would be able to take them on tours. I know you would not want everyone coming at once, so we could arrange for a few each day, some in the morning, some in the afternoon and some in the evening.'

Iris had never seen her mother be quite so ruthless, and her mouth fell open in amazement, causing her mother to put her hand under Iris's chin and push it shut.

'That most certainly will not be convenient,' the Earl said, speaking slowly through a clenched jaw. He drew in a long, slow breath then just as slowly exhaled. 'All right. If that will be the end of it, I will dine at Lady Walberton's tonight.'

'Oh, good,' her mother said, stirring her tea with satisfaction and ignoring Iris's look of disapproval. 'I'm sure you will thoroughly enjoy yourself and it will be the beginning of some long-lasting relationships.' She sent Iris a triumphant smile. 'With your neighbours, I mean.'

Chapter Ten

Theo would not have thought it possible, but the mother was even worse than the daughter. She was even more relentlessly cheerful, even less capable of grasping the basic concept that she and her daughter were not welcome in his home, and now this ridiculously joyful woman was seeing him as a potential husband for her daughter.

At least the daughter did not have such aspirations, if the constant squirming in her chair and occasional huffs of disapproval were anything to go by. That was one thing in Lady Iris's favour. He was pleased to note that she was not a husband-hunter.

But if agreeing to attend a dinner at the Walbertons' would get rid of them once and for all, unfortunately the best course of action was to grin and bear it. Well, he doubted he would spend much time grinning, but he would have to bear it. He would endure just about anything if it meant he could be left in peace. Now that the mother had what she wanted, he waited with as much patience as he could summon for them to make their much-anticipated farewells.

No such farewells came.

'Oh, you have not drunk your tea and it must have gone cold by now,' Lady Springfeld chirped instead. 'We must call for more.'

'That's quite all right. I didn't actually want any tea,' he cut in, wanting to add, *and I didn't want this visit either and the sooner you leave the better.*

The swish of moving fabric signalled he had his wish. Thank God for that. He stood up and reached out for the bell to summon Charles to escort them out. His hand found only empty space. Then he heard the tinkling of a bell. His bell.

That infernal woman had crossed the room and taken his bell from his table. She wasn't leaving, merely taking over and ordering his servants about.

Charles appeared as commanded.

'You called, my lord?' he said.

'No, I called you, Charles,' the mother replied before he could speak. 'The Earl's tea has gone cold. Could you fetch him another cup, please?'

'Very good, my lady.' It seemed Charles had decided he now took orders from this unwanted visitor.

'The Earl said he didn't want any tea,' Lady Iris said in a quiet, impatient voice. It was a pertinent comment. One that was ignored by her mother. Instead, the mother merely shuffled her way back across the room and sat down.

Apparently, he and Lady Iris now had one thing in common. They were united in their annoyance with her mother. No, they had two things in common. They both wanted this visit to be over as soon as possible. Or was that three? Neither wanted to be married to the other.

He had little control over the first two, but he most certainly had control over the third. Lady Springfeld would not be getting him up the aisle at any time soon. And Theo could only wonder as to her motives. If Lady Iris was as sought-after as her mother claimed, why was she so keen to foist her daughter off onto a man like him? He might be wealthy with a title, but, when it came to the qualities that a mother looked for in a husband for her daughter, blindness and hideous scarring were not usually high up on the list. But it mattered not what the mother was thinking. She would not be marrying off her daughter to him.

He sat back down, resigned himself to tolerating the two ladies' company a little longer and tried to blot out the sound of the mother as she resumed her cheerful chattering.

Charles arrived with yet another unwanted pot of tea, removed his cold cup and replaced it with a fresh one, which Theo would also be ignoring. The murmuring of thanks, clinking of cups and stirring of teaspoons signalled that the two ladies were also having a second cup. Theo swallowed a sigh of irritation.

'Has your family lived in this area long?' Lady Springfeld asked. A polite question, which every member of the aristocracy knew was full of intent when asked by the mother of an unwed daughter. She was really asking, *How long is your lineage, are you a well-established member of the aristocracy and what will our family gain by joining with yours?*

'Quite some time,' Theo answered vaguely, not wanting to encourage her by mentioning that his family tree went back to before the time of the Tudors. A family tree that would end with him. He had no intention of bringing children into a world such as this. Instead, his cousins would inherit the estate, and Theo did not care one bit.

'And it looks as if you own an extensive estate, and it is a rather beautiful one, I must say,' the mother continued.

Theo merely nodded his agreement, wondering whether she wanted him to get out his financial records so she could inspect how much he was worth.

'We had such a lovely walk over here, did we not, Iris?'

'Oh, yes,' said Lady Iris. 'And perhaps we should take our leave and walk back to the Walbertons' now. I'm sure the Earl has much to do and we've taken enough of his time.'

Sensible, sensible girl. She too could see the pointlessness of her mother's matchmaking. Or, even more likely, was horrified with the prospect of her mother trying to hitch her up to a man like him. Memories of last night's encounter crashed back into his mind and Theo moved uncomfortably in his chair. Of course she would not want to marry him. What woman in her right mind would want to marry a man who cried out in his sleep, a man she believed needed to be comforted like a child? Presumably Lady Iris had not passed this rather unfortunate bit of information on to her mother. If she had, he doubted she would be so keen to have him as a son-in-law.

'I wouldn't want to keep you any longer,' he said, hoping the mother would take his not-so-subtle hint and leave him in peace.

But no, Lady Springfeld's prattle continued as she asked interminable questions about the house's history and the surrounding countryside, and at every possible opportunity managed to make a comment about how beautiful and talented her daughter was.

Each question was answered with as few words as possible, while comments on Lady Iris's beauty required no response at all. He cared nothing of what she looked like. Why would he? He was blind, for God's sake. And surely the mother must be aware of that. Lady Iris could bear a passing resemblance to a gargoyle and he would neither know nor care. In fact, that might endear the daughter to him much more than all her supposed good looks ever could.

He knew from experience how fickle beautiful women were, how self-serving and how they used their beauty for their own advancement. Although, to be fair, Lady Iris did not really fit into that pattern. She was a young woman and not yet wed. As her mother had said, she was sweet, well-mannered and, he reluctantly had to agree, some would consider her rather charming. If she had good looks as well, and the sizable dowry that her mother had hinted at, there was no reason why she should not be married advantageously already. Perhaps there was something amiss with Lady Iris that he literally and figuratively could not see.

Finally, after an interminably long time, Lady Springfeld began to chatter about returning to the Walbertons' house. He stood up before she had a chance to change her mind.

'I hope you have a pleasant walk home,' he said.

And I hope you leave now and never return.

'Oh, we will, we will,' the cheerful woman said. 'And we will look forward to seeing you tonight, do you not agree, Iris?'

'Yes, I'm looking forward to it with as much anticipation as the Earl,' Lady Iris said, almost causing Theo to smile.

'I don't believe that could be possible,' he said instead with a bow. 'Until tonight, Lady Springfeld, Lady Iris.' With the greatest of pleasure, he rang the bell and Charles came to escort them out of the room.

The two women bustled their way to the door, followed by the traitorous Max, who reluctantly came to heel at the flick of Theo's fingers. When the door closed Theo collapsed into his chair, relieved to finally be alone again. All he had to do now was suffer one tedious social evening and his life could return to normal, the way it had been before the perpetually sunny Lady Iris and her equally irritating mother had burst into his life.

It had been a long time since Theo had dressed in formal evening wear. He had once enjoyed the ritual of preparing for an evening out and had done so full of anticipation of the pleasures to come.

But not tonight. Having to shave for a second time that day and change into his evening suit was a rigmarole he had avoided for the last six years, and now all he could think was that it was more effort than it could possibly be worth.

Damn woman. Damn daughter. The sooner this evening was over the happier he would be. He'd much rather spend the evening in front of the fire with his faithful companion, Max.

Well, his companion who was usually faithful. When the dog was in Lady Iris's company, he immediately forgot who and what he was. He ceased to be a noble, faithful Irish wolfhound and became a doting lapdog called Maxie-Waxie.

'Maxie-Waxie, indeed.'

'I beg your pardon, my lord?' his valet asked.

Theo was shocked that he had voiced his annoyance out loud. Those women really were getting under his skin. 'I'd appreciate it if someone could take Max for his evening walk tonight, as I will be otherwise engaged,' he said, to cover his awkwardness.

'Very good, my lord,' James said, and continued to brush down Theo's jacket. 'I'm pleased to say, my lord, the suit still fits you perfectly,' he added.

Theo could tell from his voice that James was now standing back and admiring his handiwork. He could also detect that the man had been smiling while he made that observation. What on earth did the man have to smile about? Why should he care about the way his master was dressed? He could not have fallen under Lady Iris's spell the way Max had so easily done, could he? Or was it merely that he was pleased that Theo was attending a social event after all these years?

Whatever it was, James had better enjoy it while he could, because after tonight he would not be going out into Society again, and he hopefully would not be seeing Lady Iris or her infernal mother again either.

Six years ago he had turned his back on a life that included endless dinner parties, balls, nights at the theatre and other such fripperies. It was a life that had eventually brought him nothing but disappointment and pain. He gritted his teeth together to push away all memories of his life before the accident. He had once lived in a delusional bubble, where he had not known what people were really like, what coldness could lie behind a pretty face and an enchanting smile.

No, he would not be returning to that false world. The neighbours now knew better than to disturb him—he just had to get the same message through to those infuriating women. They had to be made to understand that tonight would be an aberration, one that would not be repeated.

The valet carefully tied Theo's bow tie.

'You look quite your old self, my lord,' James said, 'if I may be so bold as to say so.'

Theo was tempted to tell him that no, he should not be so bold, but he knew the man meant well. It was hardly James's fault that Theo was in a bad mood that was all down to Lady Iris, her mother and this damnable dinner party.

'Thank you, James, that will be all,' he said instead, dismissing both his valet and the man's unwanted good mood.

James handed him his cane, top hat and gloves, then left.

Theo counted his steps towards the door, down the hallway, the stairs and the route out of the entrance hall. Using the snorting of the horses to guide himself to the carriage, he waved away the help of the coachman, and climbed up the steps. Then, with an exasperated sigh that no one would hear, he sat down and tapped his cane on the roof to signal to the driver he was ready to depart.

He rarely carried his cane. He knew every inch of his home and was familiar with the estate and surrounding area, so could easily find his way around, but he had not been in the Walbertons' home since the accident, so he would need it this evening. He had been a regular visitor to the house when he still had his sight, so knew the layout well, but he knew from bitter experience that when he was out of his own environment there were myriad obstacles that could trip him up, and he was loath to make even more of a spectacle of himself tonight than was absolutely necessary. That meant he would still have to draw attention to himself and his infirmity by finding his way with the aid of a walking stick.

Damn that as well.

He did not need his neighbours treating him in a pitying manner, did not need to hear the condescension in their voices, did not need to experience the indignity of their rushing to the aid of the poor cripple. He would not allow them to feel sorry for him, to judge him, to see themselves as his superiors.

His teeth grinding together, his muscles clenched tightly, he cursed Lady Springfeld for inflicting this torture on him.

Chapter Eleven

Lady Iris paced up and down outside the entrance hall and scanned the driveway for the sight of the Earl's carriage. Her anxiety wasn't for herself—of course not. Nor was she worried that the Earl would be unable to cope in an unfamiliar house. She was sure he'd cope admirably. After all, he appeared to cope admirably with everything…everything, that was, except her mother.

But at least her mother had been able to get him out of the house, something Lady Walberton said no one else had been able to do for many years, and she was most impressed that her friend had done something so many others had tried and failed to do. The Earl had been extended countless invitations by the Walbertons and other neighbours, but he had declined them all.

Yes, her sweet, cheerful and always friendly mother could be a force to be reckoned with when she set her mind to something.

And for some reason she had got it into her head that the Earl would make a perfect husband for her second daughter. It was most unlike her mother to be so determined when it came to marriage. Previously she had been happy for nature to take its course in the hope that Iris would meet a suitable man before it was too late. Why she had set her sights on the Earl, Iris could not imagine, but she had certainly been none too subtle in front of him. It had all been so embarrassing.

And it was that reason, no other, that had her anxiously waiting for the Earl's arrival. She merely wanted to inform him at the first opportunity that all this matchmaking was completely her mother's idea. As tactfully as possible, she intended to tell him that he had nothing to worry about. She had as much interest in marrying him as he had in marrying her.

He had made it blatantly clear that he did not want her, even if her mother had missed or ignored all his hints. And Iris had no intention of marrying a man who was a grumpy recluse who thought laughter and having fun were beneath him.

She stopped her pacing and looked up the driveway again. Was he going to be late? Was he even going to come to the dinner? Iris's hand flew to her chest, where her heart had given a peculiar jump. That was a possibility she hadn't considered until now. Perhaps he had merely agreed to attend so he could stop her mother from badgering him, but had never intended to actually do so. Could he be that rude? Iris suspected he could be—after all, being rude was his speciality.

There was no point waiting if he wasn't going to even bother to come. She looked up at the steps leading back into the house. This was a waste of time. All her anxiety had been for nothing. He wasn't even coming.

With a resigned sigh she walked up the steps, then took one last look up the driveway before entering the house. And there he was. His carriage had just turned in.

Like an excited child she skipped back down the steps, and actually waved her hand above her head, then remembered he couldn't see her.

Thank goodness for that, she thought, then pulled herself up for being uncharitable. He was blind, and she should not see his inability to see her making a fool of herself as a good thing.

The two-horse carriage drew up in front of the entranceway. She brushed down her pink silk gown, the one she had chosen because everyone said it flattered her complexion, and patted her hair to ensure every strand was still in place. What was wrong with her? The Earl was the one man who would not care what she looked like, but she patted her hair again anyway.

'Good evening, Your Lordship,' she said as soon as the liveried footman opened the carriage door and lowered the steps. 'I'm so pleased you actually came. If you hadn't my mother would have probably dragged me over to your house for another visit. And neither of us would want that. Would we? Certainly, I wouldn't.' She laughed lightly, embarrassed that she was burbling. He had made it perfectly clear when she was at his house that he did not like it when she did that, but she found it impossible not to chatter at the best of times, and the intensity of her burbling became even worse when she was nervous. And the Earl did make her nervous, as much as she wished that wasn't so.

'But I had to catch you before you entered the house,' she rushed on. 'I just had to let you know that none of this was my idea. It was all my mother's. So please, do not think that I put her up to this.'

She looked up at him expectantly. He didn't respond. Merely climbed down the steps and, using his silver-topped cane, tapped his way towards the steps.

She hovered around him, unsure what she was supposed to do or say now.

'You may take my arm, if you wish,' Iris said, extending a bent arm in his direction.

'That will not be necessary.'

'No, but it might be good manners,' Iris said, somewhat affronted. It was all but unheard of for a woman to offer her arm to a man, and the least he could do was to graciously accept it.

He paused, then extended his arm for her to take. She hooked hers through his and placed her gloved hand on top of his. Since her debut she had walked arm in arm with many a man, but for some reason with the Earl it felt like a much more intimate act, one that had set off those strange reactions. There it was again, that odd trembling that came from deep within her body. And there was that fluttering in the middle of her chest, the one she kept experiencing when she was in his house. This should not be happening. He was just a man after all, and one she didn't particularly like. There was no reason for her to either tremble or flutter just because he had taken her arm.

Perhaps it was because of all they had shared when she had spent the evening at his house, or because she knew this was the man her mother wanted her to marry. Whatever it was, it was making Iris almost light-headed, and ridiculously conscious of how close he was to her.

They walked slowly up the steps, his cane tapping out in front of them. When they reached the top the footman bowed and opened the large doors that led into the well-lit entrance hall.

'Everyone is in the main drawing room having drinks before dinner,' she said as they walked through the entrance hall.

'Everyone?' He stopped walking and inclined his head. 'I was under the impression it would merely be you, your mother and Lord and Lady Walberton. Didn't your mother say the other guests had left?'

'She said most of the guests had left. There are only a few still remaining, and Lady Walberton decided to invite a few local people as well. I think there are about twenty for dinner.'

He clasped his cane more tightly and drew in a deep breath.

'They're all very friendly,' Iris quickly added,

trying to reassure him. 'And I'll be here along with my mother. You've got nothing to worry about.'

'I am not worried,' he retorted. 'I merely do not like being deceived. Your mother gave me the impression that this would be a small dinner party.'

'Well, my mother probably does consider twenty guests to be a small dinner party.'

He exhaled loudly. 'So be it,' he said and commenced walking.

Iris put her other hand on top of his to halt his progress. 'And... I also wanted to warn you.'

'Warn me?'

'Um...yes. For some reason my mother has got it into her head that you would make a good husband for me, so she might be a bit... I'm sorry... I honestly have done nothing to encourage her.'

He removed her hand from his. 'Yes, I'm well aware of what your mother wants.'

'But honestly, it's just my mother. I don't want to marry you.' Her hand shot to her mouth. 'Not that there's anything wrong with you. But it's not as if we're...you know... I...um...'

She waited for him to say something, anything, to save her from this embarrassing moment. He said nothing. Was he deliberately waiting for her to dig herself into an even deeper hole?

'I just wanted to say, please ignore my mother,' she added quietly.

'I intend to do so,' he said and recommenced walking.

'Good.' She nodded rapidly, her cheeks burning, partly from yet again making a fool of herself in front of him, but also because of her disloyalty to her mother. After all, her mother always did what she thought was in her children's best interests. It was just that in this case she was terribly misguided.

They reached the drawing room and a footman opened the door. The guests had already assembled and were chattering amiably as they partook of their pre-dinner drinks.

The moment they stepped into the room the polite chatter died a sudden death and everyone in the now silent room turned to stare at the Earl.

Iris glared back at them, shocked by their bad manners. She looked up at the Earl, trying to think of something she could say to make this better. But no words came. All she could think was how rude they were all being and how bad she felt for the Earl.

'Whatever you're wearing tonight, Lady Iris, you appear to have shocked the guests into silence.' His comment was for her ears alone.

Her eyes grew wide as she continued to stare up at him, trying to read his expression. Was he making a joke? As far as she knew, the Earl never made jokes. Never laughed. His posture did not suggest it had been said in jest. His chin was tilted upwards, and, if he had been able to see, he most definitely would be looking down his nose at the other guests.

But it had to be a joke. And he was right, the best way to handle this situation was to make light of it. 'Well, as my mother kept trying to tell you, I'm a rare and exquisite beauty that no man can resist,' she said, forcing a laugh.

'One who is also reputed to be charming, sweet-natured, a natural mother and well adept at running a household efficiently, if I remember correctly.'

'And don't forget my highly skilled embroidery and watercolours,' she said, her laughter becoming genuine.

'Oh, who could forget those? Your mother made sure I never would by repeating your list of accomplishments over and over again. And now we can add to the list that you cause both men and women to become mute by your mere presence.'

'Yes, I'm one of a kind, that's for certain,' Iris said, pleased that quiet chatter had finally resumed among the guests, although quite a few were still staring in the Earl's direction, some discreetly and others quite openly.

Lady Walberton and Iris's mother emerged from the crowd, walked across the room to the doorway and joined them, smiling enthusiastically the entire time. 'I am so pleased you accepted my invitation, my lord,' her mother said.

'And I'm delighted to see you again,' Lady Walberton added.

The Earl paused and Iris was sure he would point out that he had been given no option to attend and the Walbertons' drawing room was the last place he wanted to be, but instead he merely bowed his head politely.

'So, I am sure you want to meet everyone present and reacquaint yourself with some old friends,' Lady Walberton said. 'Iris, will you please introduce the Earl to the other guests? I have…things to attend to.'

She sent Iris's mother a knowing look, which was returned with an equally conspiratorial smile.

'That won't be necessary,' he said with finality.

'Yes, it will,' Iris's mother said, her tone cheerful but showing she would allow no objections. She nodded to Iris to do as she had been instructed, and wandered off to talk to a group of older women standing by the ornate fireplace, while Lady Walberton halted the progress of the nearest footman and took him aside, as if she had something vital she needed to tell him, all the while keeping her eye on Iris and the Earl.

'It's either me, my mother or Lady Walberton,' Iris whispered to him.

He raised his eyebrows. 'And presumably you see yourself as the lesser of three evils.'

'No, but I suspect you do. Lady Walberton appears to be in on the marriage-making plans, so if you don't want to be subjected to another list of all the reasons why I would make a perfect wife, I think you had better let me do the introductions.'

He gave a small huff that almost sounded like a laugh but nodded his agreement.

She took his arm again and led him across the large drawing room to where the guests had gathered.

'Lord Hamilton, may I present Theo Crighton, the Earl of—?'

'Theo and I are old friends,' he interrupted. 'So good to see you again.'

Theo bowed his head. 'Lord Hamilton.' Then took Iris's arm to indicate he wanted to move on. She sent the surprised Lord Hamilton an apologetic smile and led the Earl to the next group.

'May I present Lord and Lady Smythe?'

The couple smiled at Theo, and he sent them a curt nod.

'Theo, my boy,' Lord Smythe said. 'Haven't seen you in a month of Sundays—what have you been up to all this time?'

'I have been busy on my estate. Now, if you'll excuse me, I believe there are others I must meet.'

And so it continued with each person he was introduced to. The Earl showed more politeness to those he had never met before than he did to his old friends, all of whom he dismissed with a brusque reply. Many tried to ask questions and to make overtures of friendship, but each person was rebuffed, often with little more than a one-word answer.

The Earl was making it very clear that he might be attending a social event, but he had no intention of actually being sociable.

They made it back to where they had started

in what must have been the fastest circuit of a room Iris had ever witnessed, and stood apart from the other guests.

'Well, you've got that out of the way,' she said. 'Now I suppose you can stand in the corner and scowl at everyone all night.'

The furrow in his brow deepened. 'I do not scowl.'

Iris couldn't help but smile. 'So what do you call it when someone is standing on the edge of a room full of people and frowning as if he's willing every possible misfortune to befall the assembled guests?'

'I wouldn't call it a scowl,' he said, and Iris almost detected movement in his lips. Was he about to smile? No, the frown remained in place. 'I simply have no interest in making polite chit-chat and I certainly have no interest in discussing what I have been up to since I last spoke to these people, something in which they are all inordinately interested.'

'Perhaps they just care about your well-being?'

'Nonsense, they're just being nosy.' Any hint of a smile had disappeared, and his expression could now most definitely be called a scowl.

'When I ask someone about their health, or

what they have been doing, it's because of concern for them, or because I'm taking an interest in them, not for nosiness's sake.'

'That's you, not everyone.'

Iris didn't know whether to be pleased that he had singled her out as different, or annoyed that he should be so dismissive of other people. It was that sort of dismissiveness that had led to his being a recluse, and it really was quite unfair. Everyone in the room appeared to be pleased to see him again. Even the guests' apparent rudeness when they had first entered she now suspected was merely surprise that he was actually attending a social function.

'Well, you're here now, so you might as well at least talk to some of these people,' she said.

'I'm talking to you, aren't I? You're one of these people, aren't you?'

So much for being special. She was now being classed as 'one of these people', and, as he was scowling at 'these people', it was unlikely to be a compliment.

'Well, I suppose it's making my mother happy that we're spending time together,' she said. 'And I know how much you like doing that.'

He gave another huff that almost, *almost*, sounded like a laugh. 'What would make your mother happy would be to marry you off. So perhaps you shouldn't be wasting your time talking to me. Isn't there another man here whom you can captivate with your charm and beauty?'

He had a way of making charm and beauty sound like the least attractive attributes that a woman could possess.

She looked over at Lord Pratley, a man who took every opportunity he could to praise her, for real and imagined qualities. If Lord Pratley mentioned her charm and beauty it most certainly would not sound like an insult. Lord Pratley raised his glass at her and smiled. Iris swallowed a sigh but nodded in acknowledgement. 'No, there's no one here who is capable of appreciating me in quite the way you do,' she said, not bothering to keep the facctiousness out of her voice.

'I doubt that to be true.'

She looked up at him. Did he think she was serious? And was that an insult or a compliment? It was so hard to tell with him. She turned back to face the room. It was probably safer to assume it was an insult.

'Anyway, there is no one else here that I have the slightest interest in marrying, so I might as well talk to you as to anyone else.'

'I'm flattered. I suppose that was what your mother would describe as part of your delightfully endearing manner.'

She laughed at yet another insult. 'I must admit, it's rather agreeable to be able to talk to someone who doesn't expect me to be polite or amiable,' she said, realising just how much truth that statement held. Since her coming out five years ago she had been expected to play the role of a pretty, agreeable and well-mannered young woman. After all, that was all that was expected of a débutante. She had been doing it for so long it had become a part of who she was. But with the Earl of Greystone, she was finding that another side of her personality was emerging. It was all rather interesting.

'You had better be careful,' she continued. 'If you stay talking to me all night it won't be long before I become downright rude.' She really was enjoying this. 'Then you'll be damn sorry.' Oh, yes, this was fun. When had she ever used a word like damn in public? Never, was the simple answer to that. It was tempting to say it again just to hear the word out loud.

'I look forward to it. And presumably you'll extend the same courtesy to me and allow me to be downright rude back to you.'

'Well, I haven't been able to stop you so far, have I?'

My goodness. He actually did it. He actually smiled. And oh, what a smile. He certainly should smile more often. Iris stared at him as if transfixed. Those full lips had parted to reveal perfect white teeth. Lines had crinkled around his eyes, suggesting that he had once smiled a lot. And oh, my, he actually had a small dimple. Who would have thought the grumpy, reclusive Earl of Greystone would have something as cute and adorable as a dimple on his left cheek?

Warmth flooded through her and she was tempted to hug him, that smile was making her so happy. Then, as quickly as it had appeared, it vanished, like a dream upon waking, and the frown reappeared. It was as if he had caught himself doing something he knew to be forbidden. But it was too late. She had seen it and would never forget it. She now knew he was capable of smiling, possibly even laughing. And she intended to make him smile and laugh again, as soon and as often as possible.

She looked around the room, trying to think of something else she could say that would make him smile again, but nothing came to mind. The chatter in the room had gone back to the same level as it was when they had first entered, although the frequent glances in their direction did make her suspect that the Earl was still a topic of conversation.

Before she could think of anything else to amuse him, the room unaccountably descended once more into silence, and every head turned towards the open door. Iris looked around to see that Lady Estelle and Lord Thaddeus Redcliffe had entered. As one the heads moved from the couple at the door to the Earl, then back again, as if following a rather slow tennis match.

What on earth was going on? wondered Iris. Why would Lady Estelle and Lord Thaddeus Redcliffe cause the same reaction as the entrance of Theo Greystone? They had been guests in the house since the beginning of the week, they were well-known to most of the people in attendance, and their entrance had never caused this reaction before.

Lady Redcliffe certainly looked stunning tonight, but then, she always did. She was indisputably the most beautiful woman Iris had ever seen, with her striking violet-blue eyes, thick black hair, porcelain skin, and tall, elegant figure. She was also the epitome of charm and grace.

Despite the somewhat startling reaction of the guests, she was smiling at them as if their stunned silence was only to be expected. Her gaze swept grandly around the room then halted at Theo and Iris.

'Apparently, we're not the only ones to cause a stir tonight,' Iris said. 'Or at least I'm not the only one to cause men and women to become mute.'

He inclined his head towards her as if asking for an explanation, but before she could think of a witty way to explain the Redcliffes' entrance she saw Lady Redcliffe murmur something to her husband and gracefully glide across the room towards them.

'Lady Iris,' she said with a small curtsy. Then she turned her full attention to the Earl, and her beautiful smile became even more radiant. 'Theo,' she said, her voice full of affection. 'I didn't know you would be here tonight.'

With each word Lady Redcliffe said more colour drained from the Earl's face. His body became increasingly rigid and his teeth were clenched so tightly the muscles on the sides of his jaw stood out.

'It's so wonderful to see you again,' she continued as if impervious to his shocked reaction and his lack of reply. 'So much has happened since I last saw you, we must take some time to chat, but I see my husband wants me to join him. Until later, then.'

With that she swept her way across the room, followed by the eyes of everyone present, including Iris's. Only one person was not following her progress. The Earl of Greystone, who was standing stock still, his chin lifted, his hands curled into fists at his sides.

Her heart pounding furiously within her chest, Iris flicked her glance between the stern man standing beside her and the beautiful woman chatting to her husband and smiling as if she did not have a care in the world.

It was obvious that something had happened between these two, something that virtually everyone else in the room knew about. Was Lady Redcliffe the reason why he had secreted himself away in his castle? Was she the reason why he was so hostile to the world? Had he once been in love with Lady Redcliffe? Was he still in love with her?

A pain gripped her stomach and the tightness in her chest was making it hard to draw in a breath. She tried to tell herself she was merely upset because of the obvious distress that the Earl was in, but knew that was a lie.

This pain was not just sympathy for another person's agony. As much as she was loath to admit it, this reaction was personal and it felt suspiciously like jealousy.

Chapter Twelve

Theo struggled to breathe. He struggled to keep his equanimity. He would not let anyone know how much Estelle's presence had affected him, not these guests, not Estelle or her husband, and not Lady Iris Springfeld. Although he had already failed when it came to Lady Iris. He could tell she was staring up at him. What expression was on her face? Was it pity? Was it curiosity? Was it amusement? No, he doubted the last. She did not strike him as the sort of woman who took enjoyment in other people's suffering.

'Lady Estelle and I are old acquaintances,' he finally said to satisfy what he assumed would be her curiosity. 'But we parted many years ago and have not seen each other since.' He hoped his voice sounded sufficiently brusque so it would eliminate any pity she might be feeling.

'More than just acquaintances, I suspect.' Her terse voice held none of the laughter that was usually present. It seemed she too was affected by his reaction to Estelle's presence. Perhaps she was feeling pity for him after all.

He shrugged, aiming for nonchalance. 'Perhaps, but that was a long time ago, before she married the Earl of Redcliffe.'

He braced himself for a bombardment of questions, ones he was going to have to deflect with his practised acerbity. He would not be explaining how Estelle had destroyed him, how she had been the love of his life and she had turned her back on him when he needed her most. He would not be telling Lady Iris how Estelle had taught him the fickle, fraudulent nature of love.

But no questions came. Good. For once she was silent. He waited. Surely she was going to say something? She was rarely quiet, and certainly not for this long.

Normally he would be silently begging for her to stop her constant chatter, her teasing and her jokes, but now these things were exactly what he wanted. Anything was better than this silence that had fallen between them. Anything would be welcome that would take his mind away from thoughts of Estelle and her husband.

He waited for her to say something, to tease, to make one of her little jokes, but still she remained silent.

'I'm sorry if you're upset,' she finally said, quietly. 'When my mother invited you, she would not have known that any of the guests would cause you such disquiet.'

'It makes no difference to me who the guests are,' he fired back. That was quite clearly not true, but his reaction to Estelle's presence was not something he wished to discuss with her or anyone.

They sank back into silence, something he was usually comfortable with, but not tonight.

'Lady Redcliffe and I were once engaged,' he finally said, surprised that it should be he who broke their uncomfortable silence and even more surprised to find himself doing exactly what he had vowed he would not do, explaining his reaction to Estelle's presence.

'I see,' she murmured.

He waited for her to ask questions, to make comments, to give her opinion. She said nothing. Was 'I see' all she was going to say?

'But it was a long time ago,' he repeated,

despite himself. Was he about to become the one who burbled uncontrollably?

'She is very beautiful,' Iris said, her voice still quiet.

'Yes, she was, and presumably she still is, but that hardly matters to me now, does it?'

'No, I suppose not. If you'd like to…' He heard a deep inhalation. 'If you'd like to go and talk to her, please feel free. You don't have to stay with me.'

'I'm happy with the present company.' Theo frowned, realising that there was indeed some truth in his statement. As much as he was loath to attend this dinner, he had no objection to Lady Iris's company. 'But if there is anyone else you wish to talk to yourself, please, do not let me keep you.'

'No.' She paused. 'I've spent all week with these people, and most of them have attended various balls and other social occasions with me throughout the last five Seasons.' Her voice had almost gone back to its usual cheerful tone. 'I doubt if there's anything new we have to say to each other.'

He suspected her joviality was forced, but he was grateful for it. He wanted to put all thought of Estelle Redcliffe out of his mind, but he also did not want Lady Iris to be upset, as she had so obviously been. He paused to absorb that unexpected reaction. Why did he suddenly care what Lady Iris was feeling? Previously, all he had wanted was for her to leave him alone. Now he was pleased to have her company.

'So I have novelty value?' he said in jest, before he could analyse this change in opinion too deeply.

She gave a little laugh and he had to admit he was pleased to hear it again. 'I suppose you could say that. You're certainly different from everyone else here.' Her laughter suddenly halted. 'I mean… I don't mean…'

He patted her arm in reassurance. 'I know what you mean.' His hand lingered. Her arm was bare above her gloves, her skin soft and supple. The desire to run his hand up her arm, to see if her shoulders were equally naked was an almost overwhelming temptation.

He quickly withdrew his hand as if he had placed it too close to the fire. What on earth was wrong with him? He may have become resigned to Lady Iris and her relentlessly cheerful nature, might even have come to appreciate it, at least when it provided a diversion to his thoughts of Estelle. But that was all. He did not want Lady Iris. He was not attracted to her, and most certainly did not want to do anything to encourage her mother in her marriage-making plans. The last thing he should be doing was touching her in any manner that could be misconstrued as affection.

It was not that he could find any real fault with her, unless one regarded a pleasant disposition and a tendency to being over-talkative as faults. He was sure many a man would be more than happy to have her as his wife. Just not him. He did not want anyone. He turned his head in the direction that Estelle had gone in when she walked away from him. He did not want anyone ever again.

And Lady Iris did not deserve him. She did not deserve a damaged man, one who was still foolishly in the thrall of another woman, a woman who quite sensibly had made it clear she did not want him. Lady Iris deserved a man who was capable of loving her wholeheartedly. And that was simply not him.

Chapter Thirteen

The dinner gong sounded and Lady Iris slid her arm through Theo's, taking him by surprise.

'I'm not offering you my help,' she said, her voice containing a hint of censure as if trying to stop him before he made another objection. 'You can be a gentleman and escort me into dinner.'

'I'd be honoured,' he said with a bow of his head. He had not intended to offend Lady Iris, neither the first time she had taken his arm, nor this time. And she was right. Taking her arm was merely the polite thing to do, although it had been a while since he had felt the need to be polite to anyone. Not since the last time he had been in company, and he was somewhat rusty.

But she had been wrong about the reason for his surprise. While he did object strongly to anyone who dared to see him as in need of their help, if he had shown any reluctance it was because when he had touched her naked arm, when his fingers had felt her bare skin, he'd had a somewhat disconcerting reaction, one which he did not wish to experience again.

They formed a line of couples, then paraded out of the drawing room, down the hallway and into the dining room. Lady Iris led him to their chairs and he was pleased to discover they were seated together. No doubt that had been arranged by the mother.

He tilted his head and concentrated, listening carefully until he detected Estelle's sweet voice from the end of the table, chatting happily, presumably to her husband.

Bitter bile rose up his throat. He should not have done that. He did not need to be reminded that she was now happily married. The pain she had caused him meant nothing to her. She had moved on with her life and left him far behind, discarded and forgotten.

If he was to survive this dinner party he was going to have to do his darnedest to ignore Estelle's presence.

Taking his napkin, he flicked it hard, then, gripping the edges, placed it on his lap, trying to blot out the sound of her voice.

But that was impossible. It was as if all his senses were focused on Estelle. The sound of her laughter rose above the cacophony of voices, causing him to wince. Once that laughter had brought him so much joy. Now it cut through him like a lance.

'I'm sorry you have to endure this,' Lady Iris said quietly. 'I don't know what has happened between the two of you and I don't expect you to tell me, but I can see that this is causing you pain, and I am sorry you were forced to attend this dinner party.'

He shook his head. 'It is of no mind.'

'Please be assured, my mother is not a cruel woman. She would never do anything to anyone that she thought might hurt them and would never have expected you to attend this dinner if she had known it would cause you to suffer such distress.'

He could point out that her mother had all but threatened him, had given him the option of attending this dinner party or having to suffer the horror of a constant stream of visitors, but Lady Iris was trying to be kind and was showing remorse on her mother's behalf.

'You have nothing to remonstrate yourself for.' And in that he was not merely being polite. This dinner party was not her fault.

Estelle's presence was not her fault. And he had to admit, having her at his side was at least making something that would otherwise be intolerable, almost bearable. It was as if there was someone on his side, and for that he appreciated her.

Perhaps he had somewhat underestimated Lady Iris. He had dismissed her as a mere chatterbox with a perpetually sunny disposition, but there was much more to her than that. She had shown bravery when she had entered his room, and now he could see that she also had a sensitive, compassionate nature. She had also refrained from asking him about his reaction to Estelle's presence. He had expected her curiosity to get the better of her and for her to at least ask some subtle questions to prompt him into revelations, but she had not even hinted that she expected him to reveal all. He knew from experience that young women loved to gossip, but maybe this young woman was the exception.

That was something else he should perhaps apologise for. He had unfairly misjudged her when she had entered his life, dripping wet but still cheerful. Yes, there was certainly more depth to the young lady than he had at first assumed.

The first course was served and Iris made the required polite conversation. Theo forced himself to make equally polite responses—after all, as he'd already conceded, none of this was Lady Iris's fault. In fact, she was giving him every impression that she had his best interests at heart, something he had not experienced for a long time, if ever.

So the least he could do was be civil and polite, even if what he really wanted to do was leave this damn dinner party and escape back to his sanctuary, away from these people, away from Estelle and away from the reminder of what he had once had.

When the next course was served, Lady Iris turned from him to speak to Lord Pratley, while Theo made murmured agreements to the lady on his left while she twittered on about the weather and the highlights of the Season, the favoured conversation topics of Society ladies.

Rising above the politely murmured conversation, Theo could hear Lord Pratley talking to—or should that be talking at?—Lady Iris. His conversation appeared to consist entirely of compliments, telling Lady Iris how beautiful she looked tonight, how her pink gown flattered her complexion, a complexion he compared to the pink blush on a white rose, how her blue eyes were sparkling like sapphires, and her beautiful blonde hair was like rich, creamy buttermilk.

In response to each compliment, Lady Iris merely said a polite, almost bored thank-you. Could the man not tell that his compliments were not having the desired effect, that the recipient was not enjoying his flattery? A lack of vanity was another of Lady Iris's more admirable qualities, or at least she was not susceptible to flattery the way so many other young ladies were.

In that way she differed remarkably from Estelle, who could never get enough compliments. And when he had been with Estelle he had indulged her vanity at every opportunity. Had he sounded as pitiful as Lord Pratley did right now when he had showered Estelle with compliments? That was not what Theo had thought at the time. All he was aware of was the wonderful fact that he was engaged to the most beautiful woman he had ever seen, a woman who was desired by so many men. She had never tired of hearing how beautiful she was and he had never tired of telling her so.

He had to admit that sometimes it had been as if he was praising his most prized possession, and the compliments were for himself and his ability to attract the attentions of a woman so many other men wanted. Like a puffed-up ass, he had thought being the fiancé of such a beautiful woman somehow reflected on his prowess as a man. He had enjoyed being the envy of other men and had been proud to have Estelle on his arm. Such conceit now seemed so petty and pointless.

But he had loved Estelle, and deep down, despite what had happened between them, that love had never died.

Lord Pratley's loud voice interrupted his thoughts. He had now moved on to Lady Iris's lips, which he was comparing to rosebuds, rich claret and ripe strawberries. Then he went back to her eyes. Apparently sparkling sapphires weren't enough, because Pratley believed they also bore a striking similarity to the sky on a summer's day, and to cornflowers and borage. Borage? Was that even blue? Theo had no idea.

Instead of encouraging more of his compliments, as he knew Estelle would have done, Lady Iris turned the conversation to Lord Pratley's planned fishing trip to Norway. As the Viscount talked about all the salmon he planned to catch, where he would be staying and the adventures he and his friends were expecting to have, Lady Iris merely made murmurs of interest. Theo wondered what the expression on her face would reveal. Was she bored? Her responses had been polite but showed no real enthusiasm. Or was she enjoying the Viscount's company?

'It's a shame you can't come with us,' he heard Lord Pratley say. 'But maybe you will next year?' Pratley gave a loud guffaw, which drowned out any response Lady Iris might have made.

Theo gripped his knife and fork more tightly. The audacity of the man. Was he assuming that he would be married to Lady Iris before next year's fishing season? She had said nothing about Pratley being her intended. Her mother had said Lady Iris received many offers each Season, and Pratley's clumsy attempt at courting suggested that she did indeed have at least one conquest this year, one she was evidently not particularly interested in.

Theo had to wonder why not. Why would Lady Iris not be interested in a courtship with Pratley? Theo thought him a buffoon, but he was a good catch for any unmarried young lady. He was from a distinguished lineage, was known to have a substantial estate and income, and, as far as Theo knew, had all his faculties. So why was the mother interested in Theo when Lady Iris already had an equally, if not better, catch already on her hook?

Although the question he should be asking himself was, why did he care? Lady Iris was merely a casual acquaintance, one who meant nothing to him. Her mother might be seeing him as a potential husband, but neither he nor Lady Iris saw it that way. Why should he care what was happening between Lady Iris and Lord Pratley? But still, the impertinence of the man made his blood boil.

'Sir, may I remove your plate? The next course is about to be served,' a footman said close to his ear, interrupting Theo's thoughts.

He released the tightly held knife and fork and sat back in his chair while the servants shuffled round them, serving the next course.

'Oh, salmon, lovely—my favourite,' Lady Iris said in her usual sunny voice.

'Well, you'll be able to catch all the salmon you want next season, won't you?' he said, his voice more curt than he'd intended. 'Enjoy fishing, do you?'

'Were you eavesdropping on my conversation with Lord Pratley?' she said, a teasing note in her voice.

'I could hardly avoid hearing Pratley prattle on, could I?' he said quickly, to cover up any embarrassment over being caught doing something that might suggest he cared about her relationship with another man.

'Hmm, well, in answer to your question, I have no idea whether I enjoy fishing or not because I've never tried.'

He wanted to say that would make her unique among young ladies. She might not have tried salmon fishing but fishing for a suitable husband was a sport most young women excelled at. He knew from bitter experience what it was like to be reeled in by a beautiful woman. Men could be so ridiculous at times. Just like Pratley, he had once thought he was the one who had done the chasing, but he had been skilfully landed like a helpless fish at the mercy of an accomplished angler.

'Perhaps when you're married to Pratley and he whisks you off to Norway you'll be able to find out,' he bit out.

What on earth was wrong with him? Why should he care whether she married Pratley or any other man? The strain of the evening was having more of an effect on him than he had realised. The sooner this evening was over and he could return home the better. In the meantime, he needed to rein himself in and adopt a more composed manner.

She laughed lightly, but made no comment. But why should he expect her to tell him what her arrangement was with Lord Pratley? He had no more right to ask her about Pratley than she had to ask him about Estelle. And, he had to admit, she had been a lot more restrained than he was in that regard.

'Eat your food—it will be getting cold,' he said to cover his discomfort. He lifted his wine glass and was pleased that the weight showed the footman had refilled it.

'Well, it's actually a salmon mousse, so I don't think there's much danger of its getting cold.' She gave another of her little laughs. Did this young woman laugh at everything? 'And you had better drink some more of your wine. It's probably in equal danger of getting cold.'

'As you command, my lady,' he said, taking a long quaff.

He was being unfair to her and he knew it. It was hardly her fault if Pratley had intentions towards her. And it mattered not a bit to him whether she had intentions towards Pratley or not.

He needed to settle down, stop being a cad

and go back to making polite conversation like the well-bred gentleman he had once been.

He racked his brain for something polite and pointless to talk about, but nothing would come. Once he had been the master of making small talk. Using a lot of words to say virtually nothing had become second nature to him, honed over years of attending dinner parties such as this and seemingly endless balls. But now he was out of practice and could think of nothing trivial to say.

Before any witty comment or pithy observation could occur to him the sound of Estelle's tinkling laugh rose above the polite murmur of the other guests' voices again. Lady Iris appeared to have heard it as well, as the sound of her knife and fork on her plate ceased. Although why Estelle's happiness should affect Lady Iris he did not know. But then, neither did he know why Pratley's assumption that he would be marrying Lady Iris should affect him the way it did.

Estelle's joyful laughter rang out yet again, cutting him to the quick, and causing every muscle in his body to tense.

He grabbed his glass, lifted it to his lips and was annoyed to discover it empty. With a tap on the glass, he signalled to the servant that he needed more wine *now*. The man instantly leant over him and refilled the glass.

Theo drained it, trying to steady his mind and relax his body. He knew from experience wine could not anaesthetise pain, but tonight he was going to give it another try.

Iris looked down the table, to where Lady Redcliffe was seated. She was smiling brightly, laughing loudly and talking animatedly, as if she was having the best time of her life. And yet, she kept flicking quick glances in the Earl's direction as if to reassure herself that she had his attention.

Her husband gave the appearance of either being oblivious to this behaviour, or enjoying it, sitting across the table from her, looking as proud as a peacock. Every man around her was focused on Lady Redcliffe and she was glowing, revelling in being the centre of attention.

Iris wished Lady Redcliffe would stop laughing so loudly and drawing attention to herself. Iris rarely cared about such things. After all, her family could get raucous at times and she herself was known to laugh loudly on occasion, even when she knew such behaviour was deemed unacceptable for a young lady. But even though she wished it wasn't so, Lady Redcliffe's laughter was grating on her nerves. Was it because it sounded so false, or was it because of the effect it was having on the Earl? Or, much worse than either of those reasons, was it simply that she was jealous because Lady Redcliffe was drawing the Earl's attention away from her? Was she that self-centred? The poor man was suffering and she was being a vain and frivolous woman, wanting to keep his attention all to herself.

Yes, she was pathetic, and not particularly nice. It was the Earl that was being forced to endure something which was causing him great anguish, and here she was feeling sorry for herself.

He should never have been forced to attend this dinner party. If it weren't for her and her mother the Earl would be at home beside his fire with Max. She looked down to the other end of the table, where her mother was sitting beside Lord Walberton. Her mother sent her a sad smile. Lady Redcliffe's behaviour and the Earl's reaction had not been missed by her ever-astute mother.

'I'm so sorry,' Iris murmured.

He shook his head. 'You've nothing to be sorry for,' he said, raising his hand to signal the footman. 'And certainly not for this rather fine Bordeaux.'

He lowered his glass and drew in a deep breath. 'Lady Iris, really, you have nothing to apologise for,' he repeated, his voice conciliatory. 'I'm a grown man and I'm perfectly capable of looking after myself, but I thank you for your concern.'

She looked at his wine glass and frowned, hoping that wasn't the way he thought he could look after himself.

'You don't appear to have eaten your salmon,' she said.

'No, I have no appetite,' he said sharply. Then in a softer voice he continued, 'It's a shame Max isn't here. Living on my own, I have got into the bad habit of giving him anything I don't eat myself.'

Iris smiled, pleased that he was no longer speaking in such a terse manner and pleased that Lady Redcliffe's laughter was no longer filling the air.

'He's such a lovely dog,' she said. 'As much as I adore Sookie, I must say I'm rather taken with Maxie-Waxie.'

'And him with you. I've never seen him latch on to anyone as quickly as he did to you. It almost made me jealous.'

Iris winced slightly at the mention of jealousy and cast a quick glance in Lady Redcliffe's direction. Catching the lady's eye, Iris quickly looked away.

The salmon course was removed, the dishes hardly touched by either the Earl or Iris. With reluctance she turned back to Lord Pratley and braced herself for another round of compliments. Surely the Viscount must have run out of flattering things to say by now. After all, how many comparisons could he make to her eyes, hair, lips and skin? Perhaps he'd now move on to her nose, telling her it was like a tulip bulb, a potato or a mushroom.

She smiled to herself, which was a mistake as the Viscount thought she was smiling at him and instantly launched into complimenting her teeth.

'Lady Iris,' he said, raising his glass as if in toast. 'You have the most beautiful smile I have ever seen and it's an honour to be bathed in its glow. Your teeth are as white as snow and as straight as...'

He paused to think and Iris was tempted to supply him with a few comparisons. As straight as a row of tombstones in a graveyard...as straight as the cutlery on this table... as straight as the pickets in a cottage fence.

Unable to think of anything which he felt best described her teeth, he went back to complimenting her lips, and Iris drifted off, merely providing the occasional 'mmm-hmm' for the sake of politeness.

Why men thought women required constant flattery about their appearance Iris would never know. She looked over at the Earl. He had absolutely no idea what she looked like and that was rather wonderful. She could be a breathtaking beauty or as plain as a pikestaff and it would make no difference to him whatsoever. And yet, he had been engaged to a beautiful woman. Was this before or after he had lost his sight? Iris wondered. Was it something other than her beauty that had attracted him to Lady Redcliffe? He couldn't see her now, and yet she still had a strong hold over him, so presumably it wasn't just her beauty that he adored.

Once again she caught Lady Redcliffe's eye, and once again Iris quickly looked away as if being caught doing something shameful.

The footmen removed their plates, the dessert was served and with relief Iris turned back to the Earl.

'So I hear that you have teeth as white as snow and they are as straight as something unimaginable,' he said, causing Iris to smile. She looked over at Lord Pratley to make sure he hadn't heard.

'I'm starting to build up an interesting picture of you,' the Earl continued. 'You have eyes like sapphires, a strawberry for a mouth, skin like a rose and teeth like snow. You're quite an unusual-looking woman, I must say.'

Iris started to giggle. This really was rather rude but also rather funny. His voice was still stern, and she wasn't sure if he was joking or merely being rude and mocking Lord Pratley, but it was funny all the same. Iris had an image of herself with stones for eyes, strawberries for lips and a mouthful of snow.

'It could be worse,' she added quietly. 'I could have teeth as yellow as buttermilk.'

'Which might be better than teeth like borage and skin the colour of claret and the texture of a strawberry.'

Iris put a hand to her mouth to stop her laughter from getting louder. Now she was sure he was joking, or at the very least making fun of Lord Pratley and his pretentious attempts to woo her.

'Your mother was right,' he continued. 'You are an unsurpassed beauty, or, at least in Lord

Pratley's opinion, you're an unsurpassed collection of random pieces from the natural world.'

Just as Iris was starting to relax and enjoy herself, Lady Redcliffe's laughter again cut through the air, louder and more forceful than before, destroying the light moment they had been sharing. She looked along the table and saw the Countess was staring straight at them. While she was smiling as if she was having the most delightful time, her eyes were boring straight into Iris, and they most certainly were not smiling.

This was all very peculiar. What was wrong with the woman? She was no longer engaged to the Earl, was married to someone else. It was obvious to Iris that she was deliberately trying to draw the attention of the Earl, but why? She was a married woman, for goodness' sake. Why did she find it necessary to play these games? Why did she wish to toy with the Earl?

As intended, the Earl too had heard the laughter and that now familiar frown had returned. Iris wanted to tell him just to ignore her. She wanted to tell him that she was sure Lady Redcliffe was merely toying with him. But she knew nothing of the Earl's past, knew nothing about what had happened between him and Lady Redcliffe, knew nothing at all really about the Earl, except that he lived in an ancient home, had a dog called Max, was a recluse and had experienced at least one nightmare.

Oh, and that he looked rather magnificent when he was less than formally attired, but the last one was something she really should not know.

The dessert plates were removed and Lady Walberton stood up to announce that the ladies should leave the men to their brandy and cigars. With much scraping of chairs everyone around the table rose. The ladies lined up according to rank and in a straight line exited the dining room. Before she left Iris took a backwards glance at the Earl, and a surprising sense of loss washed over her. He hadn't wanted to attend this dinner party, and there was no denying it had been a fraught one. She just hoped he had at least enjoyed the time they had spent talking together. Iris knew that she certainly had.

Chapter Fourteen

'You and Lady Iris seem to be getting on rather well,' Lord Pratley said when the rustle of the women's gowns had died down and the door had shut behind them.

'Yes,' was Theo's terse reply.

'You know she's my almost intended,' Pratley added.

Theo was tempted to point out to him that there was no such thing as an *almost* intended, but what was the point? If Lord Pratley was in pursuit of Lady Iris, it was hardly any concern of his.

'She's been out now for several Seasons and I've finally got my chance to do what so many other men have tried to do and failed,' Pratley continued. 'And it would be bad form for any man to do anything to upset another man's chances. Don't you agree, Greystone?'

The brandy decanter was passed his way. He poured himself a drink and stifled a bored sigh. 'I dare say that would be the case, if the man actually did have a chance.'

'Now, steady on, Greystone.'

'I'm not your competition, Pratley,' Theo said, swirling the brandy in his glass and savouring its rich aroma.

'Well, I should hope not, but I could see the way Lady Iris was looking at you. If it had been pity I could see on her face I would have understood—after all, she does have a compassionate nature—but it wasn't like that. She actually appeared to be rather taken with you. So I'd appreciate it if you did nothing to encourage the girl's attentions.'

'Believe me, I have done nothing to encourage Lady Iris.'

'Good. After all, she's a bit wasted on you, isn't she, old boy?' The Viscount chuckled at his own joke. 'She's a damn fine woman to look at and you can't actually see her, can you?' He chuckled again, as if Theo's blindness was a source of great amusement. 'You're hardly in a position to appreciate just what a beauty she is. She was the best available in her first Season, and no one yet has been able to outshine her, that's for sure. Whereas, for you, it hardly matters now whether she's a looker or not.'

Theo gripped his glass tighter, then swallowed his brandy along with his anger. He tried to focus on the burn of the rich liquid as it moved down his throat while attempting to blot out the insulting nonsense Pratley was spouting.

'You don't need her dowry either, do you?' the Viscount continued, either oblivious of or unconcerned by the offence he had just given. 'Which, between you and me, is rather a generous one. Nor do you need her father's contacts, as I hear tell you live like a hermit these days. So, you should leave her to someone who can fully appreciate all that she has to offer.'

Pratley sat back in his chair and sighed, as if to signal that he had said what he wanted to say, and that was the last that needed to be said on the subject. Theo knew he should just let it go. He had no interest in Lady Iris and was certain that an intelligent woman like her would have no interest in this buffoon, but he couldn't. He could not let this self-satisfied oaf talk about Lady Iris as if she were a commodity, a prized possession that this fool was proud to have won.

'Is that all Lady Iris is to you? A pretty face and a sizeable dowry?'

'Well, no, certainly not,' Pratley said, sounding affronted. 'She's a lovely young woman, just lovely. All I'm saying is she'd make a man like me an attractive wife, and what man doesn't want an attractive wife on his arm? Makes him feel, well, more of a man, doesn't it?'

Theo grimaced. Did he really have any right to judge Pratley? Hadn't he been exactly the same? Hadn't he been so proud, strutting about with Estelle on his arm? He'd been full of smug self-satisfaction because he had the woman that every other man wanted. What a fool he had been. What a fool Pratley still was, and Lady Iris deserved so much better. Better than Pratley, better than himself.

'And Lady Iris is interested in what *you* have to offer, is she?'

'What?' Pratley shuffled forward in his chair. 'Well, she hasn't told me that in so many words, but then she's just playing a bit hard to get, isn't she?' He huffed out his indignation. 'After all, she's a fine-looking gel, so she's entitled to play a few games with a man, isn't she? Makes 'em an even better prize when you finally do catch 'em.'

In that Pratley was right. Young ladies often

did play games. Hadn't Estelle played games with him? Games that went from playful to cruel. But he doubted Lady Iris was the sort to dally with a man's affections and Pratley had no right to talk about her in that way. And he doubted she actually was toying with Pratley. Their conversation had suggested she had absolutely no interest in the man—quite the opposite. This so-called almost courting was purely in Pratley's mind.

Theo was confident that Lady Iris had better taste. But that did not mean the mother did. His confidence evaporated. The mother had set her sights on Theo, but Pratley was an even better catch for a mother in search of a husband for her daughter. Perhaps the mother had given Pratley reason to hope.

'And what of Lady Springfeld?' he asked, trying to keep his voice as nonchalant as possible. 'Have you broached the subject with the mother? Is she agreeable?'

Pratley huffed. 'That one. A most unusual woman, I have to say. Anyone would think she doesn't want the gel to wed. She does nothing to promote her cause. I've had so many other mothers approach me this Season, encouraging me to show an interest in their daughters, but from Lady Springfeld, nothing.'

Interesting. That was not the impression Theo got. His presence here tonight was testament to how much the mother wanted the daughter to be wed. He took another drink, pleased that Pratley had confirmed his suspicions. The man did not stand a chance with Lady Iris, as neither the young lady herself nor her mother saw Pratley as a marriage prospect. He doubted he was the only gentleman Lady Springfeld had tried to interest in her daughter, but Pratley was not under consideration. Good. He would hate to see Lady Iris married off to this self-serving ass.

'But not to worry,' Pratley continued, pouring himself another brandy. 'Lady Iris has shown no interest in any other man this Season, or any previous Season, and I hear tell that the mother is not pursuing any other possibilities either. So it's an even playing field, as they say, and I've got more chance than most.'

That was even more interesting. What on earth was the mother playing at, then, setting her sights on Theo when there were so many other, better prospects for her daughter? Sometimes the workings of a woman's mind were beyond him, and he would never solve the conundrum of why women did what they did when it came to selecting a suitable husband.

All Theo needed to be aware of was, even if the misguided mother was trying to pair him off with her daughter, neither he himself nor Lady Iris had any interest in such a match.

'Then I wish you every luck in your pursuit,' he said to Pratley.

'Thank you, Greystone, mighty good of you,' he replied, oblivious to Theo's lack of sincerity. 'Not sure why I was so worried,' the Viscount said, and dragged on his cigar. 'After all, we all know that no attractive woman would want to be with a man like you. Lady Redcliffe made that clear, didn't she?'

Theo's right hand curled into a tight fist. His muscles clenched. His body burned with rage and the desire to drag Lord Pratley outside and give him a sound beating became all but overwhelming.

With as much control as he could muster, Theo placed his brandy balloon on the table and leant in close to Pratley. So close he could smell the cigar smoke and drink on his breath. 'You do not know what you are talking about,' he said through gritted teeth. 'You don't know anything about me and Lady Iris, and you know even less about what happened between me and Estelle.'

'That's not… I didn't mean… I just meant…

It's as if history has repeated itself, that's all… isn't it? You were engaged to the most beautiful woman available six Seasons ago, and now you've attracted the attention of the most beautiful one available this Season. I was just saying… I mean, I'm sure Lady Iris isn't interested in you…and Lady Redcliffe…' His choked voice came to a halt.

'You're despicable, Pratley. No wonder you've never made it further than *almost* courting. Lady Iris is clearly far too sensible to be attracted to you.'

'But not so sensible as to show interest in a blind recluse,' Pratley said, his voice starting to rise. 'At least Lady Redcliffe had more sense.'

Theo gripped the edges of the table, holding himself back. He might not be able to see Lord Pratley but that did not mean he could not do considerable damage to the man's smug face.

'I hope you're not discussing my good wife,' Lord Redcliffe called from the end of the table. 'That would be in very poor form indeed.'

'We were merely saying she has made a good marriage,' Pratley said, his voice ingratiating.

'Indeed, she has. The lady made the right choice,' Redcliffe replied. 'In the end,' he added, a noticeable level of hostility in his voice.

The boisterous conversations from the men seated around the table suddenly fell silent, the only sound coming from the footmen moving quietly round the room refilling glasses, and a few men shuffling uncomfortably in their seats.

The tension in Theo's jaw intensified. He could hardly object to what Lord Redcliffe had said. Estelle had been completely within her rights to choose Lord Redcliffe over him, and she had indeed made the right choice. After the accident, what could he have offered her? Marriage to someone who was now half a man? That was no life for someone as beautiful and vibrant as Lady Estelle Redcliffe. Or Lady Iris. Pratley was right on that point as well.

He reached out for his drink, something he desperately needed. His hand slipped. The drink overturned, liquid sloshing across his fingers. A footman stepped in, his cloth at the ready. If Theo needed a reminder of how enfeebled he was, this accident would provide it. He couldn't even help himself to a glass of brandy.

He flapped the servant's cloth away and gripped his now refilled glass. A smattering of voices began to fill the silence, then a few more. Soon the room was alive with the sound of men drinking, laughing and trying to outdo each other with their witty comments and boasts.

While the noise of the men circled around him, Theo sat in silence, nursing his drink and his anger. This evening had not been the disaster he had imagined it would be. It had been worse. All it had done was reinforce that he was not the man he had once been and never would be again. He was now half a man, a blind man who had once courted the most beautiful woman of the Season, who had been the envy of all other men, but was now a pitiful, bumbling idiot. But at least this damnable dinner party had achieved one thing. It had reminded him of why he did not go into Society and had strengthened his resolve to never do so again.

As Lady Estelle Redcliffe glided across the room Iris couldn't take her eyes off her. She really was stunningly beautiful. Iris didn't usually compare herself to other women, but Lady Redcliffe was making her feel somewhat dowdy.

Lady Redcliffe had been a guest at the Walbertons' home for several days. They had spoken a few times, exchanged a few polite words, but Iris had never noticed before that she was so remarkably attractive.

Much to her annoyance, Iris knew she was now looking at Lady Redcliffe in a different light because she had once been engaged to Theo Crighton. She also knew she was being ridiculous. Of course the Earl would have women in his past. He was an attractive man, and with his title and large estate he was in many ways the perfect catch.

But even more annoying was that uncomfortable, gnawing feeling in the pit of her stomach, the one she knew to be caused by the fact that the Earl had shown he still had feelings for Lady Redcliffe, the one she knew she had no right to feel.

Lady Redcliffe took the wingback chair beside Iris and smiled. It was a smile that made her beautiful face even more radiant. And yet, Iris couldn't help but wonder whether it was genuine. She pushed that uncharitable thought away. It was an unkind thought which presumably was a product of those annoying feelings she was not allowed to have. For politeness' sake, she smiled back at Lady Redcliffe.

'Aren't you the brave one?' Lady Redcliffe said as she stirred sugar into her tea.

'Brave?' It was the second time in the last few days that Iris had been described in that manner and she still did not believe it was an apt description of her behaviour.

'Inviting Theo Crighton to this dinner party,' Lady Redcliffe added.

Iris shook her head in confusion. 'I didn't invite him, my mother did, and I don't quite see how inviting him would make someone brave.'

She smiled, as if Iris had made a joke that they both understood, then leant closer and lowered her voice. 'Aren't you put off by all those scars?'

Iris sat up straighter in her chair, fighting to stop her voice from rising. 'No, why should I be?'

Lady Redcliffe took a sip of her tea, observing Iris over the rim. 'Well, I suppose they're not as bad as they were when he first had his accident, but it's hard not to notice them.'

Iris bit her bottom lip to stop any censure of Lady Redcliffe from escaping. She had noticed the scars when she'd first met the Earl, but now she was hardly aware of them at all. She even tended to forget at times that he was blind, as there were so many other things about him that she did notice.

'As I said, you're very brave.' Lady Redcliffe took a sip of her tea. 'So, are you and he courting?'

Iris was about to make a denial, then thought better of it. What right did this woman have to question her? And what business was it of hers what was or wasn't going on between her and the Earl? So instead of an answer, she gave what she hoped was an enigmatic smile.

'Well, that is a surprise,' Lady Redcliffe said, placing her teacup on the table. 'After all, you are rather attractive, you know.'

She slowly looked Iris up and down, as if taking an inventory of her figure and her face, causing Iris to bristle.

'Yes, rather attractive,' Lady Redcliffe said, her voice overly sweet. 'I suppose you do know that Theo and I were once engaged...that he was hopelessly in love with me.' She smiled and lightly patted her hair. 'And I suspect he is still a little bit in love with me.'

Iris very rarely took a dislike to anyone, but she was starting to take a strong dislike to Lady Redcliffe.

'So why did you not marry?' she asked, horrified that her question came out sounding like an accusation.

Lady Redcliffe's eyes grew wide and she

glared at Iris as if she'd just asked why she had
not run off and become a clown in the circus.

'Do you really need to ask that?'

Iris held her gaze, her look saying, *Yes, I do.*

'Well, I hardly need to mention his facial
deformity, nor his affliction. He appears to be
able to hide it well, but you do know he's completely blind, don't you?'

'Yes, I had noticed,' Iris said, fighting to
keep her voice as neutral as possible so she
would not reveal the level of her anger.

'Well, there you are, then,' Lady Redcliffe
said, picking up her cup and taking a small sip.

'So why didn't you marry him?'

Lady Redcliffe's eyebrows drew together
and she tilted her head, as if trying to work out
whether or not Iris was a simpleton.

'Like you, my dear, when I was an unmarried young lady I was considered an exquisite beauty. Some say I still am.' She smiled
at Iris and paused as if giving space for the
expected compliment. When none came, she
frowned slightly then continued. 'Until the accident, Theo was the ideal husband, the man
that every young woman that Season was hoping to catch. He was handsome, wealthy, well-
connected, perfect in every way.' She sighed
lightly. 'Yes, I was disappointed that the fire

ruined him. My husband is perhaps not as exciting and attractive as Theo was, but it is a good marriage and I am content.'

Iris wanted to condemn Lady Redcliffe for her callousness, but how could she? Young women were expected to make the best marriage they possibly could. Love rarely entered into it. Her parents were in love, as were her married sister, Hazel, and her husband, Lucas Darkwood, but they were the exceptions. Marrying for love was not what women of her class were expected to do. They were expected to marry well, and if they were also in love, that was simply all good and well, but most certainly not the aim of the union. Lady Redcliffe had done no less than was to be expected of her.

'Although, between you and me,' Lady Redcliffe said, leaning forward, 'it was rather wonderful for a man to have made such a romantic, such a heroic gesture.' She sat back and smiled. 'It is something I'll always cherish.'

'I don't understand.' Iris both wanted and did not want to know what she was talking about. Did she really want to hear what the hopelessly in love Earl of Greystone had done to show the depth of his admiration for another woman?

Lady Redcliffe tilted her head and sat up straighter in her chair, still smiling wistfully. 'Oh, do you not know what caused his scars? He was saving me. He was so in love with me that he risked his own life to save me from a burning building.'

Iris stared back at her in shock.

'Oh, it's true,' she simpered. 'The man was besotted with me. He was staying at my family home the night the fire broke out. He immediately ran to my room and carried me out in his arms to safety.' She smiled and placed her hands on her heart. 'Then he went back in to rescue some of the servants who were trapped upstairs. Something happened, I'm not sure what—a burning beam fell or something—and that's how he got those burns across his face. The servants ended up having to save him in the end. It was all very dramatic.'

'That's terrible.'

'Oh, it was. The damage to the house wasn't too bad and was easily repaired, and everyone got out safely, but Theo was never the same afterwards. His scarring was frightful to begin with, even worse than it is now. No one knew whether he'd make a full recovery and it was immediately apparent that he'd never see again. Lord Redcliffe had proposed to me earlier in the Season and I'd turned him down because I had much preferred to marry Theo, but under the circumstances I thought it best to accept Lord Redcliffe. And it seems I made the right choice, as Theo has never really recovered, and I don't just mean his appearance. He retreated to his home and has become quite the hermit, I hear.'

Iris hardly knew what to say to this woman. Lady Redcliffe had no understanding that anyone would find what she had just said objectionable, that she had done anything wrong, that she had hurt and mistreated a man who loved her and had risked his own life for her.

Lady Redcliffe shook her head, her big blue eyes sad. 'I could never live like that, and really, my dear, as an older, more experienced woman, I counsel you to consider whether such a life would be right for you either.' She smiled at Iris and gently patted her arm. 'After all, you are a pretty young woman. You want to attend social functions where people can appreciate your beauty. You want to spend your time mixing with fashionable Society, not be stuck away in the country, having no fun whatsoever.'

Arguments spun round in Iris's mind. She wanted to tell Lady Redcliffe that if she loved a man she would not care about such things.

But was that true? Hadn't she already decided that she could never love a man like the Earl, a man who did not laugh, who shunned Society and gave every appearance of disapproving of people who liked to enjoy themselves? And yet she wanted to defend him, to insist that he would make a wonderful husband, and was a man it would be easy to love.

Instead, she merely furrowed her brow, trying to organise her thoughts and digest what Lady Redcliffe had said.

The doors opened and the men entered the drawing room, bringing with them a waft of cigar smoke and the bonhomie of men who had enjoyed their brandies.

Both Iris and Lady Redcliffe continued to watch the door, even after Lord Redcliffe had entered. *Was Estelle too watching out for the Earl of Greystone?* wondered Iris. Despite all her protestations that she had made the best choice, was content with her marriage, did Lady Redcliffe still harbour some lingering affection for Theo Crighton? Or did this rather vain woman just like the thought that there was a man present who had once been so in love with her that he had risked his life to save her, and destroyed his own life in the process?

The room filled up with loudly talking

men, but there was still no sign of the Earl of
Greystone. Lord Redcliffe joined them. He sat
beside his wife then looked around the room,
smiling to himself as if proudly showing off a
priceless artwork he expected others to admire.

The remaining men joined the party but
there was still no sign of the Earl. Iris excused
herself and left the room to see what the delay
was. He wasn't in the hallway. She made her
way down to the dining room, but that too
was empty of guests, with only a few servants
clearing away the remaining glasses and putting the room back in order.

'Excuse me,' she asked one of the footmen.
'Do you know where the Earl of Greystone
has gone?'

'He asked for his coach a few minutes ago,
my lady,' the footman replied.

'His coach?' Iris stared at the footman as if
he could explain the meaning of this, but, as
she should have expected, the man's face remained impassive and he made no reply.

With a nod of thanks, she left the room and
walked down to the entrance hall. There was
no sign of the Earl or his coach. He had left
without saying goodbye. Iris remained standing at the doorway, staring out into the dark
night, unsure what to make of the Earl's sud-

den departure, but suddenly feeling very angry with everyone—with Theo Crighton, with Lady Redcliffe and most of all with herself for standing in an empty entrance hall lamenting the departure of a man who was supposed to mean nothing to her and was still in love with another woman.

Chapter Fifteen

Iris was exhausted. All the emotions that had spun through her head throughout the night meant she hardly got a minute's rest. One moment she was angry with Lady Redcliffe for her appalling treatment of the Earl. The next moment she was angry with the Earl for being in love with such a self-centred woman. Then she was annoyed with herself for getting so worked up and letting it disturb her sleep. Then she felt sorry for the Earl, for allowing his love for Lady Redcliffe to destroy his life. Then she felt intense admiration for him, for his heroism when he had rushed into a burning building. Then it was back to anger again. Anger at his treatment of her. Anger that he had left the dinner party so suddenly, without speaking to her again, without saying goodbye.

She had thought they were getting on much

better. After all, she was sure she had nearly made him smile at least once and he had almost laughed at one stage. Hadn't he? But perhaps she had been wrong. Perhaps he hadn't enjoyed her company after all. As soon as that thought entered her mind she would circle back from feeling sad and defeated to being angry again, and, in particular, angry at herself for caring whether they were getting on or not and whether he had or hadn't enjoyed her company.

And in amongst this mix of anger, admiration and sadness there was another pesky emotion that kept poking in its unwanted head. It felt a bit like anger but wasn't. And, like her anger, it was directed mainly at Lady Redcliffe. It was that horrid little green-eyed monster, jealousy. She was jealous that the Earl should be in love with a woman like Lady Redcliffe, a self-serving woman who had seen the Earl merely as a means to her self-advancement. Despite that, he had loved her. Was probably still in love with her. That was the worst emotion of all. That was the one that made her toss and turn the most, unable to shake it off. And what was worse, it was an emotion she had no right to feel. After all, she wasn't interested in the Earl, so why should she be getting so upset because he was in love with another woman?

And thoughts of love and things she should not and did not feel would unfortunately bring up the memory of how he had looked standing in front of her beside his bed, naked, his skin a warm hue in the candlelight. When those images invaded her mind, that increasingly familiar tingling would erupt deep within her body. Iris would have to jump out of bed and pace backwards and forwards until her mind moved on to something else and she could return to bed and go back to feeling angry.

After such a night, no wonder she was completely exhausted. As she dragged herself out of bed following what was at best a fitful sleep, she had to fight to stop her mind from going over and over the unsolved questions that had been whirling in her brain.

Today was a new day, she told herself, determined not to think about Lady Redcliffe or the Earl's love for her. She would focus her mind on one feeling, one less disconcerting than her anger or any of those other vexing feelings. And the chosen feeling was that of disapproval. That at least was something she was allowed to feel. Disapproval at the Earl for leaving last night's dinner without even showing the courtesy of saying goodbye to her, her mother, or the Walbertons.

Iris stood up straighter, pleased that she was now looking at things from a completely objective point of view.

It was outrageous and she had every right to be offended by such behaviour. She could forgive him for not saying goodbye to her—after all, he owed her nothing. She could almost forgive him for not saying goodbye to her mother, as her mother hadn't been the hostess, and she *had* all but press-ganged him into attending the dinner party. But she could not forgive him for being rude to Lady Walberton. That was an inexcusable breach of etiquette.

Yes, disapproval over his rudeness to Lady Walberton made much more sense than all those complicated emotions that had been warring for supremacy last night.

And she was completely within her rights to disapprove of what he had done. Being rude to one's hostess simply would not do, and someone needed to tell him so. And, as there was no one else, that someone would have to be Iris.

She tugged on the velvet cord to call for her lady's maid while she continued to seethe with self-righteousness. And that seething did not let up as Annette helped her change into her white lacy blouse and dove-grey skirt. Her emotions now had nothing to do with what Lady Redcliffe had told her, nor how the Earl felt about Lady Redcliffe, Iris reminded her reflection as Annette brushed and styled her hair.

Last night, while she was trying to get to sleep, she may have gone over and over everything that lady had said, but that was last night. In the cold light of day, she now did not care one fig if the Earl was still in love with Lady Redcliffe. That made no difference whatsoever to how she was feeling now. It was his bad manners she could not abide. Even if he was upset about Lady Redcliffe being present at the dinner party, that was no excuse for unbecoming behaviour. And this morning she would tell him so.

'It's such a lovely day. Let's go for a walk,' she said as Annette put the finishing touches to her hair. 'I don't even think I'll bother with breakfast, I'm so keen to get out and enjoy this weather.'

They both looked out of the large sash window at the grey sky and the trees bending in a stiff breeze.

'I so love walking in weather like this,' Iris

said, hoping that the dark clouds were not a signal that it was about to rain. 'It's so invigorating, don't you think?'

'Yes, my lady,' her maid replied in a voice that was somewhat less than enthusiastic. 'I'll lay out your coat and umbrella, shall I?'

'Yes, perhaps that might be wise,' Iris said, casting another glimpse at the ominous sky. Was she about to turn up at the Earl's during yet another storm? She would hate him to think she made a habit of such imprudent behaviour, but there was nothing for it. Even if it was about to rain, she needed to visit the Earl immediately so he could be informed of his appalling lapse in etiquette while it was still a recent occurrence.

Iris stood up and did a little twirl in front of the full-length mirror to view herself from every angle, then frowned at her own foolishness. Who was she trying to impress? The Earl of Greystone couldn't see how she looked and wouldn't know whether her dress was fashionable or not, whether it flattered her figure or made her look like a complete frump. And more than that, she did not care one iota about such things anyway, did she? She was not going to visit the Earl so he could show his admiration for how she looked in her pretty new outfit. She was going to visit him so she could give him a piece of her mind.

Annette helped her into her coat, and while she was putting away Iris's nightclothes Iris quickly pushed her reticule into the gap beside the dressing table.

She headed down the stairs and out of the house at a brisk trot while still pulling on her gloves, as if anxious to get outside and enjoy the bracing weather, followed by a reluctant Annette.

'Let's take the coastal path,' Iris said, striding off towards the track that would take them along the dramatic cliff top that overlooked the sea.

Iris had to admit, the wind was perhaps a little brisk to make walking entirely enjoyable. Her skirt and petticoats whipped around her legs, and all the trouble her lady's maid had taken with her hair was wasted, as it soon became tangled by the breeze. Walking into the wind, both women kept their hands firmly on their hats to stop them from being lifted off their heads and carried away, out to sea.

'I think we should stroll down to the village. It will be lovely to have a look at the shops,' Iris said, raising her voice to be heard above the wind and the sound of crashing waves hit-ting the boulders below. 'Oh—but I appear to have forgotten my reticule.' She frowned at her maid in feigned disappointment. 'Would you please go back and get it? I'll meet you at the village.'

'Very good, my lady,' Annette said and turned quickly, presumably pleased to get out of the wind.

Iris watched her lady's maid hurry back along the path. As soon as she was out of sight, she turned and headed across the grassland to the country road that would take her to the Earl's estate.

She hesitated when she reached the driveway that led up to his home, and for the first time wondered if this really was such a good idea. Forcing her indignation to reignite, she remembered sitting in the drawing room with Lady Redcliffe, waiting for him to enter, then realising he had left without even saying goodbye. It had been so rude and so insulting, and he deserved to be called out for such a complete lack of basic manners.

Her ire sufficiently rekindled, she straightened her spine and strode down the driveway.

The butler opened the door, smiled and bowed in greeting.

'Good morning, Charles,' she said, trying

not to smile in case it undermined her serious mood. 'Would you please inform Lord Greystone that Lady Iris is here to see him?'

Charles looked over her shoulder to see who was accompanying her.

'My lady's maid will be arriving shortly.'

That was another little white lie to add to the growing list. Hadn't she sworn an oath that she was finished with telling white lies? But then, she had promised she would not lie to her mother again. She had said nothing about lying to Charles. Iris wondered whether that counted, then shook her head to drive out such frivolous thoughts. She needed to focus on the task at hand, not get caught up in such nonsense.

'Very good, my lady.' Charles stood back for her to enter and walked down the hallway and into the drawing room. While she waited, Iris went over in her mind what she would say, how she would remind him of how a gentleman was supposed to behave at a social event, and how he at the very least should have shown more respect for her mother and the hosts.

Charles opened the door to the drawing room and bowed to her before departing.

The Earl was standing in the middle of the room, facing her. She stood at the entrance to the room and suddenly all her self-righteous indignation deserted her. He looked a bit too imposing, a bit too unnervingly handsome, a bit too manly for her to feel entirely comfortable about what she planned to do. Her heart beating rather faster than the easy walk should have provoked, she remained frozen to the spot, staring at him. Even with the scars distorting the skin of his forehead and across his left eye, he was undeniably breathtaking. No wonder Lady Redcliffe had once been so taken with him.

Lady Redcliffe.

Suddenly Iris's anger came back, its flames burning fiercely. That was why she was here, standing at the door of his drawing room, staring at him, awkward and tongue-tied. She wasn't here to admire his appearance. She was here to rebuke him for his behaviour last night, behaviour which had been unconscionable.

She strode into the room, her head held high. 'I've come to tell you that I was more than disappointed by your actions last evening. You were very rude to my mother and Lady Walberton.' There, she had said it. She tilted up her chin in defiance of any objection he might now raise.

His eyebrows drew together and he frowned slightly. 'Your mother? Lady Walberton? I hardly spoke to either woman, so I cannot see how anything I said to them could have given offence.'

'That's exactly it,' she said, standing up even straighter and lifting her head even higher. 'You left without saying goodbye. That was extremely rude of you.'

He said nothing. Iris stared at him and waited to hear his excuses. He still said nothing. Was he not going to respond? This was becoming increasingly uncomfortable. She forced herself to maintain her affronted posture. Forced herself to remember how ill-mannered he had been. Forced herself to ignore the way her heart was now beating even faster, and her entire body seemed to be blushing.

'I fail to see how it is any concern of yours,' he finally said, his voice low and disquieting.

'Well, yes… I mean, no,' Iris said, suddenly flailing and uncertain what it was she really wanted to say. Fortunately, he could not see her confusion as she bit the side of her lip and tried to gather her thoughts. 'No one else would tell you, so yes, I do feel it is up to me.' She nodded, confident in her assertion.

He walked towards her, and she resisted the temptation to take a quick step backwards.

'And did either your mother or Lady Walberton comment on my rudeness?'

Iris swallowed to try and relieve her suddenly dry throat.

He took another step towards her. 'Did either of them suggest that someone needed to put that ill-mannered man in his place so in future he would know the correct way to behave in Society?'

'Well, no…' Iris pursed her lips, determined not to be undermined by his close proximity. 'But then, both of them are very well-bred women, so they wouldn't, would they?' She smiled in satisfaction with her answer.

'What does that mean, Lady Iris? That you are not as well-bred as either your mother or Lady Walberton?'

Her satisfied smile died. 'No, that's not what I'm saying. Stop twisting my words. I just… It's just, I think you need to know that when you're invited to a social event it's good manners to say goodbye to the hostess before you leave. That's all. And it would have been polite to say goodbye to my mother as well, as she was the one who had extended the invitation.' She placed her hands emphatically on her hips to underline the point, even though he couldn't see how emphatic she was being.

'And perhaps a well-bred young lady should be sure of her facts before she arrives at a man's home, unaccompanied, and starts making unfounded accusations.'

'I am sure of my facts,' Iris stated, biting her lip again and trying to think what facts she actually was sure of.

'If you'd asked either your mother or Lady Walberton, you would know that I asked Lord Walberton to pass on my apologies for leaving so early.'

Oh, it was those facts he was referring to.

'You would also know that I sent over a card this morning, thanking the Walbertons for their hospitality.'

Drat. Perhaps she *should* have got her facts right.

'Would that be deemed suitably well-mannered for you? Or is there some other breach of etiquette you'd like to point out to me?'

Iris's hands dropped from her hips. She was no longer feeling quite so emphatic. 'I didn't realise.'

'No, you didn't. And perhaps I can now give *you* a lesson in etiquette. Should I remind you that young ladies do not reprimand gentlemen, particularly ones they are not related to? And that they do not arrive at a man's home, uninvited and alone? Something you appear to be making a habit of.'

'My lady's maid will be joining us shortly,' she blurted out and said a silent apology for yet another little white lie.

'Shortly?' He inclined his head. 'A lot can happen in a short time. A young lady's reputation can be destroyed in a short time. What would your mother say if she knew that you were in my home, alone? And I believe this time you are neither lost nor needing shelter from a storm.'

Iris continued staring up at his proud face, at the uplifted jaw, at the full lips that were pinched together in annoyance, and wished the fog in her brain would clear so she could think of a suitable counter-argument.

'It is rather windy outside,' she finally muttered, then cursed herself for being such a dunderhead.

He gave a small, dismissive laugh. While his laughter was something she'd longed to hear, this laugh contained no humour.

'Or do you think such rules do not apply when it comes to me?' He took hold of her arm, holding it tightly, causing Iris to gasp. 'Is that the reason, Lady Iris? Is it that, as I am a blind man, you do not see me as a real man, one that you should not be alone with?'

Iris did not move, unable to breathe, unable to talk, unable to think. All she was aware of was the touch of his hand on her arm. A touch that was burning into her, causing her skin to come alive.

And he was wrong. So wrong. Right now, there was no way she could see him as anything other than a man, a man who was so close to her she could feel the warmth of his body, could smell his masculine scent, the one she remembered so well from his nightshirt, from the night that she had held him in her arms. It would be so easy for her to reach out and touch his chest, to reacquaint herself with those hard, strong muscles. And more than that. With him so close, all she had to do was rise up on her toes and she could kiss those full lips.

She swallowed and drew in a quick breath, her hand flying to her tingling lips. This was so wrong. What was he doing? He should not be this close to her. He should not be holding her arm. And she should not be letting him do so. She should admonish him in no uncertain terms, break from his grasp and storm out of the house, never to return. But she knew she was not going to do that.

'Well?' he asked, tightening the grip on her arm.

'No… That's… It's…' Her words came to a halt. What she wanted to say eluded her, but she knew exactly what she wanted to do, what she wanted him to do to her. Her breath coming in more rapid gasps, she leant towards him, wanting him to do more than just grasp her arm, wanting him to take her in his arms, to hold her close against him, to feel her body against his chest, that strong, muscular chest that she had seen just two nights ago. She wanted him to kiss her, to caress her. But that was so wrong she shouldn't even be thinking about it.

She looked up at his implacable face, her eyes focusing on his full lips, lips she wished would kiss her, would whisper sweet, seductive words in her ear. Gasping in another quick breath, she ran her tongue along her own lips and placed her hand gently on her stomach, which was fluttering in a most peculiar manner. Was it nerves, excitement, a little of both? She didn't know.

'Have you entered my home, alone, because you do not think a blind man is capable of ruining your reputation?'

'No, no, I...' Iris wasn't sure what she wanted to say. Her heart was beating so loudly in her chest any thoughts she tried to form were drowned out by its insistent pounding.

She drew in a few strangled breaths and

tried to focus her mind. 'That's not what I thought,' she finally murmured.

When she had set off for his house she hadn't been thinking about her reputation. Now she wasn't sure what she had been thinking, or if indeed she had actually been thinking at all. She just knew she had wanted to see him again.

And now that she was here, thinking was the last thing she wanted to do. How could she possibly be expected to think of anything when her body was consumed by that strange feeling, the one that always took her over when she was in his company? But now it was even stronger, even more demanding, pulsating wildly and uncontrollably within her.

Still not thinking, she closed her eyes, her skin aching for his touch, her fingers itching to touch him. She arched her back and moved even closer towards him. He had said he could ruin her reputation and right now that was exactly what she wanted—for Theo Crighton to take her in his arms, thoroughly ruin her reputation, and to hell with the consequences.

Chapter Sixteen

She was still here. Theo had expected her to turn tail and run, never to visit his home again. But she was still here. No woman should allow a man to stand this close to her, to take hold of her arm the way he had done. If she was so damn adamant about correct etiquette, she should at the very least be objecting. She still did not see him as a threat. Still did not see him as a real man. Damn her. How dared she treat him like this, like a non-threatening child?

She was no different from Estelle. No different from everyone else at last night's dinner party who had treated him with such condescension. If she didn't leave soon, she was going to discover just how wrong she was to think he was less of a man just because he could not see.

He was so close he could almost feel her

up against him, could feel the warmth of her body and smell her scent of orange blossom and rose water.

It was an enticing scent. He inhaled deeply, letting it fill his senses. It was also the scent that had woken him from his last nightmare. He had awoken to find her holding him, like a child who needed comfort. She had even told him that she was doing exactly what her mother had done when she was a little girl and had a bad dream. That was how she saw him, as a child who needed to be coddled.

He exhaled loudly to rid himself of the effect her scent was having on him and to focus on his anger.

No matter what she thought of him, he was still a man, damn it. A man who had once been admired. A man who had been at the very pinnacle of Society. He was not a cripple to be pitied by everyone, including Lady Iris Springfeld. And if she didn't leave soon she would discover that he was definitely not a helpless child, and coddling was the last thing he was after.

'Do you make a habit of this?' he asked, pleased that his voice contained a significant degree of menace.

'Habit of what?' He could hear the trepida-

tion in her voice. Good. She was starting to realise what a mistake it was to arrive at a man's
house unaccompanied.

'Of reprimanding gentlemen.'

'Um, no, but…' He could hear her breath,
coming in short, rapid gasps. She was frightened of him. He loosened his grip on her arm,
suddenly ashamed of what he was doing. He
did not treat women like this. This was rep-
rehensible.

'No, I don't usually, but I made an exception
in your case.' Her words cut through him. He
was an exception. He was different from other
men. He was a child to be both comforted and
chastised according to her whim. He increased
the pressure on her arm. She needed to know
the folly of what she was doing.

'So why am I singled out for this attention?'
Go on, say it, damn you. Because I'm a cripple.

'Well, because…' She drew in a deep breath
and exhaled slowly. 'I don't know. I suppose I
made a mistake.'

He reached out and took hold of her chin,
tilting up her head. 'Yes, you did. And you
made another mistake today.'

She swallowed. 'I did?' Her voice was quiet,
breathy.

'As I said, a well-bred woman does not visit

a man's home on her own.' He waited for her to make another joke, to let him know that she saw *him* as a joke. 'Not unless she cares nothing for her reputation.'

She still said nothing, but he could hear her breath, loud and fast. But she still hadn't left, still hadn't put up any sort of protest. She still did not see him as a man, as a threat to her reputation. Well, he was going to have to show her how wrong she was.

'Young ladies do not enter a man's house alone, unless this is what they are after.' His hand slid quickly around her waist and pulled her towards him. 'Any man would be forgiven for thinking this is what you came here for.'

He heard a quick gasp just before his lips found hers. He had given her ample warning but she had refused to take him seriously. Now she would discover how wrong she was to not see him as a real man. And he would not kiss her gently. He would teach her that she had no right to toy with him, to pity him, to coddle him.

His tongue parted her lips and he entered her mouth, tasting, probing, plundering. His hand moved further round her slim waist as he pulled her closer, her soft breasts pressing against his chest, her thighs against his legs. If she had any doubt that he was a man, she would now feel it, hard and urgent, up against her.

He continued to kiss her while waiting to feel her hands on his shoulders, pushing him away. Soon she would do what he expected, —slap his face, and flee from his house.

None of these reactions happened. Instead, her rigid body went soft, moulding against him, and she kissed him back.

What was he to make of this? Did Lady Iris want his kisses? While his mind tried to analyse this surprising behaviour, his body just reacted to having her in his arms. His hand ran slowly down her spine, loving the feel of her curves, loving the way she moved sensually under his touch.

Her lips parted wider, tempting him, enticing him. This was more than he could stand. She wanted his kisses and he wanted her. But this was not right. He should stop. He should, but he couldn't.

His hands moved lower down her body, cupping her lovely round buttocks and pulling her in hard against him, wanting her to relieve the pounding desire he had for her.

Surely, now that she could feel how she was affecting him, feel his hard arousal pressing into her, she would finally take control and push him away. But she did not react with the expected horror to the hardness of his manhood, pushing urgently against her. Instead, she arched her back and rubbed herself against him, increasing his desire for her and making him wild with need.

A low moan escaped his lips. He was now completely lost, unable to think, unable to reason, only able to act. His lips moved from her lips to her neck, kissing and nuzzling, loving the touch, the taste of her silk-like skin.

She tilted her head back and moaned quietly, driving him mad for her. He had to have her now. Grasping her blouse, he freed it from the skirt and slowly slid his hand up inside. Slowly, teasingly, his hand moved up over her corset, to the thin material of her undergarment. He could feel her heart pounding fiercely, her chest rising rapidly as she continued to gasp in quick breaths.

He paused, waiting for her to object. Instead, her moans continued, getting faster and louder.

His hand cupped the soft mound of her breast, still covered by the flimsy material. She gasped loudly. He stopped, pulled his hand away. Was she finally going to tell him to stop? Was she finally going to do what she should have done when he had first kissed her?

But no, her hand took his and she placed it back on her breast as her gasping breath resumed, coming faster and faster.

She had given him permission to do whatever he wanted to do, and every ounce of his being wanted to accept that invitation. He grabbed the thin fabric of her undergarment and roughly pulled it down, causing a button to pop off, but releasing her full breasts to his appreciative touch.

He cupped the beautiful soft, silky mound, kneading it, loving the way it filled his hand. The nipple hardened under his touch as he rubbed his thumb over her, filling him with a sense of satisfaction.

His lips found hers again, kissing her with such urgency it was almost desperation. And she kissed him back with equally unfettered passion. Her hands entwining themselves in his hair, holding him tightly against her, she ran her tongue along his bottom lip, then slowly entered his mouth, licking, tasting, exploring.

As he continued to caress her tight nipples, she broke from his kisses and placed her head on his shoulder, her gasps becoming slow moans, getting louder with each caress. If he had had any doubts, they were now gone. This woman wanted him. She did not pity him. She wanted him as a woman wanted a man. She was ripe for the taking and there was nothing to stop him from taking her, right here, right now.

He moved to her other breast, cupping it in his hand and stroking the nipple, harder and faster, making her writhe with pleasure.

She was now as caught as he was, lost to reason, only capable of feeling. There was nothing to stop him now from lifting her up, placing her on the table, parting her legs and taking her. Her panting breath, her burning skin and the way her body was moving sensually against him told him that it was what she wanted as well. And what he wanted, what his body was demanding from him, was to bury himself deep within her, to fully satisfy his demanding need for her.

He had wanted to teach her that he was a man and should be treated as such, not as a child. He had wanted her to see that she could not presume that she was safe to visit him, unaccompanied, simply because he was blind. And that was exactly what he was doing. Teaching her that he was a man.

She was now his for the taking. He could now complete what he had threatened to do to her before he had taken her in his arms. He could ruin her.

Ruin her.

Those words cut through the fog in his head. What was he doing? He was about to ruin her. She did not deserve this. As if his hand were on fire, he quickly released her breast and took a step back. This was unconscionable. She was a sweet, lovely, innocent young woman and he was about to ruin her.

'You should go,' he said, his voice coming out in a husky rasp he hardly recognised. 'Fasten your blouse and leave.'

Iris fought to get her breathing under control as she emerged from her dazed state. What had just happened? She looked up at the stern man standing in front of her, then down at her bunched-up blouse. It was obvious what had just happened. And if she couldn't tell from her blouse, then her sensitised breasts, her pounding heart and that intense throbbing between her thighs made the answer abundantly clear. The real question she should be asking herself was, *How had that happened?* One moment she was trying to rebuke him for his behaviour, the next moment she was acting like some woman she didn't know, a wanton woman who was allowing, indeed encouraging, a man to take liberties with her.

What on earth had she been thinking? That question also answered itself. She had not been thinking. The moment he had touched her arm her mind seemed to cease to work and she had lost the ability to think.

And then his touch had moved to a kiss. If she actually had been capable of thinking before she felt his lips on hers, his kiss would have certainly put an end to that particular skill. In fact, after what had just happened, she was unsure whether she'd be able to think in a rational manner ever again.

She ran her tongue along her bottom lip and sighed. While she might have lost the ability to think, she certainly hadn't lost the ability to feel. Her entire body had come alive under his touch, as if every nerve end from the top of her head to her smallest toe had been stimulated and aroused. She closed her eyes and sighed again. She had not known it was possible to feel that way, and she had loved every second of it. Had loved the intensity of the emotions that had coursed through her when he took her in his arms, had loved the passion his caresses had aroused deep within her, had loved the sense of abandonment, of giving herself over to him.

She opened her eyes and looked up at him,

desperate for him to hold her close once more, to push his hard chest up against her soft, yielding body, to touch and caress her.

Iris sighed again and smiled. She had no regrets. How could she possibly have any regrets over what had happened? It had been wonderful. Her only regret was that he had stopped when he did, leaving her wanting more, so much more.

He, on the other hand, did not appear to feel the same way, if one was to judge by the serious look on his face. But Iris knew that was a deception. He might be trying to look as if he was unaffected by what had just taken place, but she knew differently.

He had been just as lost in the moment as she had. Well, almost as lost. He had managed to pull back, something she knew she would have been incapable of doing. Something he, unfortunately, *had* been capable of doing.

'Well, I'm not sure who should reprimand whom on that little breach of etiquette,' she said with a small laugh. 'Or whether we're equally guilty.'

'I think you should leave, Lady Iris,' he said, his voice back to its brusque manner, his lips drawing into a thin line.

'No,' she said, causing him to look even

more affronted. 'I think we should talk about what just happened.'

He exhaled loudly. 'Yes, you are right. I apologise. What I did was unforgivable. I should not have taken advantage of you.'

'You didn't.'

'I did. I should never have kissed you, never have…' He paused and tilted up his chin, as if unable to even discuss what had just happened between them. 'For that I am profoundly sorry.'

'But I kissed you as well.'

He paused, his chin still lifted, his body rigid. 'But I did more than just kiss you.'

Iris smiled. 'Mmm, yes, you did.' She bit the edge of her thumbnail and smiled, pressing her arm against her still sensitive breast. 'And I let you, wanted you to. You have nothing to rebuke yourself for.' *Except perhaps for stopping when you did.*

'You are an innocent young lady,' he said, his voice starting to rise as if angry that she was not allowing him to completely abase himself and wallow in guilt like a conscience-stricken penitent.

'Not quite as innocent as I was when I woke up this morning,' she said, unable to resist the jest.

'And for that, too, I apologise.'

She rolled her eyes and sighed. He really was determined to take all the blame, wasn't he?

'Theo…' She paused. 'I suppose I can call you Theo now. After what happened I think we can probably drop the formality of using titles.'

He nodded but his expression did not soften.

'Theo, if I don't blame you then there's no reason why you should blame yourself.'

She looked at him, imploring him to believe her. His face remained fixed and he gave no sign that he would accept that he was without guilt.

'And anyway, no one knows what happened between us. I don't intend to tell anyone, and I assume you won't either.'

'That goes without saying,' he said, his voice offended.

'Good. Well, no one knows, so my reputation has not been ruined. As long as no one finds out, no harm has been done.'

He slowly shook his head. 'You really are a unique, remarkable young woman,' he said, his voice appearing to be full of awe.

Iris shrugged. Nothing she had said seemed particularly remarkable to her. 'And you're rather remarkable yourself,' she said with a smile, slowly looking him up and down.

He merely replied with a humph, as if that

was something else he would not accept. Iris wanted to list all the ways in which he was remarkable. He was brave, handsome, more honourable than she wished him to be, but the most remarkable thing about him was the way he made her feel when he touched her. Until he had kissed her, caressed her, she had not known it was possible to feel such intensity, such passion. Yes, it really was all rather remarkable.

She looked down at his hands, those strong, slender hands with the tapering fingers, and wished he would touch her again. But she knew that was not going to happen. He was adamant that what he had done was wrong, and, judging from the way his body was still clenched so tightly, it was unlikely he would commit another wrong very soon.

Damn him, she said to herself, sighing.

At least her reputation was safe, although that felt like a very small consolation for what she had missed out on.

'I suppose you're right. I suppose I should go,' she said, disappointment clearly showing in her voice.

'Yes, I believe that would be for the best,' he said, his voice still formal. 'I shall call for my carriage to take you back.'

'No, that will not be necessary. After all, if we're to keep all this between the two of us it would not do for me to arrive at the Walbertons' in your carriage.'

'You are right. And I am sorry you are going to have to walk back alone.'

'Again, not your fault. I came here alone. I'm perfectly capable of walking back alone.' She looked down at her dishevelled blouse. 'But I had better tidy myself up first.'

'Of course.' He turned his back on her as if giving her privacy, although, as he couldn't see her, that was a pointless gesture. Or was it a symbolic gesture? Was he telling her that he was turning his back on her, rejecting her?

As she fumbled with her blouse she hoped not. She tucked it into her skirt, and something dropped out from under her clothing and bounced on the carpet. She bent down to pick it up and discovered it was a small button from her chemise.

It was such an innocent little thing, but its presence in her hand was the result of something far from innocent. She smiled as she placed it in her pocket, as if saving a souvenir, a memory of what had happened between them. She was going to have some explaining to do to Annette when she discovered the missing button, but she'd think of an excuse later.

'Right, then, I'll say goodbye,' she said, brushing down her skirt.

'Goodbye, Lady Iris,' he said, turning back to face her. 'And once again, I cannot apologise enough for my behaviour.'

'And once again, you have nothing to apologise for.' She continued to stare up at him. She really did not want to leave. Did not want to just walk out of his house, out of his life, and pretend nothing had happened, but that was what they had agreed. For the sake of her damn reputation, they would act as if the most wonderful thing she had ever experienced had never actually happened.

She looked towards the door, the one through which she should be departing, and then back up at him. Would it be completely unacceptable if she rose up on tiptoes and gave him a quick kiss goodbye? After all, she wouldn't be doing anything they hadn't done already, and what harm could one little kiss do?

She swallowed down her reservations and took a step towards him, wondering how he would react. Hopefully in a manner very similar to the way he had reacted last time they had kissed.

'Goodbye, Lady Iris,' he said firmly. As if reading her mind, he took a step backwards and reached out for the bell to summon Charles, but before he could do so there was a knock on the door.

As if caught doing something she shouldn't, Iris jumped back. They both stood up straighter, the very picture of propriety—or was that the very picture of guilt?—and turned towards the opening door.

Chapter Seventeen

'Enter,' the Earl said, his voice overly terse.

Charles came into the room, followed by Iris's mother, who hadn't waited to be introduced.

'Lady Springfeld, my lord,' Charles said, looking slightly affronted at the older woman's boldness as she pushed past him.

Theo made a low bow and greeted her mother, while Iris quickly scanned down her dress to make sure all was in order, and patted her hair. At least she could blame any escaped strands on the windy walk over to the Earl's home. Then she beamed a smile at her mother, as if delighted to see her. But she was no actress and her mother was not convinced. She looked from Iris to the Earl then back to Iris, her raised eyebrows and wide eyes causing increased heat to rise on Iris's already warm cheeks.

Iris drew in a deep, steadying breath, still

smiling as brightly as she could. If ever there was a time for a white lie it was now, and hang any punishment the gods planned to send down on her. She doubted any retribution they could dish out would be worse than her mother's wrath if she ever found out what had just happened between her and the Earl.

'Mother, how wonderful to see you.' White lie number one. 'I was out for a little walk and decided to call in on the Earl.' White lie number two. 'We were just discussing how much fun last night's dinner was.' White lie number three. Or was that lie actually white? Given what had really happened, claiming they had merely been talking was at the very least a bit grey around the edges, and possibly even heading towards a rather black lie. Iris forced herself to hold her smile, even though her cheeks were now starting to ache.

Her mother's eyebrows moved slightly higher up her forehead. 'Indeed,' she said, drawing the word out so that it spoke volumes. She slowly looked the Earl up and down, and Iris was certain that he would be as grateful as she was for his long frock coat, which covered up any incontrovertible evidence of what they really had been up to.

'I discovered Annette in quite a fluster,'

her mother said as she slowly turned her attention back to Iris. 'She said you had sent her back to the house to retrieve your reticule, but she could not find it. Then she was supposed to meet you in the village. Not at the Earl's home.'

'Oh, yes, I got a bit lost, yet again.' Iris pulled a little moue, as if to say silly old me. It was another white lie, but she had lost count and now had no idea how many they tallied up to. 'And then I found myself in the vicinity of the Earl's house, so I couldn't really pass without popping in and saying hello.'

'And I assume you have said hello by now?'

'Mmm, yes, I have.' And what a way to say hello. Iris's forced smile became genuine and she had to suppress a little giggle that was threatening to escape.

'Would you like some tea, Lady Springfeld?' the Earl said, showing surprising hospitality, particularly under the circumstances.

'No, thank you. I believe my daughter has intruded long enough,' her mother said, showing an uncharacteristic lack of friendliness.

'Then I will call for my carriage to take you home,' he said.

Her mother waved her hand in dismissal. 'No, thank you. Iris and I have much to discuss and I think a nice walk back will be the perfect time to have that discussion.'

Iris fought hard to hold on to her smile. *Much to discuss?* She didn't like the sound of that. Not one little bit.

Iris and her mother walked along the now familiar country lane between the Earl's house and the Walbertons'. The wind had dropped and the walk was rather pleasant. Or at least it would have been if Iris weren't dreading what her mother was going to say about her latest lapse in propriety by turning up at a man's house uninvited and unaccompanied. And that was just the impropriety her mother knew about.

As they strolled along, her mother commented on what she was seeing, admiring the trees, the small cottages and the well-tended hedges that lined the road. Iris started to relax and enjoy herself. She had got away with it, she thought with a satisfied smile.

'I am not naïve, my dear,' her mother said, suddenly changing the subject from a discussion on the delightful cottage gardens.

Her sense of satisfaction, along with her smile, disappeared. 'No one has ever suggested you were.'

Her mother sent her a sideways glance. 'You might be surprised to know this, but I am very familiar with how a woman looks when she is impassioned, and even more familiar with that state in a man.'

Iris grimaced—partly because it was now obvious she had not got away with it, but mainly because she'd rather not think about how her mother knew what a man looked like when he was impassioned. No one ever wanted to think about one's parents in that way, and Iris was no exception.

'I know exactly why a woman gets that flush on her cheeks and her neck, and it is certainly not because she's been discussing what happened during a dinner party which I believe for the Earl was anything but fun.' Her mother stopped walking and turned to look at Iris. 'And her lips do not usually get quite so swollen and her eyes are not usually glazed because she has had a pleasant conversation.'

'Oh,' was all Iris could think to say.

'Oh, indeed,' her mother replied.

They continued walking, this time in silence. Iris suddenly felt rather guilty. Not because of what she had done, but because she did not want to upset her mother, and most certainly did not want her mother to be ashamed of her.

'You are in love with him, my dear,' her mother finally said, breaking the silence in a most unexpected manner. Her voice was quiet, but the words hit Iris as if she had shouted them from the rooftops.

Iris came to a sudden halt. 'In love? With the Earl? No, I am not.'

Her mother smiled. 'Yes, you are. I have watched you with all those young men who have tried to court you. You have been friendly. You have even flirted on occasion. But you have treated all of them as if they were nothing more than friends. None of them has affected you the way the Earl of Greystone has.'

Iris stared at her mother, taking in the implication of her words. No, it couldn't be true. She could not be in love with the Earl. She could not be in love with a grumpy recluse, even if he was handsome and his kisses could make her forget what day it was, who she was and what she was doing.

Slowly Iris shook her head, which caused her mother to smile.

'I suspected you held the Earl in high regard the first time you mentioned his name. Your voice softened. A sure sign that you had feelings for him. And then every time you mentioned his name after that you reacted in some way—either you softened your voice, you looked flustered, or as if you were deliberately trying to act normally. It has all been rather entertaining, actually.'

Her mother pushed a wayward strand of hair back off Iris's face. 'I would have preferred you to have fallen in love with another man, but so be it.'

Iris bristled and she glared at her mother in shock. 'Why? Because he's blind? He might be blind but he's more capable than most sighted men, and certainly a lot braver than any man I've ever met. I would have expected better from you, Mother.'

'Oh, get off your high horse, Iris. No, it is not because he is blind. You know as well as I do why it would be a lot easier if you had fallen in love with one of the other men who have pursued you.'

Iris sighed and her shoulders slumped. 'Lady Redcliffe?'

Her mother nodded. 'Yes, Lady Redcliffe. Lady Walberton told me last night all about the Earl and Lady Estelle, as she once was. It would definitely be better if you had fallen in love with a man who was not still in love with another woman.'

'But I'm not in love,' Iris said again, her voice sounding defeated.

Her mother merely rolled her eyes, something Iris doubted she had seen her do before, and they commenced walking, although now Iris was finding it all but impossible not to drag her feet.

Was she in love with the Earl? Was that why he had taken over her thoughts every waking hour and was even invading her dreams? Was that why she was going out of her way to see him, even if it meant breaking all the rules of polite society? Was that why she was so desperate to have him kiss her, and once in his arms wanted him to do so much more than just kiss her? Perhaps her mother was right. She was in love with the Earl of Greystone, a man who was in love with another woman.

'But all is not lost,' her mother said, returning to her usually cheerful manner. 'Even if the Earl is in love with another, there is nothing to stop him falling in love with you and forgetting all about Lady Redcliffe. There is no denying he feels something for you, or my eyes are starting to deceive me, which I know they are not.'

Iris made no answer, reluctant to explain

to her mother that even though the Earl had kissed her it hadn't been due to passion but to teach her a lesson about the dangers of arriving unaccompanied at a man's home. Then he'd rejected her. He had been more than capable of controlling himself, even though she hadn't been. She doubted that he would have behaved in that manner if he'd had Lady Redcliffe in his arms. No, her mother meant well, but this was a lost cause and the sooner Iris put that kiss behind her the better. She sighed loudly. That was something she knew was going to be an all but impossible task to accomplish.

'We are just going to have to make him realise that his love for you is much greater than anything he may have felt for Lady Redcliffe,' her mother continued in a voice full of confidence.

Iris gripped her mother's arm and stopped her in her step. 'Mother, you can't make someone fall in love,' she stated emphatically. Iris knew that from personal experience—hadn't enough men over the last five Seasons tried to convince her that she was in love with them, and they had all failed? The Earl was in love with another woman and nothing was going to change that. His rejection of her was all the proof she needed.

'Yes, you can,' her mother said, still smiling and not the slightest bit discouraged. 'Your father didn't realise he was in love with me until I convinced him of that fact. Then all I had to do was act terribly surprised when he finally proposed, as if I had never even considered him as a possible husband.'

'But I thought your marriage was arranged.'

'Yes, it was. Arranged by me. I have not told anyone this, Iris, so please keep this just between the two of us.'

Iris nodded.

'Without being too obvious, I managed to convince my parents and his parents that our marriage would be advantageous to both families. Then I convinced your father, who until that point had not even noticed me, that he was hopelessly in love with me. They all thought it was their own idea and that innocent little me had nothing to do with it. So, if I could convince two well-established families and a stubborn eldest son who was certain he wanted to remain single that our marriage was exactly what they all wanted, then convincing the Earl of Greystone that he loves you should be no problem whatsoever.'

Iris stared at her mother. In awe? In horror? In admiration? She wasn't sure.

'Oh, refrain from looking at me like that, my dear. You know this is exactly what you want. It is what you wanted from the moment you met the Earl.'

'It was not and it still is not.' Iris shook her head. 'I didn't like him when I first met him. He was rude and bad-tempered, plus he's a recluse and, as we both know, in love with another woman. I could never be married to such a man.'

Her mother rolled her eyes again. That unfamiliar gesture was almost becoming a habit. 'You can lie to yourself, Iris, but you can't lie to your mother. The Earl is the man for you.'

Iris was tempted to inform her that she had now lost count of the number of white lies she had told, but thought it would be in her best interests to keep that to herself.

'When you lie, you blink your eyes repeatedly. You have done it ever since you were a little girl,' her mother continued. 'When you said you had a headache I knew you were lying, but, as I also knew you wanted to escape from Lord Pratley and his relentless courting, I said nothing. Although I did not think you would be silly enough to go for a walk when there was a storm coming and stay out all night. That did take me rather by surprise. Then the next morning when you started telling me about the Earl of Greystone you started blinking hard enough to generate your own storm. All I could think was, oh, this is interesting. That was why I had to meet the Earl. And that was why I took the liberty of inviting him to the dinner party.'

'You're so wrong, Mother,' Iris said, holding her eyes open as wide as she could, so she wouldn't blink.

Her mother laughed and patted her gently on the arm. 'Anyway, I know you want to marry the Earl and I think he would make an excellent husband for you, so that is what is going to happen. And after what I witnessed this morning, I would be well within my rights to insist that he do the honourable thing and marry you.'

'No, please, Mother, no,' Iris gasped out, trying to form the words in her head that would explain that what had happened between them was not the Earl's fault, that he had shown a greater level of restraint than she had been capable of, and he did not deserve to be punished for his actions.

'Oh, cease your worrying. I would not do that.' She patted Iris's arm in reassurance. 'I do not blame you and I do not blame the Earl.

These things happen when young people fall in love. Their passions can get the better of them and they forget all the rules that Society places on them.' Her mother sighed lightly and looked off into the distance. 'I know exactly how it feels. Before we married, when your father and I were still courting, we too often—'

'Yes, Mother, I get the idea,' Iris cut in, horrified at the thought of what her mother was about to reveal.

Her mother merely laughed. 'All I am saying is that it happens, and I am not one to judge. Nor will I make the Earl feel any obligation towards you. We do not want him thinking he has been forced into marriage. That is no basis for happiness. This all has to be the Earl's idea, or at least he has to think it is his idea.' She looked at Iris and gave her a conspiratorial smile, although to Iris's mind there was no conspiracy—this was all her mother's idea.

'So, to that end, I will ask Lady Walberton if we can extend our stay for another month. That should give us enough time to make the Earl realise just how much in love with you he actually is.'

Iris continued to stare at her mother, her mouth open but unable to speak. Unlike the mothers of so many other débutantes, her mother had never taken an overly active role as matchmaker. But she appeared to be making up for that now and Iris did not know whether that was a good or bad thing, for her or the Earl, or whether she was now about to be punished for all her lies and all her bad behaviour, and was about to suffer a complete and utter humiliation.

Chapter Eighteen

Lady Walberton was delighted that Iris and her mother would be staying longer and not the slightest bit surprised. It was all so mortifying, the two ladies conspiring together in their hopeless quest. She could almost understand her mother's delusions—after all, she hardly knew the Earl—but Iris would have expected Lady Walberton to be aware just what an impossible task her mother had set herself.

But there was nothing for it. It had all been agreed, and they would be staying for at least another month. And if Iris was being honest, she did not mind. The balls, parties, dinners and picnics remaining on this Season's social calendar no longer held any appeal, so she might as well stay in the country and make the best of things.

And, if she was being *really* honest with

herself, the fact was she did not want to return to London, knowing it would possibly mean never seeing the Earl again. And what would be the point in participating in the rest of the Season? She had no interest in any other man, had never had the slightest interest in any man, until she met the Earl. And now that he had kissed her, she was certain no other man would interest her ever again.

It was a cruel trick of fate. After having rejected so many men over the last five Seasons, she had fallen in love with a man who did not want her.

And what was worse, she had been given a taste of what the Earl could offer, had sampled his kisses, and then it had all been taken away from her.

Even thinking about that kiss was torture enough, albeit an exquisite torture. It had been unlike anything she had ever experienced, and he was unlike any other man she had ever met. It hadn't been her first kiss, but it was certainly the first time she had been affected so completely.

Many a man had stolen a quick kiss, and the most it had elicited from her was a giggle. None had caused a tempest to erupt deep within her, an insatiable, burning desire to consume her, leaving her demanding more, much more, and none had left her with such a desperate sense of loss.

Was it simply because his kiss had been unlike those quick, passionless pecks she had experienced in the past? There had been no playfulness to his kiss, not even any gentleness. He had kissed her with such force it had overwhelmed her, swept her off her feet and left her defenceless. Was that a good sign or a bad one? Iris had no way of knowing. She wanted to ask someone, but most certainly was not going to ask her mother. She suspected her mother would know the answer, but it would be far too embarrassing to talk to her about such things. She could ask her married sister, Hazel, but that would mean writing a letter and Iris wasn't sure how to put her confusion into written words. And even less sure if she wanted to commit such thoughts to paper. What if the letter fell into the wrong hands? That too would be more mortifying than she could imagine.

So Iris was left wondering about that kiss, wondering about the Earl, and wondering about her mother's determination that Iris and the Earl would soon be marrying. Her mother had promised that she would be subtle and the Earl would not feel as if his hand had been forced, but when her mother announced that the Earl would be hosting a county fête, she had to suspect some not so subtle hand-forcing had come into it.

Her mother had convinced Lady Walberton that a village fête should be held in the next few weeks, that it should have a medieval theme, and that, as the Earl of Greystone's home still contained parts of the original castle, it would make a simply splendid backdrop.

Lady Walberton could only agree and commend Iris's mother for such a clever idea. Then she busily gathered all the local ladies to form an organising committee.

Somehow, Iris doubted the Earl had seen the idea as either commendable or clever, but according to her mother he had agreed immediately.

Iris suspected her mother was now telling her own white lies. When she questioned her mother about this, Iris had been horrified by the answer.

'My dear, when it comes to the Earl, he will do exactly what I ask.' She had sent Iris a knowing smile. 'He is not a stupid man. He kissed my daughter and will know that I am quite within my rights to demand a lot more of him than hosting a local fête. This will be a very small price to pay for the liberties he has taken.'

'You mean, you blackmailed him?' Iris asked. Her mother was constantly surprising her, and not in a good way.

'No, not blackmail, dear. All I did was politely ask him to host a fête that will be of benefit to everyone in the county and he graciously accepted.'

Graciously? Iris doubted that very much.

'So you have nothing to worry about,' her mother added, then left the room, humming the 'Wedding March' to herself.

Iris watched her leave, suspecting she actually did have a great deal to worry about.

On the day of the fête, it was as if he had been caught up in a storm, one far worse than the one that had blown Lady Iris into his life. This storm was called Lady Springfeld and was creating havoc in his life and in his house.

Only a few short weeks ago he had lived alone, just him and Max, and had hardly seen his neighbours in years. Now it was as if the entire county had congregated on his grounds and were making themselves entirely at home.

It was most definitely not what he had wanted, but Lady Springfeld had given him no choice. That joyful, sunny lady had a dark side and was a master in the nefarious art of blackmail. When suggesting that he host a fête she had managed to casually drop in a series of threatening words, such as 'kisses', 'impropriety', 'reputations' and even that fateful word 'marriage'. She may not have said it outright, but she made it clear that she knew what had happened between him and Lady Iris and that she had every right to demand that he marry her daughter. And on that point, unfortunately, Theo knew her to be right. Lady Springfeld now had him at her mercy.

He supposed he should be grateful that she was not completely outraged on behalf of her daughter, but instead of being completely incensed she seemed rather pleased about it. They really were a rather peculiar family.

If she had insisted that he marry Lady Iris he would have consented—after all, it was no less than would be expected in the circumstances. His behaviour *had* been unacceptable. If he'd been forced to justify what he had done, he would have said that he had never expected her to actually allow him to kiss her. But that really was no justification at all. A gentleman should never have behaved in the way he had towards a lady unless he was prepared to accept the consequences.

And for him the consequences would at least be a fête, not a marriage—a small price to pay for a kiss that, he had to admit, had left him reeling. Not only had he not expected her to allow him to kiss her, but neither had he expected her to kiss him back, and to do so with such ferocity. That had most certainly taken him by surprise and continued to take his breath away, every time he thought about it. And, unfortunately, he was thinking about it rather more than he wanted to. Despite his determination to put Lady Iris out of his mind, he kept remembering her soft lips on his, the feel of her satin-like skin, and those glorious, full breasts filling his hands.

He shook his head, as if to physically drive out that thought. It was the last thing he should be thinking of, particularly when the mother was somewhere in the vicinity and his estate was full of milling hordes.

He settled down in his chair and scratched Max's head. But at least nothing more was expected of him than letting the county loose on his grounds. He could hide away in his drawing room until it was all over, and life returned to normal.

He rang his bell so he could ask Charles to inform him of all that was going on at this infernal fête. Charles entered and the ringing continued, even though the bell had been returned to the table. Most odd.

'What's that noise?' he asked, moving his head from side to side to try to find the source of the continued tinkling.

'I'm afraid it's me, my lord,' Charles said just as the ringing stopped. 'It's the bell pads round my shins. You did say we were to do whatever the organising committee required of us, and when they found out about my little hobby they insisted I dress in costume for the entire day.'

'Your little hobby?' What on earth was the man talking about?

'Yes, my lord. I'm a Morris dancer, and the committee has asked me and my fellow Morris dancers to put on a performance at the end of the day.'

Theo turned his head in the direction of his butler. Charles was a secret Morris dancer— who would have thought it? He'd known the man for more years than he could remember but never knew that about him. This must be what comes from having servants with not enough to do, he decided. They take up unusual little hobbies.

He closed his mouth, which had fallen open in surprise. 'I see,' he said, not sure he really understood at all. 'And do the organisers of the fête have everything they need?' *Please say yes*, he silently implored his butler. The last thing he wanted was to be bullied around by the ladies of the committee, who over the last few weeks had acted as if they were organising a military campaign and not a simple county fair.

'Yes, the ladies appear to have everything under control. It's quite a spectacle, really. They've organised court jesters, jugglers, acrobats and men dressed as knights to entertain the crowds, along with Morris dancers, of course. We're going to provide the grand finale.'

Theo could hear excitement starting to rise in his butler's usually emotionless voice.

'There are stalls selling everything you can think of,' Charles continued. 'Herbal concoctions, ale, elderberry wine, flowers, vegetables, baking. And, if I do say so myself, our servants have done us proud. The gardeners' flowers and vegetables are among the best on show, and no one can beat Cook's gooseberry pie. That's sure to win a prize.'

Now the man was getting rather more animated than was seemly for a butler.

'In that case, you had better take the rest of the day off so you can join them and do your dancing or whatever it is you do.'

'Thank you, my lord,' he said, the ringing of bells presumably signalling a bow. 'But Lady Springfeld would like a word with you. Shall I show her in?'

Theo suppressed an annoyed sigh. Being left alone inside his own home would have been too much to hope for. 'Yes, show her in, then go off and enjoy yourself.'

'Very good, my lord,' Charles said, and jingled his way out of the room.

Lady Springfeld burst in the moment Charles departed. 'Lord Greystone, this simply won't do. You must go outside and circulate. It's expected of the host.' She lowered her voice. 'And I know you want to do what's right.' There it was again, that veiled threat.

He heard another woman enter the room, somewhat less boisterously. Lady Iris. He'd recognise her scent anywhere, and the way she moved. It was that youthful yet gracious swish of her skirts that gave her away.

He bowed to the two women. 'If you insist, Lady Springfeld,' he said, reminding himself that it was at least a better option than being dragged up the aisle.

'Oh, good,' the mother trilled, as if she had given him a choice. 'You can take Iris's arm and she can escort you. I'm far too busy with the organising.'

'Delighted,' he said, offering his arm and feeling anything but delight at what was expected of him. He would do a quick circuit then retreat and leave the rest of them to their merriment.

'Oh, and we will expect you to present the prizes, so do not disappear, will you?' Lady Springfeld said as she bustled off, no doubt to boss around some other poor, helpless dupe.

Theo stifled a sigh and with resignation escorted Lady Iris out of the room. Not that he had any reservations about touching her again or having her close beside him. After all, that had been something he had been thinking about constantly, but when he had fantasised about having her in his arms again it had most certainly not been under circumstances such as these.

'I'm sorry about all this,' she said as they walked down the hallway, followed by Max, who, once they reached the front entrance to the house, skittered past them and out through the door, excited by the prospect of so many people and so much activity.

'None of this was my idea. It was all my mother's doing,' she added.

'I do not doubt it.' The mother was a force of nature and he'd already suspected that when she got an idea in her head nothing could stop her.

They walked outside and he was hit by a cacophony of sounds. Laughter, loud talking, shouts from conjurers and men trying to interest passers-by in the stalls, people spinning a tombola and balls being thrown at the coconut shy, along with the sounds of children at play, and more of those jingling Morris dancers' bells.

They entered the nearest tent and he heard Tom, his head gardener, loudly declaring that the secret to growing successful vegetables was the right combination of horse manure and straw, followed by a murmur of approval, presumably from the other gardeners.

The conversation came to a halt.

'Please, carry on,' he said. 'We're just here because Lady Iris really wants to see the vegetables.'

'Oh, yes, I do, indeed,' she said, following his lead. 'And I'm particularly keen to see the turnips, which I hear were a bumper crop this year.'

That was enough to start all the gardeners talking at once and giving their opinion on how to grow the biggest and the tastiest turnips.

Lady Iris made the appropriate responses, then nudged him lightly as a signal that they could now move on. A good idea, as the gardeners had gone back to arguing over which manure was the best and how thickly it should be spread.

They entered another tent, causing conversation to once again come to an abrupt halt. The shuffle of cotton fabric suggested that numerous women had just curtsied.

'My lord, Lady Iris, it is so good to see you,' his cook said.

'So, I hear you're in line to win a prize for the best gooseberry pie,' Lady Iris said.

'Thank you, m'lady. I do hope so.' Theo could hear the justified pride in her voice.

'And the best scones,' the kitchen maid added.

'Oh, I don't know about that, Lottie,' the cook replied with false modesty. 'There's going to be a lot of competition from the cook at the Walberton estate.'

'Oh, you're too kind,' a woman said, presumably the Walbertons' cook.

'And then there's Polly Smith from the Redcliffe estate...' She halted and there was much shuffling of feet. 'Polly's a fine cook as well,' she added quickly. 'Although I'm not too sure I agree with the temperature she has her oven and she does add a little too much fruit.'

'Nonsense,' another cook shot back. 'The higher the temperature the better and you can never have too much fruit.'

'Well, good luck to you all,' Theo said, leading Lady Iris out of the tent. Did everyone at this fête know about him and Estelle and were they all feeling sorry for him? Even the servants? Was it any surprise that he did not want to mix with his neighbours when they were all discussing his misfortunes?

At the next tent they were hit by the scent of flowers. They were introduced to the competitors, all of whom had their own ideas on the best way to grow the perfect blooms, and how to create the most attractive arrangements.

And so it went. Lady Iris led him into tent after tent, where he was greeted with enthusiasm as if he were some long-lost traveller finally returning home. Apart from their sometimes uncomfortable attempts to avoid mentioning Lord or Lady Redcliffe, he had to admit their kind wishes and cheerful greetings were somewhat heartening, and despite himself, as the day wore on, he was starting to slowly relax.

And having Lady Iris on his arm was certainly adding to the cheerful nature of the afternoon. For once her happy disposition was an asset rather than an annoyance as she conversed with all the locals and accepted their constant offers of cups of tea with a natural graciousness.

As she continued to chat away, he could hear their voices turn from polite and guarded, as one would expect when talking to an earl's daughter, to comfortable and natural as she put them at ease with her genuine interest in what they were saying and with her happy disposition.

And, he had to admit, she was also putting him at his ease. He had expected there to be a certain awkwardness between them, after what had happened, but there was nothing awkward about Lady Iris.

Yes, she was making today quite tolerable— more than tolerable—but that did not mean he wanted her, or anyone else, in his life. Once the fête was over, once these tents were packed up and gone, it would be back to his old life as if none of this had ever happened.

A pain hit him, like a punch to his stomach. Back to his own life, of being alone. He drew in a deep breath and exhaled slowly. What was wrong with him? That was the life he had chosen for himself, and the one he would continue to live, the one he wanted.

'Are you all right?' Lady Iris asked, concern in her voice.

'Perfectly all right,' he shot back.

She didn't answer and he could tell she was staring at him with concern, but what could he say, when he didn't know himself what had caused that strange reaction?

'Oh, there you are,' Lady Springfeld said, interrupting his thoughts.

As if he would be anywhere other than exactly where she had insisted he be.

'Don't wander off or disappear, will you?' she added, her voice cheerful, even though Theo knew it was bound to contain some threat or other. 'Remember you're still going to have to present the prizes.'

'No, I hadn't forgotten,' Theo responded, trying and failing not to sound annoyed.

'It could be worse,' Lady Iris said with a smile in her voice. 'At least all you have to do is present the prizes. It would be so much worse if you had to be one of the judges. I suspect they'll have to make a hasty retreat once the results are announced.'

Theo smiled, remembering the animated discussion on manure in the gardeners' tent. By the time he and Lady Iris had crept away they were almost coming to blows over the merits of horse manure versus cow manure.

'And I suspect a few of the losers will be drowning their sorrows in Myrtle Williams's elderberry wine,' she said.

'I noticed you were more than happy to try a few samples of that yourself,' he added, causing her to laugh.

'Yes, about the judging,' Iris's mother cut in. 'There was some disagreement over the impartiality of the fruit pie judge, and it resulted in a bit of unpleasantness between the competitors.'

Theo joined Iris's laughter. That didn't surprise him in the least. While the cooks had been polite to each other in his company, their compliments had all had a slight competitive edge to them, and he suspected once he and Lady Iris had left their tent the disagreements had got as heated as that of the gardeners.

'It has been decided that Iris would judge the appearance of the scones,' Lady Springfeld said, causing Theo to smile at her unfortunate predicament. 'And you will judge the taste and texture. So make haste—they're expecting you at the baking tent.'

The mother rushed off, leaving a stunned Theo reeling in her wake and wondering whether that woman would ever stop tormenting him.

'I'm sure it won't be too bad,' Iris said, suspecting it probably would be. 'Although perhaps we should have asked Mother what happened to the last judge.'

'Tarred and feathered probably,' he said, looking as worried as she felt. 'Or perhaps buttered and floured would be more appropriate.'

She smiled, pleased that at least he could joke about it. 'Well, there's nothing for it,' she said, taking his arm. 'Once more into the breach and all that.'

They walked towards the baking tent, with as much trepidation as if they were about to face a firing squad.

'I think we had better try to smile,' Iris said. 'Otherwise they might be able to sense our fear.'

He smiled down at her. 'How does this look?'

'Perfect.' And it was. He had such a wonderfully perfect smile, she just wished he would show it more often.

They entered the tent and once again all conversation stopped.

'I believe you'd like His Lordship and me to judge the scones,' Iris said, trying to keep her voice calm.

'Yes, my lord, my lady,' Theo's cook said. 'That last judge, he didn't know a thing about gooseberry pies. Wouldn't be able to tell a good flaky pastry if it bit him on the...anyway, we're sure you'll do a much fairer job.'

'We'll do our best,' he said, his voice sounding more confident than she was sure he was feeling. 'Now, lead me to all your tasty scones.'

Iris looked along the line of jam, date and sultana scones. They all looked equally wonderful to her: golden-brown, plump and either perfectly round or precisely square.

Theo broke open the first one, took a bite and chewed, his brow furrowed in thought.

'Light, good texture and an excellent balance of flavours,' he declared, causing the women to smile in approval and the cook responsible to puff herself up, just like her well-risen scones.

He moved down the line, his face maintaining that look of intense concentration, and each comment he made not only flattered the cook, but also surprised Iris in his ability to think of something new and apt to say.

When he came to the last scone, Iris could see he was about to be presented with a challenge. These scones were not golden, nor were they perfectly round or square, and did not even look like scones, but more like some sort of misshapen rocks containing bits of burnt fruit.

The scullery maid from Theo's house was smiling fit to burst, proud of what presumably was her effort.

With some force Theo broke the scone open, tried to take a bite, then managed to rip some off with his teeth. Iris watched in amazement as his expression did not change. He kept that thoughtful look on his face throughout the chewing. It took some time to consume the morsel, then eventually she watched a lump travel slowly down his throat.

'Unique flavour, interesting use of the ingredients and an enterprising interpretation of a traditional recipe,' he said, amazing Iris with his tact. The scullery maid smiled with pride while the other cooks either raised their eyebrows or bit their smiling lips.

'Perhaps I could have a cup of tea,' Theo asked, obviously still trying to swallow the last offering. Once he had finished his drink the cooks all leaned forward, their eyes fixed on Theo in anticipation.

'You haven't made it easy for me, have you, ladies?' he said, to much murmuring and shuffling from the assembled cooks. 'Allow me to consult with Lady Iris for a moment and I'll give you my verdict.'

Iris led him to the corner of the tent and they huddled together.

'I've no idea,' she confessed quietly. 'They all look excellent to me—well, apart from that one exception. What are we going to do? We have to choose one.' Iris looked over her shoulder at the faces of the cooks, staring at her with narrowed eyes and set mouths. 'Perhaps we could say there's a six-way tie.'

Theo laughed. 'Whatever fate awaits us, we'll just have to face it together,' he said, giving her hand a reassuring squeeze. 'But at least no one can accuse me of bias. This truly has been a blind tasting and I have no idea who made which scone.'

She squeezed his hand back. 'Good luck,' she murmured. 'And if they turn nasty, I recommend we try and make a run for it.'

She was pleased to see he smiled at her little joke.

'Right, let's do this,' he said and they returned to the waiting competitors.

'After a thorough discussion on the merits of each scone with my fellow judge, and taking into account the colour, taste, lightness, and texture of each scone, we have to declare the date scone as the winner.'

The cook from Walberton Estate clapped her hands together and smiled at the other cooks in satisfaction.

'Well, my scones used to be the best in the county,' Theo's cook said as the other women gave their guarded congratulations to the winner. 'But I'm a bit out of practice, what with not having guests any more.' She sent Theo a withering look, then smiled at Iris. 'But perhaps that's going to change soon and by next year's fête I'll have once again perfected my recipe.' She looked at the winner. 'Then we'll see who's got the best scones in the county.'

'I don't know about that,' the winner said. 'Mine had the best texture, lightness, taste and colour. The Earl said so.'

Theo and Iris quietly backed out of the tent as the argument continued and voices grew louder. Once they were outside, they both broke into laughter.

'I don't think we should linger,' Theo said,

taking her hand. 'It won't be long before rolling pins start being thrown and we don't want to get caught in the crossfire.'

He led her away from the tent and complete pleasure consumed Iris. Spending the day with Theo was such fun. *He* was such fun and she hoped he was enjoying himself as much as she was.

They walked arm in arm through the crowds, with everyone saying hello, smiling and giving Iris knowing looks. The Earl's cook apparently was not the only one who believed Iris would be a part of Theo's future. And she had never seen him look more content. It made her think that maybe, just maybe, the cook was correct, and she was about to get plenty of practice making prize-winning scones.

The sound of the bustling crowd was suddenly drowned out by the jingling of bells, and like the rest of the revellers they turned and headed over towards the music.

'That will be the Morris dancers,' Theo said. 'Another activity that one of my servants has got caught up in, but hopefully Morris dancing won't be quite as combative as scone-baking.'

They arrived at the courtyard where the dancers were flinging themselves in the air and waving white handkerchiefs. And, right in the middle, there was the usually ever-so-professional Charles, a wreath of flowers on his hat and a big smile on his face.

'This is wonderful, just wonderful,' Iris said. 'I would never have thought Charles would have such a playful nature.'

'Neither did I until today,' the Earl replied, slowly shaking his head. 'Now I'm beginning to wonder about the secret lives of all my other servants.'

Iris laughed and clapped along to the accordion, being played by a rather jolly man with a shiny red face. 'Come on, join in,' she said, nudging Theo lightly in the ribs.

He looked sideways at her, his eyebrow raised, but began clapping along to the merry tune, and soon he was smiling as widely as Iris. When the dancers finished, they both clapped enthusiastically and cheered their appreciation along with the rest of the crowd.

The Morris dancers jingled their way off to the nearest tent, where ale was being served, and the gusto with which they accepted their tankards did rather suggest that the ale and the camaraderie were as much an attraction as the dancing.

Iris took Theo's arm again and led him back through the crowd. 'Shall we see what the rest of your servants are up to? If Charles is a Morris dancer, heaven only knows what the rest of them are capable of.'

'Good idea,' he said, still smiling. 'I've always thought the housekeeper was a bit of a witch. Maybe we'll find her reading tarot cards somewhere. One of my footmen has a habit of dropping plates. Perhaps he's been using the china to practise his juggling routine.'

She looked up at him and smiled. 'If I didn't know you better, I would swear you were actually enjoying yourself.'

'It's good, then, that you do know me so well. I wouldn't want you to get the wrong impression,' he said, his smile contradicting his stern words.

Iris leant in closer to him, certain that there was nothing wrong at all with the impression she had of the Earl.

Chapter Nineteen

Enjoying himself? Theo wasn't sure. It had been such a long time since he had enjoyed himself, he no longer knew what enjoyment actually felt like. All he knew for certain was the fête wasn't as bad as he had expected, but, as he had expected it to be completely intolerable, that wasn't really saying a lot.

'Good, there you are,' the dreaded mother said, suddenly appearing beside him like a premonition of doom. Whenever that woman appeared it always resulted in Theo being strong-armed into doing something he did not want to do.

'The prizes are about to be presented, so we need you over at the podium.'

Theo nodded. That wasn't so bad. He'd already been warned about being expected to perform that particularly unwanted duty.

'And you're going to have to make a small speech,' Lady Springfeld added. There it was, as expected. Theo nodded with a resigned smile—after all, he knew it would not be up for negotiation and there was no point trying to argue with his blackmailer.

Accepting his fate with as much dignity as he could, he took Lady Iris's arm and she led him to the podium, where the crowds had already started to gather.

When the chattering had settled down, he stepped forward. 'I'd like to officially welcome you all to my home and hope you have all had an enjoyable day.'

Despite the fact that I was blackmailed into hosting this event and am looking forward to you all leaving, he added to himself.

'I've sampled some delicious food today, and been reliably informed that the vegetables, flowers, and crafts are exquisite.'

Not that I can possibly see any of them.

'I believe I can confidently say that the produce from this area of Cornwall is the best in the county, and, as Cornwall is the best county in all of England, that means it is the best in the entire British Isles.'

This rather over-generous boast was greeted with a loud cheer of approval.

'Everyone present deserves to be commended for their sterling efforts, but unfortunately only some can receive the prizes. So, let's get on with presenting these ribbons and cups, shall we?'

'And we're all pleased to see you again, my lord,' a voice called out from the back of the crowd. Followed by countless men calling out, 'Hear-hear!' and then a loud round of clapping and cheering.

'I believe you have been missed,' Lady Springfeld said as Theo took in the surprising jubilation from the crowd.

When the cheering finally settled down, the prizes were presented, the happy revellers departed, and the tents were packed up. Theo had expected that to be the end of it. He had paid his ransom to his blackmailer. Now Lady Iris and Lady Springfeld could also depart and leave him in peace.

But no. Apparently, it was essential for Lady Walberton and the other members of the organising committee to hold a post-mortem, right now, inside his home.

'Oh, but we won't need you,' Lady Springfeld said, much to Theo's relief. 'You and Lady Iris can retire to your drawing room while we have our discussion in the blue room.'

She headed off down the hallway with the other ladies, all chattering at once. Leaving him and Lady Iris standing in the hallway.

Gracious of you, Theo thought, to let me know which room in my house I can use. But there was no point arguing, so he merely took Lady Iris's arm and retreated to the room that had been assigned to him.

The door clicked shut behind them and Theo wondered at Lady Springfeld's motives. Was she assuming that if she left Theo alone with Lady Iris he would not be able to contain himself, that he would inevitably kiss her and then Lady Springfeld would have him just where she wanted him?

Well, she was wrong. He was more than capable of keeping himself in check, and how dared she think otherwise? Had he not proved himself today? Despite having her on his arm, despite being able to inhale her delightful scent of orange blossom and rose water and being disturbingly conscious of her warm body so close to his, he had acted at all times in the manner of the honourable gentleman he knew himself to be. He'd had one lapse a few weeks ago in an otherwise unblemished life. That did not make him some sort of beast.

He led Lady Iris to where he knew the arm-chairs had been placed.

'Well, that was so successful I suspect Lady Walberton will be suggesting that a fête be hosted here every year,' she said, her voice teasing as she collapsed into a chair.

He took the adjacent armchair. Not if he had anything to do with it, he wanted to reply, but didn't want to ruin her good humour. It wasn't her fault that her mother hid a devious mind behind a sunny, cheerful façade, so he merely made a non-committal *hmm.*

'You don't need to sound quite so excited by the prospect,' she said with a little laugh.

He heard a light tap on the door and the door slowly creaking open.

'Excuse me, my lady, Lady Springfeld sent me in. I'll just sit over in the corner, shall I?'

Lady Springfeld obviously did think him a beast who could not be trusted to be alone with her daughter. Presumably, she expected Theo to try and ravish Lady Iris the moment they were alone and had decided he needed to be watched constantly.

'Thank you, Annette. Yes, that will be perfect,' Lady Iris replied to her lady's maid. 'Did you have an enjoyable day?'

'Oh, yes, thank you. It was just lovely,' came the enthusiastic response from across the room.

Theo tried to suppress his irritation at the maid's presence. After all, it was right and proper and did not necessarily mean that Lady Springfeld did not trust him. But he could not deny that deep down he had been anticipating, with some pleasure, spending time alone with Lady Iris, even if just briefly. Not that he had intended to kiss her again, but her presence was not entirely offensive to him, and he was even getting used to her constant chatter and laughter.

But at least with a chaperone in the room, Lady Springfeld would not be able to accuse him of taking liberties. Thank goodness for that. He hated to think what she would expect from him if he did kiss Lady Iris again— hosting the local hunt perhaps, a masked ball, a weekend party or two.

Lady Iris moved in her chair to turn towards her lady's maid, and the gentle rasp of silk stockings moving against each other assaulted his ears. He moved uncomfortably in his seat. The last thing he should be thinking about right now was Lady Iris's legs encased in silk, or any of the other soft parts of her body he had unforgivably touched.

As she continued to talk to the maid he sat up straighter in his chair and coughed to clear an annoying lump in his throat. He must not think about that kiss, must not think about his hands caressing her body. Such behaviour had already got him into enough trouble, and he did not need any more problems in his life. Although he had to wonder, would hosting a hunt or a ball in exchange for another kiss be such a bad deal?

What on earth was he thinking? As tempting as it was, the price was far too high. He had no intention of kissing Lady Iris again. Just as he'd had no intention of kissing her the first time he had taken her in his arms. Somehow, it had just happened, but it must never happen again.

The door squeaked open again and Charles entered, this time thankfully minus his dancing bells, but followed by an exhausted Max, who, after receiving his expected greeting from Lady Iris, slumped down at Theo's feet and instantly started snoring lightly.

'Shall I serve tea, my lord?' Charles asked, once Max had finished with his grand entrance. 'And the cook asks if you'd like some scones. There's a new recipe she's anxious to try.'

'No!' Theo and Lady Iris cried out in unison. Then they both laughed at their equally vehement reactions.

'Thank you, Charles, no,' he said, in a more serious manner. 'But you might like to serve scones and tea to Lady Iris's maid and the organising committee.'

'And your Morris dancing was such a joy,' Lady Iris added. 'Wasn't it, Annette?'

'Oh, yes, it was grand,' the lady's maid said from across the room, her voice strangely abashed. 'Best I've ever seen, and you looked right dashing in that costume.'

Were Charles and Annette flirting? Was Lady Iris matchmaking between their servants? This really was all getting a bit too familiar.

'That will be all, Charles,' he said, hoping his voice conveyed that he for one was not going to condone this level of informality.

'Very good, my lord. I'll be back presently with the lady's maid's tea.'

'Or perhaps Annette would like to take it in the servants' quarters,' Lady Iris said. 'You can come back when you've finished, Annette. I'm sure you won't be long, and Charles can leave the door open so there will be no impropriety.'

Was Lady Iris in collusion with her mother? Were they both trying to get him in a compromising position? Theo knew he should put up an objection. Even if the door was open, even if the maid was only gone for a brief moment, there was still the danger that he would again find himself in a position to be blackmailed.

But he remained mute as the maid and Charles left the room together. What was wrong with him? Was he losing his sense of self-preservation?

'Don't worry,' she said with another small laugh. 'I know my mother threatened you so you would host this fête, but she's not a vindictive woman. She wouldn't make you do anything she thought you'd really object to.'

Was she serious? He would have objected strenuously to hosting this fête if he had been given an opportunity to do so.

'Oh, don't look so affronted,' she said. 'You know you enjoyed yourself today. And isn't holding a fête so much better than having to marry me?'

'I… Well… I…' Theo didn't know what to say. She was right, he didn't want to marry her, but that didn't mean that being married to her was an abhorrent fate that all men would want to avoid. It was just one that *he* wanted to avoid, and not just to her, but to any woman.

'Don't worry. I'm just teasing you,' she said.

'But Mother would never have forced you to marry me. Can you imagine my lovely mother making anyone do anything they don't want to?'

'She made me host this fête,' he stated bluntly, finally finding his voice.

'Yes, and you had an enjoyable afternoon, didn't you? Go on, admit it.'

Theo huffed out a loud breath.

'Go on, say it—you had fun. I know you did,' she continued in that teasing voice.

'Oh, all right. Yes. It wasn't as dreadful as I had expected it to be.'

'And?'

'And, yes, all right—at times it was almost enjoyable.'

'That wasn't so hard to admit, now, was it?'

He was about to object to her teasing tone, but instead smiled. She was right. It wasn't that hard to admit. 'Well, a glass of Myrtle's elderberry wine certainly took the edge off the day.'

'One glass?'

He shrugged. 'All right, several glasses. I must order a barrel or two for the wine cellar so I can cope with next year's fête.'

What was he saying? He shouldn't even be joking about this. He had no intention of hosting another fête. The elderberry wine must be having more of an effect on him than he'd first thought.

'I'm sure the locals will be delighted if you do,' she said. 'They were all so happy to see you again. It was obvious how much you were missed.'

He huffed a dismissal. 'I'm the local Earl—they could hardly behave in any other way, could they?'

She lowered her voice. 'You don't need to do that, you know.'

'Do what?'

'Push people away. Everyone was pleased to see you at both the fête and the dinner party. And you *did* enjoy yourself today so that proves that you don't need to hide yourself away.'

'I am perfectly aware of the fact that I do not *need* to hide away,' he said, more loudly than he had intended. 'I live this way out of choice. If you consider that to be hiding myself away, then so be it.'

'But today you were so happy, you smiled and even laughed, whereas I don't believe the way you usually live is really making you happy,' she said, her voice still quiet and no longer teasing.

'Nonsense.'

He expected her to put up a barrage of arguments to counter his claim, but she said nothing. She did not remind him, yet again, that he had enjoyed himself today. And about that she was surprisingly correct. Once the initial shock of having so many people on his grounds had worn off it was actually quite pleasant to meet the locals again. And despite himself, he had to admit, it had been heartening the way they had greeted him, as if with genuine affection.

'All right, yes. I had a good time today, but that does not mean I wish to change the way I live my life. As I said, I'm perfectly happy the way I am.'

'Hmm…' was all she said in response.

He waited for her inevitable lecture, for her to argue that if he was so damn happy, then why was he always so bad-tempered? He even thought she might insult him by saying that hiding away was the behaviour of a coward. But after that small, murmured *hmm*, she kept uncharacteristically quiet.

'All right,' he said again, in answer to her unasked questions. 'Perhaps it doesn't necessarily make me happy. But it is the way I choose to live my life and that is an end to it.'

She said nothing. He tapped his hand repeatedly against the arm of his chair, his irritation growing with every second she remained silent. He knew she was still present, could hear her soft breathing, could still smell her enticing scent, so why didn't she speak? After all, chattering incessantly was something she was so good at. Why didn't she start blathering on about the weather, or start cooing over Maxie-Waxie, or say something, anything, other than criticising the way he lived his life?

'All right,' he repeated, to fill the annoying silence. 'So, you think I've acted like a coward, do you? Buried myself away because I can't face the world? Retreated in defeat?'

'I don't think you're a coward,' she said quietly. 'After what you did no one would ever consider you a coward.'

He huffed out his annoyance. 'I'm not talking about the fire. That night I merely did what any man would do. I'm talking about how I've lived since then.'

'So am I,' she responded. 'Your world as you knew it was destroyed that night. You did what you did to protect yourself. That's not cowardly...that's survival.'

What on earth was she blabbering on about? Protect myself? From what? From whom? From the world? From those people at the fête who acted as if overjoyed to see me again? From Estelle? Nonsense. None of those people frightened him. Nothing frightened him.

He gripped the sides of the armchair, his irritation continuing to grow. Or did she think he was protecting himself from her? From the potential pain of her rejection? From the pain of being rejected again? That too was nonsense. He did not want her or any other woman and he did not appreciate this line of questioning.

'You were hurt,' she said. 'It's natural to want to hide away while you heal.'

Would she never stop with this absurd balderdash? He wanted to shout at her in a most ungentlemanly manner. It was time to nip this in the bud, to let her know that she had no right to talk to him like this—after all, she meant nothing to him.

'Need I point out, Lady Iris, that you are overstepping what is considered appropriate behaviour from a young lady when in the company of a gentleman?' he said through clenched teeth. 'Twice you've come into my house uninvited, and the last time you did so it was to reprimand me for an impropriety which I hadn't committed. Now you feel you're within your rights to question the way I live my life.'

This elicited a hearty laugh from Lady Iris,

one much louder than would normally be acceptable in polite society, and certainly not the reaction he expected.

'And need I point out to you, my lord, that said gentleman has perhaps lost the right to point out to said lady what she should or should not do or say? Not when he's kissed that young lady and has actually had his hand up her blouse.'

Theo froze in his chair. How could she talk about what had happened between them in such an open, teasing manner? Most women would be too contrite to even mention it, never mind joke about it. He could only hope no one was listening at the doorway.

'And I suppose you believe that intimacy we shared gives you the right to comment on the way I live,' he said in a lowered voice.

The tantalising sound of silk caught his attention as she moved in her chair. He tried hard not to be distracted by it and to focus on her annoying words.

'It's one thing to hide away when you first need to heal—that's only natural—but you don't need to do that any more. You should get out into the world. You should socialise with other people. You had been happy before and you can be happy again, but that isn't going to happen if you hide yourself away.'

'Next you're going to be suggesting that I should marry, have a family, become part of the community.'

'Would that be so bad?' she said softly.

Theo was silent for a moment, unable to formulate all the reasons why that was indeed *so bad*. It had once been what he wanted but not now. And if little miss Lady Iris had thoughts in that direction then they needed to be quashed immediately.

'Yes, it would. I have no intention of marrying anyone, ever. And I would appreciate it if you would keep your opinions to yourself. Yes, we shared a brief intimacy, but that gives you no more right to question the way I live my life than I have the right to question the way you live yours.'

'You're right,' she said softly. Theo knew he was being cruel and for that he felt bad, but he could not abide having her suggesting that he should make changes just because she didn't approve of his solitary existence.

'It is none of my business,' she said, her voice no longer teasing. 'I suppose I'm a bit like my mother. We just want everyone to be happy.'

He scoffed his disagreement. 'And, like your mother, you want to interfere in people's lives.'

'Yes, I suppose we do,' she said, not sounding as if she had just been insulted. 'But only when we think it's for the best.'

The only response he could give to that was another humph.

'And we do want what's best for you,' she continued, her voice taking on a soft, soothing quality, as if she were talking to a child. But he was not a child and he would not be spoken to in this manner.

'Blackmail, forcing me to open up my home to all and sundry, forcing me to attend dinner parties where I have to endure...when I have made it clear that I don't want to go. If that's what you and your mother consider helping someone, I'd hate to see how you behave when you've got a vendetta against some poor man.'

'Yes, the dinner was perhaps a mistake, but an unintended one.'

The memory of Estelle's laughter and her flirtatious voice crashed unbidden into his mind. *A mistake.* That dinner had been more than a mistake—it had been a disaster, as had every encounter he had had since this overly joyful, overly meddlesome Lady Iris had entered his life. A woman who thought every problem could be solved by laughing and making a joke about it. Well, she could not solve the world's problems just by making people laugh. She could not change his life just by tricking him into attending a dinner party and hosting a fête.

'I know it's not my place to give an opinion,' Lady Iris continued, shuffling in her seat.

'Well, it not being your place hasn't stopped you before.' He sat back in his chair in preparation for her latest ludicrous pronouncement.

'I know Lady Redcliffe hurt you,' she continued. 'But you don't need to continue to punish yourself for the way she treated you. None of it was your fault and you deserve to be happy and to live a full life.'

His chest tightening, his breath caught in his throat. 'You're right,' he gritted out through clenched teeth. 'It is not your place to give an opinion, and I'd appreciate it if in future you would keep them to yourself.'

'I just…'

'Yes, you *just*,' he hissed. 'You just want to make everything better, make everyone happy, make the world a place full of sunshine and joy.' He cut her off before she could impart any more of her unwanted advice or misguided opinions.

'No, I just…'

'Now that you have finished telling me how I should live my life and how I should be feeling, I think you should go and join that coven of women who have invaded the blue drawing room.'

Before she could speak again, he grabbed the bell and rang it hard and long.

'You rang, my lord,' Charles said, presumably an ironic comment as his master was still shaking the bell vigorously.

'Yes, Charles,' he said, placing the bell back on the table with a decisive clunk. 'Lady Iris is leaving now. Please show her to the blue drawing room, as it is past time that she, her mother and that organising committee departed.'

'Very good, my lord.'

Max's tail started thumping as Lady Iris patted him on the head and said goodbye. Although that was a pleasantry she reserved for the dog alone. When the door shut behind her, Max emitted a little whimper.

'Oh, don't you start,' he said to his dog. 'You were content enough before she came along. You don't need her in your life, so just get over it.'

Max settled down at his feet but continued with his sad whimpering.

Chapter Twenty

Iris had no regrets over what she had said to Theo Crighton. No, that wasn't entirely true. She did regret ruining the companionship they had shared throughout the day. And she regretted that he had pushed her away. But still, if she could take back time she would still have said everything that she had said to him. Someone needed to.

It broke her heart that he was wasting his life, locked up in his castle. He was a good man and he deserved to have a good life, to be loved and to be in love. It wasn't going to be her he loved—that was becoming increasingly obvious—but he did deserve to meet someone and that wasn't going to happen if he never left his home, and never let anyone close to him. Nor was it going to happen if he continued to cling to his love for Lady Redcliffe. It made her seethe every time she thought of that woman. Not because the Earl loved her—well, not *just* because the Earl loved her—but because she did not deserve his love, not after the way she had treated him.

She entered the blue room and her mother looked in her direction, her face expectant. Iris gave a small shake of her head and her mother shrugged and went back to discussing whether they should have a skittles competition at next year's fête and whether donkey or pony rides for the children should be included.

Iris sat quietly in the corner while the animated discussion continued and was soon joined by her smiling lady's maid. Annette appeared to have had more success in her romantic pursuits than Iris had, although, as they would soon be returning to London, Annette also was about to experience disappointment.

When the discussion finally came to an end, with no resolutions to the various contentious issues, only an agreement to meet again for further talks, the women gathered themselves up to leave.

They all headed off down the hallway to say goodbye to the Earl, still arguing about donkeys versus ponies. Iris's mother suggested that

Iris join them. When she declined her mother sent her a questioning look.

'I've already said goodbye. It would look a little odd if I went back in and said goodbye again,' she explained to her unconvinced mother, but she followed on behind and waited outside the door, while the other women gushed over the Earl, telling him how grateful they were, what a success the day had been, and hinting that it should happen again next year.

The terse replies from the Earl suggested his bad humour had not improved, but the ladies were undaunted and their spirits were just as high when they left his drawing room and fluttered off towards their waiting carriages.

'A very satisfying day, all round,' Lady Walberton said as she, Iris and her mother climbed into their carriage for the return journey.

'It was an excellent idea to host the fête at the Earl of Greystone's home,' Lady Walberton continued. 'And he did seem to be enjoying himself today.' She smiled at Iris. 'And I believe we have you to thank for that. I think the Earl is quite taken with you.'

Iris forced herself to smile back.

'Hopefully, that means he's put his past behind him and is now ready to re-enter Society, and maybe we'll be having a wedding in the county soon.'

Iris continued to smile, even though her jaw was now starting to hurt, while the satisfied Lady Walberton's smile beamed out, encompassing both Iris and her mother.

When they reached the house, Iris's mother took her arm and with great haste rushed her up the stairs to her bedroom. The fête wasn't the only thing that needed to be discussed, picked over and analysed. Her mother wanted to know everything that had happened between her and the Earl when they had been alone together in the drawing room, everything that had been said, and every gesture he had made.

Iris tried to repeat everything that had happened, what she had said, what the Earl had said, and in what tone. 'I'm afraid I undid any good will between us that had been built up during the fête, and now it's a rather hopeless cause,' Iris said when she'd finally relayed the entire conversation to her mother.

'Not necessarily,' her mother replied, her lips pursed in concentrated thought.

Iris had to admire her mother's optimism, even if it was a bit misplaced. But then, she hadn't been the one to be ejected from the Earl's drawing room.

'He kissed you and he was thoroughly enjoying your company today,' her mother said. 'We just need to contrive some more ways to put the two of you together so he can see how much in love with you he really is.'

Iris couldn't help but sigh. 'Mother, we've already stayed an extra three weeks at Lady Walberton's. We can hardly move in permanently.'

Her mother waved her hand in front of her face as if that was no problem. 'I'm sure Lady Walberton will not mind in the slightest.'

'But what about the rest of the family? What about the rest of the Season? I've got no interest in attending any further balls, but Daisy might want to, and someone needs to accompany her. And surely Father is missing you.'

'Getting your sister to attend a ball is becoming an almost impossible feat, so I've all but given up on that, and should a miracle happen your brother can escort her. And your father can always come down here and visit us. No, I sense that a marriage to the Earl is imminent, so we shouldn't give up now when it's all so close.'

'But he doesn't love me,' Iris said, despair in her voice.

'Yet,' her mother replied emphatically. 'He

doesn't love you yet, Iris, always remember that. Some men just take a bit more persuading than others. Your father was such a man and so is the Earl.'

Iris collapsed down onto her bed while her mother paced back and forth, thinking of strategies to turn a heart of stone into one that was warm and cuddly. Something that was much more of a conundrum than whether one should have donkey or pony rides at a fête.

'Perhaps we need to host a ball, here at the Walbertons'. Or maybe if we—'

'No, Mother,' Iris cut in. 'I know you mean well, but there's no point. You can't make a man love you. He either does or he doesn't. And the Earl most decidedly doesn't.'

'But your father, he thought he didn't...'

'No, Mother, you're wrong. Father would have fallen in love with you no matter what. I'm sure, no matter what you think, the moment he met you he was smitten. It's different with the Earl. This is all just a waste of time, and frankly rather embarrassing.'

'Oh, my dear,' her mother said, sitting down on the edge of the bed. 'I never intended to upset you.' She wiped away the tear that had inexplicably appeared on Iris's cheek. 'If it's upsetting and embarrassing you, then of course I'll stop.'

'And can we just return to London and forget all about this?'

Her mother gave her a long, appraising look. 'If that is what you wish, my dear, what you really, really wish?'

'It is,' Iris said, nodding with determination. It wasn't entirely what she wanted but it was what she was going to have to accept. Despite her mother's claims, she knew that a man could not be forced to fall in love. And she was also certain that she did not want a man's love if he had to be tricked and cajoled into giving it. It was better just to accept the reality that Theo Crighton, the Earl of Greystone, was not in love with her and there was no amount of fêtes, balls, picnics or whatever that would change that.

Theo raged, and he fumed, and he argued repeatedly with her in his head. Who did she think she was? Coming into his life, trying to change everything, trying to change him? Did she think one kiss gave her the right to tell him how he should live his life? Well, it didn't, and thank goodness he had put her straight about that.

Since he had all but ejected her from his house, he had heard nothing from Lady Iris or her interfering mother. He had expected more unwanted invitations, more veiled threats that if he didn't attend this or that social event he would be strong-armed into a marriage he didn't want. But no invitations came. The blackmailing appeared to have ceased.

Good. Finally, both mother and daughter had got the message. Life could return to normal. All he needed now was to get her out of his head and he would be free of her.

He resumed pacing up and down, all those ridiculous things she had said running repeatedly through his mind.

'Hiding away,' he said out loud. He turned and walked back along the well-worn track down the middle of his drawing room.

How *dare* she tell him he was hiding away? How *dare* she call him a coward?

He paused in his walking. No, she hadn't actually said that, had she? She'd said he wasn't a coward. But she had said he had been hiding because he needed to heal, as if he were some sort of sick animal. He resumed his pacing. How *dare* she compare him to an injured animal?

He clenched his teeth together tighter, his

jaw aching from tension, tension that little miss Lady Iris had caused him. He hadn't been tense like this before she'd come bursting into his life. She might be right that he hadn't been particularly happy, and perhaps he hadn't been content either, as he had claimed, but at least he hadn't had all this pent-up tension inside him, making his muscles ache and his thoughts a whirl of confusion. She alone was responsible for that. Before she had washed up on his doorstep, wet from the storm, he hadn't paced his room, he hadn't ranted and raved to himself like some demented madman.

And then just as suddenly as she had appeared, she disappeared from his life.

'Good riddance,' he muttered to himself. He was much better off without her coming in and giving her unwanted opinions on the way he lived his life.

Or had she returned to London? His pacing stopped. Had she gone back to the social flurry of balls, parties, the theatre, picnics and heaven only knew what other activities she should be filling her days and nights with? No doubt she was shining at them all, being fawned over by a coterie of men such as Lord Pratley. Well, they were welcome to her. And she was welcome to that lifestyle if that was what she wanted. But it was not for him. And how dared she think that it was? Just because she wanted to fill her own days with frivolous laughter and entertainment, it did not mean he did as well.

He recommenced walking the well-trodden path down the middle of his drawing room, then came to a sudden stop. And at these parties, balls and picnics, was she giving her kisses to some other man? Was some other man unleashing that untapped passion he had experienced when he had taken her in his arms? Was some other man holding her tightly, feeling her soft body pressed against his?

His hands clenched into fists so tight the nails dug into his flesh. Why should he care what she was or wasn't doing, who she was or wasn't kissing? Some other poor dupe could be blackmailed into marrying Lady Iris by that conniving mother for all he cared. At least he was safe from that dreaded fate.

Yes, it was all for the best that she was back in London, away from him, and trying to trap some other poor sap into marriage. No, that was unfair. She had never tried to trap him into marriage, and if she had wanted to she most certainly could have. And her mother could also have made him marry the girl, not merely host a fête.

But it was still good that she had gone, back to her life, and out of his.

He turned around and paused. Not that he knew for certain that she had returned to London. For all he knew she could still be staying with the Walbertons.

Hadn't the mother mentioned they were staying another month? That time had nearly passed, but they had extended their visit once before, and there was no reason why they couldn't extend it further. Lady Iris might still be staying within walking distance of his home, and he could be subjected to another unwanted and uninvited visit at any moment.

Perhaps he should find out, just to put his mind at rest. He could walk over to the Walbertons' and find out once and for all whether or not she had left the county. Then he could put all thoughts of her out of his mind and know for certain that he was never again going to be pestered by her or her mother.

Max would enjoy the walk and he could do with some exercise himself. That might be the perfect remedy for all this excess energy that was coursing through his body. He knew the path well enough and, with Max at his side, finding his way shouldn't present any problems.

Yes, that was what he would do. He rang the bell to summon Charles.

'Fetch my hat, coat and cane,' he said with new-found determination. 'I'm going to take Max out for a walk.'

'Very good, my lord,' Charles replied. 'But you have a visitor. Should I send her in first?'

Chapter Twenty-One

'What?' Theo asked, even though he had heard Charles clearly.

Charles coughed slightly. 'It's Lady Estelle Redcliffe, my lord.'

As if his lungs had been punctured, Theo's held breath escaped and he gasped in another.

'Please show her in, Charles,' he said, surprised that his initial shock quickly changed to disappointment. He had expected Lady Iris, but how could he possibly be disappointed? He had waited for this moment for six years. When Charles left, he walked across to his chair, grabbed his jacket, pulled it on and waited.

The last time Lady Redcliffe had been in his house she had still been an unmarried woman, and he'd been happily anticipating their wedding, their honeymoon in Italy and their future together.

It had been a different time and he had been a different man. And now she would see what he had become. A pitiful invalid, a recluse, a man who had never recovered from the pain of her desertion. A man who, as Lady Iris had said, had hidden himself away to tend his wounds, too broken to return to Society.

'Theo, it's so good to see you again.' Her voice was just the same. Just as light. Just as carefree and musical. It was a voice that had once entranced him.

'Lady Redcliffe,' he responded with a low bow.

'I'm so sorry to come uninvited but I was sure you wouldn't mind. Are you going to ask me to sit down?'

He gestured to the chair beside the fireplace, the one that had been placed so Lady Iris could get close to the fire when she had arrived at his house wet and bedraggled. The one she had sat in when she had questioned him about the way he lived his life. The chair from which he had all but ejected her and then made it plain he did not want to see her again.

'I'm visiting neighbours of yours, so I thought I couldn't possibly not come and see you while I was so close by,' she said as she sat down.

Theo wondered whether he should point out

that she did not live so very far from him and had managed to avoid visiting him for the last six years. Six years when he had desperately hoped that she would come.

'You are most welcome, Lady Redcliffe,' Theo said, unsure if that was still the truth.

'Oh, please, call me Estelle, and please, sit down. Or do you require some assistance?' He heard the rustle of her skirt as she stood up.

'No, I'm perfectly capable,' he said, taking the seat opposite her.

'Yes, you are, aren't you?' She paused, as if taking the time to assess him. 'And it was *so* good to see you again at the Walbertons' dinner party and I hope you were pleased to see me as well.' She paused again, then laughed. 'Well, you couldn't actually see me, could you, but you know what I mean.'

He suppressed his irritation at her attempt at humour and merely nodded in acknowledgement.

'It is good to see you again, Theo. You are looking well, I must say. Much better than I would have expected.'

She moved in her seat, satin crinkling. 'But you always were a handsome man and the scarring is hardly noticeable now.' Her voice was now closer to him as she leaned forward.

'It's nowhere near as bad as I had been led to believe.'

'I have no idea how bad my scarring is. As you pointed out, I can't see.' Why he should be so irritated by Lady Redcliffe he had no idea. Was he such a curmudgeon that he couldn't even stop himself from being annoyed with the woman he had once loved to distraction? A woman he hadn't stopped thinking about for the last six years. He revised that thought. She was no longer on his mind quite so much. For the last few weeks Lady Iris had also intruded on his thoughts, often driving out all memories of the woman to whom he had once pledged his undying love.

'Well, believe me, it's not too bad at all, in fact.'

And yet you can't stop talking about it.

'And you appear to be coping very well with your handicap,' she continued.

'I cope. But what about you? I take it that marriage and being a titled lady is everything you hoped it would be.' He was curious to know but also wanted to shift the subject from his infirmity.

She shuffled in her seat. 'That is partly why I'm here, Theo. I wanted to apologise for choosing Lord Redcliffe over you.'

It was Theo's turn to move uncomfortably as he crossed his legs and sat back in his chair. He did not want to rake over old ground. Did not want to be reminded of that terrible time when she had abandoned him when he needed her the most.

'I really did believe at the time that it was the sensible thing to do,' she continued, her voice beseeching. 'The only thing I *could* do. I hope you understand, Theo.'

He hadn't understood at the time and was unsure whether he did now.

'But that is not what you asked me, is it?' she said. 'You asked me if my marriage and my title are everything I hoped they would be.'

'And are they?'

'Well, I have to admit I love being a married woman—it gives one so much more freedom— and I love having a title...love the status that being the wife of an earl gives me.'

'So you have everything you want. Few people can say that.'

'But I do miss you, Theo,' she said, her voice quiet as if her head was lowered.

Theo could say that he had missed her terribly as well. For the last six years he had constantly imagined what his life would have been like if he had not been burnt in that fire.

How he would have been married to a beautiful woman whom he adored. How they would have lived a charmed life. How by now they would have children. Instead, he was living alone with his misery, knowing that the woman he loved was with another man.

'And I hope you missed me as well, Theo.'

'I missed you terribly,' he said in all honesty. 'But what's done is done.'

'But it doesn't have to be the end of things,' she said, urgency in her voice.

Theo frowned. Of course it was the end. She had married someone else.

She lowered her voice. 'As I said, married women have certain freedoms. I have done my duty by my husband and provided him with two fine boys. Now he allows me the same freedoms that he has also exercised throughout his married life. Freedoms that I wish to take advantage of. With you.'

Theo said nothing, surprised by this turn in the conversation.

'You know what I'm talking about, don't you?'

Still he made no response.

'Are you going to make me say it?'

She waited, but he chose not to answer.

'Oh, Theo, can't you tell, you silly man? I'm offering to become your mistress.'

Again, he chose not to respond.

She laughed lightly. 'That's if you'll have me.' Her laughter made it clear she expected him to agree wholeheartedly. So why was he hesitating?

'If you're worried about people finding out, you don't need to be,' she rushed on, assuming that was why he was unresponsive. 'No one need know. I visit Lady Walberton on a regular basis, so it would work out perfectly. We could be very discreet.' She lowered her voice. 'I know how much you wanted me, Theo—still want me. Now you can have me.'

'I don't believe that would be the right thing to do, Lady Redcliffe,' he said, surprised at his own reaction.

She laughed, a laugh that was no longer melodious but tinged with bitterness. 'You don't need to be so honourable. My husband certainly isn't.'

She paused and drew in a deep breath. 'Oh, Theo, I'm so unhappy. My husband doesn't love me any more,' she said, her words coming out in a rush. 'Now that he's got the children he wants he never even touches me. When we first married, he couldn't get enough of me. He showered me with gifts and was constantly telling me how beautiful I was. Now he hardly speaks to me and I know he has a mistress in London.' She paused, and when she spoke again her voice was full of bitter defiance. 'So I don't see why I can't do the same. He certainly wouldn't care.'

Was that the role she expected him to play? She wanted him so she could get revenge on her husband for his unfaithfulness, for his lack of compliments. She wanted Theo to be the one to worship her beauty, to shower her with gifts. It was a role he had once happily played, but was it what he wanted now?

She stood up and approached his chair. 'So, do you want me to be your lover, Theo?' He made to stand but she placed her hand on his shoulder. 'Silly question. I know you want me. I saw how you reacted when we met at the Walbertons' dinner party.'

She leant down, her face close to his. 'Well, you could have me, Theo,' she whispered in his ear. 'Not as your wife, but as your lover.'

Her hand lightly caressed his cheek. 'My husband isn't expecting me back until this evening,' she whispered, her implication clear.

He took hold of her hand and stood up.

'Lady Redcliffe, you are a married woman. Your loyalty should be to your husband.'

'Married? Loyalty?' she said, her voice harsh. 'You know nothing of my life. My husband doesn't love me any more.' Her voice softened. 'But you do. When I saw you at the Walbertons', when I saw the way you reacted to meeting me again, I knew that you were still in love with me.'

She leant in towards him. 'My husband doesn't love me the way you did, Theo. The way you can still love me.'

'You made your choice six years ago, Estelle,' he said, his voice gentle.

'So, does that mean you're actually saying no to me?' She laughed at the absurdity of that possibility.

'That's what I'm saying.' Theo could hardly believe it himself. 'I am sorry your marriage is not all that you had hoped. But the time for us has passed. I think you should return to your husband.'

'What? Are you serious? I'm offering myself to you, Theo. As you know, I could have had any man I wanted when I first met you. And I'm still a desirable woman. Many a man would want to take me as his lover.'

'Then I wish you good luck in finding the right man.'

She stepped back quickly as if he had struck her. 'You've changed, Theo. That fire did more than just take away your sight and scar your face. It made you an imbecile as well.'

'I'm sorry you're hurt. That was not my intention.'

'I suppose you think that other pretty little thing who was at the Walbertons' is interested in you,' she shot back. 'Well, I very much doubt that. She's almost as beautiful as I am and is hardly likely to settle for a deformed cripple when she is sure to have plenty of other opportunities.'

'Estelle, you're angry. I think you should leave,' he said, surprised at how calm his voice was.

'Oh, yes, you're wasting your time there. She may have been paying you attention at the dinner party, but it will come to nothing. A pretty girl like that would merely be playing with you so she could incite the other men and get their attention. I know the games women play, and believe me, Lady Iris is not for you.'

Was that what had revived her interest in him? Jealousy that another woman who was reputed to be a beauty had been talking and laughing with him? Was she really that petty?

'Lady Iris was merely showing pity towards you because you're an invalid,' she continued. 'You couldn't possibly think you have any more chance of marrying her than you did of marrying me.'

'No, you're probably right,' he said.

'Well, good, then,' she said, her voice unconvinced. 'At least you're not making a complete fool of yourself over that young lady. And I know for a fact that Lord Pratley and Lady Iris are almost engaged.'

Theo gave a mirthless laugh. Last time he'd spoken to Lord Pratley they had been *almost* courting. Now they were *almost* engaged. He assumed they would soon be *almost* married.

'I don't see what's so funny about that,' she spat out. 'The only thing funny is the laughing stock you will make of yourself if you pursue Lady Iris.'

'I think it is time you left.' He reached down and gave the bell a ring.

'Would you please show Lady Redcliffe out?' he said when Charles appeared.

With a loud huff of disapproval she walked out in a fluster of rustling fabric.

Theo sank down into his chair and shook his

head slowly from side to side in disbelief. He had wasted too many years pining over something that had never existed. He had thought he was in love with Lady Estelle but had never really known her. All he had seen was her beauty and he had been blinded by it and by his own vanity and masculine pride. He had lost his eyesight in the fire, but it had taken becoming blind for him to finally see the truth.

Yes, he had wasted six years, and he wasn't about to waste another minute.

He rang the bell again so Charles could fetch his coat, cane and Max's lead. He would still walk over to the Walberton estate, but now it would be with an entirely different purpose in mind.

Chapter Twenty-Two

The Walberton estate was a hive of activity when Theo arrived at the front entrance. Carriages were lined up. Servants were stacking luggage and calling out instructions, and the horses were snorting and stomping at the ground, anxious to get moving.

Theo hoped he had not left it too late and Lady Iris had already departed. He stopped a passing footman and asked if he could take Max to the kitchen so he could have a drink of water, then asked if Lady Iris was still in residence.

'Yes, my lord,' the footman said. 'But Her Ladyship and her mother will be departing soon. That's their luggage we're loading now. They'll be taking the evening train back to London.'

Theo released his held breath. He wasn't too late.

'Would you please tell Lady Iris that the Earl of Greystone requests an audience?' The man departed and, using his cane, Theo made his way up the steps to the entrance hall and waited anxiously. When the footman returned, he led him into the drawing room.

'Lord Greystone,' said Iris. Fabric swished softly as she walked towards him. 'I did not expect to see you again. Please, sit down.'

She took his arm and led him to a chair. He waited till he heard the rustle of fabric to indicate she had sat down, then took the seat opposite her. Theo had not thought about what he wanted to say to Lady Iris, only that he needed to speak to her again, needed to be in her company again, needed to try and make things right between them, even if it was the last time he saw her.

'So, have you come to reprimand me again for my reprimand?' She gave a little laugh. He smiled. How he loved that little laugh that punctuated much of what she said.

'No, Lady Iris. I have come to ask for your forgiveness.'

'My forgiveness?' He could hear the incredulity in her voice.

'Yes, for everything I have done since I first met you.'

She made no reply and he could imagine her staring at him in wide-eyed surprise. He was not a man for apologies. At least, he had not been a man to apologise until he had met Lady Iris, and this was no easier than the previous half-hearted apologies he had made to her, but he needed to persevere. It was essential that he set things right before she left his life for ever.

'I have been rude, curt and ill-mannered, and you did not deserve that.'

Still she said nothing. Had he shocked this delightful chatterbox into silence? He hoped not.

'While I have treated you appallingly, you at all times have acted with kindness and courtesy.'

'Kindness? Courtesy? The last time we spoke I gave you a telling-off for the way you lived, and you made it very clear you did not appreciate it.'

'And for that I also apologise. Even if you were questioning my choices, I now realise it was done out of kindness, with the best of intentions. You are a lovely, warm, generous and caring woman and instead of responding to your well-meant advice as I should have, I repaid your kindness with ill temper and rudeness.'

'Well, you'll get no argument from me on

that,' she said, her voice returning to that teasing manner he was coming to adore.

He smiled, then adopted a more serious tone. He had so much more he needed to tell her and could not allow himself to become distracted by the sound of her lovely voice. 'I didn't realise it at the time, but now I understand that everything you said was true.'

'It was? You do?' Her startled disbelief made him smile again.

'Until you came into my life, I did not know how angry I was with the world,' he said. 'I blamed everyone and everything for what I had lost. What I thought I had lost. I wanted to punish the world, so I locked myself away. You made me see that the only person I was punishing was myself.' He drew in a deep breath, to drive away the anger he felt, anger that was no longer directed at the world but at himself, at the man he had once been.

'You made me realise that the only person who was being hurt was myself. I could live with that realisation, but I couldn't live with the fact that I had been rude and insulting to the woman who had the kindness and the courage to point these things out to me. So for that I apologise.'

'Oh, Theo, I don't blame you for the way

you reacted. Nor do I blame you for locking yourself away. After all, there was the fire, and, you know… Lady Redcliffe and all that.'

'Yes,' he said with a resigned sigh. 'There was the fire, Lady Redcliffe and all that. Those were the grievances that I had been clinging on to. Clinging on to so tightly that they were pulling me under and I was drowning. It was only when I let go of them that I could come back up to the surface.'

'I'm so pleased.' He could hear the smile in her voice.

'I should also thank your mother before you leave for London.'

'My mother? Do you want to thank her for blackmailing you?'

He laughed at the shocked sound in her voice. 'No, I want to thank her for forcing me to attend that dinner party. If I hadn't I would not have met Lady Redcliffe again.'

'Oh, I see.'

He could tell by the strain in her voice that she did not understand at all.

Theo paused, determined to get this right. 'When I met Lady Redcliffe again, after being apart for so many years, I have to admit, I was devastated. As you know, I had once been in love with her, had expected to marry her.

Being in her company again, and the company of the man she did marry, made me think of all I had lost and would never have.'

'I know, and I am so sorry for that, as is my mother. She didn't know about your past with Lady Redcliffe at the time.'

Theo held up his hands to silence her. 'That is not what I mean, and neither of you have anything to apologise for. Meeting Lady Redcliffe again also changed my life.'

He heard a quick intake of breath, then she quietly said, 'I see.'

Once again, he knew she did not understand, that he was not making how he felt clear to her. 'Meeting Lady Redcliffe again made me realise that I had never really been in love with her, that I had never really known what love was.'

'It did? You did? I mean, you didn't?'

He smiled at her confusion. 'I thought I was in love with her. She was the most beautiful woman I had ever met and I was dazzled by her. I now know that that was all I was in love with, her physical beauty. I also now realise what a superficial man I was. I loved having the most desirable woman of the Season on my arm and being the envy of every other man.

And for the last six years I have lamented that loss, but I had lost nothing. Certainly not love.'

He suppressed the anger he was feeling at himself for those wasted years so he could continue. 'When she rejected me because I was no longer the man I had been, when I became a blind, scarred man, I retreated into myself. I hated the fact that other men no longer envied me. After the fire I couldn't be that man so I hid myself away like a hermit, avoiding people so they wouldn't pity me. But the only person who was full of pity was myself. I was drowning in self-pity for what I had lost, without realising that I had lost nothing. I now realise that if anyone should be pitied it was that superficial man I had once been, a man who only cared about external appearances. And it was meeting Lady Redcliffe again that made me realise that, and for that I thank your mother.'

'She will be pleased to hear that. She never meant to hurt you and felt so bad about the dinner party.' She paused. 'Although that didn't stop her from blackmailing you into hosting the fête, which she probably shouldn't have done either.'

'And for that, too, I should thank her. You were right. I did enjoy the day. As much as I tried to deny it, I enjoyed meeting people again, enjoyed having the house full of laughter and activity.'

'Good, and does that mean you will now be entering Society again?'

'Yes, I hope to.'

'I am pleased. You do deserve to be happy, Theo.'

'But I didn't just come here to apologise to you and your mother,' he said. 'I also came to tell you how much I admire you.'

'You? Admire me?'

'Yes, you are a truly beautiful woman.'

'Oh, I see.' He could hear the disappointment in her voice.

'I can tell you are a beautiful woman because of the way men react to you, but that is not what I mean. I'm talking about a different type of beauty. You have a beautiful soul, a beautiful heart. You are kind, generous, forgiving and brave, and for those reasons you are the most beautiful woman I have ever met.'

'And I admire you, too, Theo,' she said, and he could hear the smile in her voice. 'For your courage and your strength.' She gave a small laugh. 'And you are still rather handsome, you know,' she continued, causing him to laugh as well. 'Not that I care about such superficial things,' she added, still laughing.

Theo had almost said everything he wanted to say to her before she departed, but there was one more thing that he wanted to get off his chest. Standing up, he crossed the short space that divided them and knelt down in front of her.

'Lady Iris. My feelings for you are more than just admiration.' He drew in a deep, steadying breath. 'I have also come to realise that I have fallen in love with you.'

He waited. She made no answer, and when she did it came as a gasp. 'You have?'

'Yes, Iris. I love you.' It felt so good to say what he had been feeling for so long but had refused to acknowledge. 'I know you are leaving for London this evening, and I expect nothing from you, but I could not let you go without telling you how I feel. Meeting you has changed me so much. You have made me a better man. You have brought light and warmth into my dark life. Meeting you was like the sun coming out on a cold winter's day. I know I am not worthy of you. I know I have no right to ask for your love in return, but because of you I will continue to strive to be a better man.'

'You are…you do…you can,' she said. 'Oh, what I'm trying to say is you are worthy of me, you do have a right to ask for my love and you have it. I think you have always had it.'

'You do? You have? I have?' he replied in the same manner, causing her to laugh again.

'Yes. I think I fell in love with you the moment I met you, sitting beside your drawing-room fire all gloomy and grumpy. I knew that under that grim countenance was a noble, wonderful man. As soon as we met something deep down inside of me was telling me that this is the man you are going to m…this is the man you are going to fall in love with.'

'Marry? Were you going to say marry?'

'No,' she stated emphatically. 'That is, unless that was what you were going to say.'

'It was what I hoped for, but never thought would be possible.' He took her soft hands in his. 'Is there a possibility that you would consider marrying a man like me? Would you consent to my courting you?'

'Oh, stop being so coy. You know that I will,' she said, and bent down and kissed him on the cheek.

A surge of happiness washed through Theo, the like of which he had never experienced before. He wanted to sing, wanted to dance, wanted the world to feel as good as he felt right now. But he did none of those things. Instead he forced himself to retain his dignity. He needed to maintain propriety.

'In that case, I should do this properly.' He lifted up her hand and lightly kissed it. 'Lady Iris Springfeld, would you do me the honour of consenting to be my wife? If you do, I promise I will do everything in my power to make you happy, to make you feel loved every day of your life, the way you deserve to be loved.'

No answer came.

'Iris?' he asked again, less assured. 'Will you marry me?'

'Oh, sorry,' she said. 'I was smiling and nodding, when what I should have been doing was saying yes, I will marry you, Theo. Yes, yes, yes.'

Theo had believed it would not be possible to feel happier when she had said she loved him, but he was wrong. Her acceptance of his proposal had caused his happiness to soar, to make him feel giddy, almost mad with joy.

'Then I shall ask your parents if they will agree to my courting you. Do you think your parents will give their consent?'

'I can say with complete confidence that my mother will agree and if she agrees then it automatically follows that my father will also agree.' She paused and he was sure she was smiling. 'But if you want to make sure, you could always kiss me again. If my mother finds out, she'll have no choice but to blackmail you into marriage.'

He laughed. It was an admirable idea, so he rose to his feet, took her in his arms and lightly kissed her, savouring her feminine taste, loving the feel of her silky skin against his.

He had meant to merely kiss her lightly, to seal their commitment, but with her now in his arms, with her lips on his, her hands around his head, he could not hold back. He pulled her tighter, kissed her harder, wanting to consume her, to make her his own. And she kissed him back with an equal ferocity. Her fingers wove through his hair, holding his head to hers, as if she feared he would escape. She had nothing to fear. Standing here kissing her was exactly where he wanted to be, exactly where he wanted to stay for the rest of his life. His hands ran down the length of her body, loving the curve of her waist, the feel of her buttocks under her skirt. How he looked forward to their wedding night when he could strip her of her clothing, could explore her body, feel, caress and kiss every inch of it.

The temptation to do so now was all but overwhelming. They planned to marry—would it be so wrong?

Behind him, as if from a long way away, he heard a door open.

'Iris, we need to get ready—' The mother's voice came to a sudden halt as she registered what she was seeing.

'Oh, Mother, you caught us…what a shame,' Iris said with a laugh in her voice, her arms still wrapped around his shoulders, her lips still close to his. 'I do believe you're going to have to blackmail the Earl into marrying me after all.'

'So I see.'

The mother rushed forward. Theo stepped backwards, expecting the worst.

'Oh, I'm so happy for both of you,' Lady Springfeld said instead, grasping both their hands. 'I don't believe I've ever seen a couple more in love and more right for each other.'

She released their hands. 'Oh, but I suppose I'd better tell the servants to unpack the trunks and let Lady Walberton know we've changed our plans yet again.' She headed to the door. 'And I suppose I'd better start arranging a wedding. In the meantime, you two just carry on as if I was never here.'

When the door clicked shut behind her, they did exactly that.

Chapter Twenty-Three

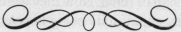

Almost immediately Iris's family arrived en masse to visit her soon-to-be husband, and Theo's house was filled with laughter and chatter.

The loud, warm, wonderful family consisted of Iris's younger sister, Daisy, who brought her bicycle with her on the train so she could explore the countryside; her older sister, Hazel; Hazel's husband, Lucas, and their daughter, Lucy—who, although only two years old, had inherited the family habit of talking constantly; her brother, Nathaniel, and her parents. The father was the only member of the family who wasn't constantly talking and joking, and he instantly became Theo's ally in this boisterous, female-dominated household.

Sookie, the little pug dog, also made a visit. As Max and Sookie were introduced, everyone held their breath, as if it was essential for these two animals to get along if Theo and Iris were to be assured a happy future together. After a few cursory sniffs, while Max worked out whether this little creature really was a dog, they started to play together and everyone released a sigh of relief. Now they were the best of friends, and despite being hopelessly mismatched spent their days playing together and their nights curled up around each other in front of the fire.

A noble wolfhound befriending a tiny pug dog wasn't the only surprising change that had happened in Theo's life since Iris and her family began spending time in his home.

Iris had taken to reading to him from her favourite books, and he discovered he enjoyed gothic novels, or at least he enjoyed listening to her reading gothic novels to him. As she recounted tales of vampires, haunted houses, and dastardly murders he found himself completely mesmerised, although he suspected it was as much that he enjoyed the sound of her lovely voice, and her sharing this simple pleasure with him, as his actual enjoyment of the stories.

But more surprising than his newfound literary tastes, even more surprising than a wolfhound and pug dog becoming best friends, or Charles's revelation that he was a secret Morris dancer, was the disappearance of his nightmares. From the moment he let go of his past and started to look forward to the future, his future with Iris, his night-time torment ceased.

And he *was* looking forward to his future life and never wanted to go back to the way he had been before Lady Iris Springfeld burst into his home. He had gone from living in almost complete silence to being plunged into non-stop noise and activity, and he loved it. He was now part of a welcoming, happy family and surrounded by love. But it was more than that. He was in love for the first time in his life, truly in love.

Sometimes that love was just there, sitting quietly in the background, and merely providing a framework for his life. At other times it would bubble up inside him and he'd have to immediately tell Iris how he felt or he was sure he would explode. If that happened when they were alone, he could let it out in a heartfelt declaration. But if he was caught unawares, such as when the family was present, he would have to be content with whispering his love for her in her ear, or merely squeezing her hand, or lightly touching her arm so she would know how deep his affection was for her.

Theo was sure that with every passing day he spent with Iris, his love continued to grow. While that was a wonderful sensation, it did mean he was also finding it harder and harder to wait for her to become his bride. Fortunately, the parents agreed that there did not need to be a long courtship. Thank goodness for that.

Then, eventually, after what felt like an interminable amount of time, the day finally arrived.

The wedding ceremony was held at the local church near Iris's family's Dorset estate, and it was agreed that the couple would stay at the family home for a few days then travel back to Cornwall. That too was something for which Theo was grateful. He did not think his control would last the journey, and he did not want to consummate his marriage in a railway carriage.

Standing at the altar as the vicar conducted the service, Theo was tempted to tell the man to hurry up. Finally, when he declared them man and wife, Theo could hardly believe such happiness was possible. That was, until he was told he could kiss his bride, and he realised he was wrong. An even greater level of happiness swelled up inside him as he leant down and lightly kissed his wife, loving the touch of her now familiar lips on his own, adoring that enchanting scent of orange blossom and rosewater.

'Oh, that was a bit tame, wasn't it?' his cheeky bride whispered, causing Theo to smile.

'It will have to do for now, Lady Greystone. After all, the vicar is watching,' he replied equally quietly, his skin softly rubbing against her cheek as he whispered in her ear. 'You'll just have to wait till I get you alone.'

'Mmm, alone and less than formally attired, I hope,' she whispered in reply, causing Theo to tilt back his head and laugh out loud, even though such behaviour was perhaps a bit raucous for the local village church.

Iris joined in her husband's laughter. *Her husband.* Was there a more wonderful phrase in the English language? If it were actually possible to die from happiness, Iris was sure her days must be numbered. But how could she not be deliriously happy when she was married to the most wonderful man in the world?

She loved Theo Crighton. Every time she reminded herself of that fact a little shiver of pleasure rippled through her, just as it was doing now.

The vicar held up his hands so the congregation would rise.

'Right, the vicar isn't watching,' Iris whispered. 'You can kiss me again now.'

'But what about your parents, your family, the guests?' he said, still laughing. 'Or do you want the entire congregation to close their eyes, along with everyone from the village?'

'I'm sure that can be arranged.'

He pulled her close and kissed her again, to the accompaniment of the cheering and clapping guests.

Taking her hand, he led her down the aisle, and out into the glorious sunshine. Then he kissed her again, this time to the accompaniment of ringing church bells and the raining down of rose petals.

'That, my dear, is going to have to do, until tonight,' he said, as his lips left hers.

Iris resisted the temptation to pout and stamp her foot. She had no choice but to wait. They had the wedding breakfast to get through, the speeches and the dances. But it would be so tempting to tell everyone to carry on without them, to inform the wedding party that they had more important things to do. But she knew she would not do that. As desperately as she wanted to be alone with Theo, she also wanted to share this wonderful moment with her family and friends.

She looked up at her adorable husband, whose wide smile was the mirror of her own. In fact, he had smiled so much since they had begun courting that it was hard to believe that a few months ago he had never smiled, never laughed and had been constantly serious and mournful. Now he was the man she had always known was hidden behind that gruff exterior. A loving, lovely man with a great capacity for happiness, for giving and receiving love.

Her family surrounded them, all talking at once, as the church bells continued to ring out, declaring their happy union. Her older sister, Hazel, looked beautiful as her maid of honour, and her younger sister, Daisy, for once was not wearing her bicycle-riding costume and had donned a lovely cream silk dress, with an appropriate garland of daisies in her hair.

As much as she believed that Daisy should be allowed to live her life the way she wanted, and dress any way she chose, she was pleased she had put up no objection to the bridesmaid's gown Iris had chosen for her.

'I'm so happy,' her mother said, kissing Iris on the cheek while her father shook Theo's hand. 'I've managed to get two daughters married. Now there's only one to go,' she added, wiping away a tear. She turned and smiled at her youngest daughter. 'And dressed like that I'm sure I'll find Daisy a suitable husband, just as I've done for you and Hazel.'

All three girls rolled their eyes in unison, then broke out into laughter. Iris did not have the heart to point out to her mother that both she and Hazel had found their own husbands. If it hadn't been for Iris wandering away from a house party in the middle of a storm she might never have met the love of her life.

Iris also suspected that Hazel was tempted to remind their mother that she had met her husband in less than conventional, and somewhat scandalous circumstances. And as for Daisy, everyone knew that she had no interest in marrying anyone. Ever. What she wanted was to be free, to be an independent woman and to explore the world from the seat of her bicycle. Although Iris knew that Daisy's claim she wanted to remain single would fall on her mother's deaf ears. As her mother had already said to Daisy, repeatedly, finding love and riding a bicycle were not mutually exclusive activities.

She turned back to her smiling husband, whose hand was being shaken by a seemingly endless line of well-wishers who wanted to congratulate him. The poor man must be getting quite worn out. And she did not want that to happen. After all, she had plans for those hands tonight.

That small shiver of pleasure rippled through her again at the thought of the night to come. They would be together, alone and married. She had just made a vow to love Theo Crighton until death did them part. Iris had once made a vow, to marry for love, and she had kept it. Now she had made another, and she knew that loving her husband until the day she died was going to be the easiest vow in the world to keep.

* * * * *

COMING SOON!

We really hope you enjoyed reading this book.
If you're looking for more romance, be sure to
head to the shops when new books are
available on

Thursday 16th September

To see which titles are coming soon, please visit
millsandboon.co.uk/nextmonth

MILLS & BOON

THE HEART OF ROMANCE

A ROMANCE FOR EVERY READER

MODERN

Prepare to be swept off your feet by sophisticated, sexy and seductive heroes, in some of the world's most glamourous and romantic locations, where power and passion collide.

HISTORICAL

Escape with historical heroes from time gone by. Whether your passion is for wicked Regency Rakes, muscled Vikings or rugged Highlanders, awak the romance of the past.

MEDICAL

Set your pulse racing with dedicated, delectable doctors in the high-pressure world of medicine, where emotions run high and passion, comfort a love are the best medicine.

True Love

Celebrate true love with tender stories of heartfelt romance, from the rush of falling in love to the joy a new baby can bring, and a focus on the emotional heart of a relationship.

Desire

Indulge in secrets and scandal, intense drama and plenty of sizzling hot action with powerful and passionate heroes who have it all: wealth, status good looks…everything but the right woman.

HEROES

Experience all the excitement of a gripping thriller, with an intense romance at its heart. Resourceful, true-to-life women and strong, fearless r face danger and desire - a killer combination!

To see which titles are coming soon, please visit

millsandboon.co.uk/nextmonth

MILLS & BOON

Coming next month

THE EARL WHO SEES HER BEAUTY
Marguerite Kaye

Dominic touched her. His finger traced the shape of her scar, from her forehead, down her brow, her cheek, to the indent on her top lip. His touch was gentle, his gaze intent. 'There is so much more to you than this, Prudence.'

No one had ever touched her in this way, yet it wasn't outrage that was keeping her silent. There was no pity in his gaze, but a gentleness that brought tears to her eyes and, to her horror, one of them escaped. 'But this is all anyone sees.'

'Not me.'

'No. I know.'

His fingers twined with hers, and she allowed him to draw her closer. His kiss was the merest flutter, the graze of his beard, the soft warmth of his lips, before he lifted his head, studying her carefully. She made no effort to break his gaze, her heart thumping, wondering if he was disappointed. Was that it?

He said her name as a question, and she finally understood that he was as confused as she was. He had kissed her. Some response was required. She leaned towards him, terrified that her inexperience would show, but more afraid that he would think she was rejecting him. Heart thumping, she put one arm around his neck, and he inhaled sharply at her touch.

'Prudence,' he said again, this time not a question but a cross between a moan and a groan, his arm sliding around her waist. 'Prudence,' he said, and she lifted her face to his.

Their lips met again. He kissed her gently, carefully, his fingers on her back stroking, and his mouth gently urging hers open. A soft, lingering kiss that became deeper, the pressure of his lips on hers making her dimly aware that she had had no idea what constituted a real kiss, but it seemed the most natural thing in the world to follow his lead. Her eyes closed and she surrendered to the sensations he was arousing in her. His tongue touched hers and they both shuddered. His hands stroked her back, curled into her hair, feathered the hot skin at the nape of her neck, and all the time their mouths clung together. And then it ended, and Prudence slowly opened her eyes before disentangling herself.

'I'm not quite sure how that happened,' Dominic said.

He looked quite dazed, and his hair was wildly rumpled. Had she done that? She couldn't recall. Her mouth was tingling. She felt tightly wound and euphoric at the same time. Nothing she'd imagined had prepared her for that. 'Do you regret it?' she asked, not because she thought he did but because she thought she should say something.

Dominic laughed gruffly. 'No, though I should.'

Continue reading
THE EARL WHO SEES HER BEAUTY
Marguerite Kaye

Available next month
www.millsandboon.co.uk